"This beautifully strange book of the mountains is alarming and inspiring. Alisa Alering's *Smothermoss* goes fearlessly toward realities dismantled by violence, and the weird, wonderful world of the woods."

–Samantha Hunt,
author of *The Unwritten Book*

"At the heart of this story are two sisters, the mountain on which they live, and the persistent question as to which is more perilous, the natural world or the unnatural. Beautifully written, tense and absorbing, *Smothermoss* is an original story from a truly gifted storyteller."

–Karen Joy Fowler,
author of *Booth*

"*Smothermoss* is rich, strange, and beautiful, simultaneously eerie and so very honest. An exciting first novel."

–Kij Johnson,
author of *The Privilege of the Happy Ending: Small, Medium, and Large Stories*

SMOTHERMOSS

SMOTHERMOSS

a novel

Alisa Alering

TIN HOUSE / PORTLAND, OREGON

This is a work of fiction. All of the characters, organizations, and events portrayed in this novel are either products of the author's imagination or are used fictitiously.

Copyright © 2024 by Alisa Alering

First US Edition 2024
Printed in the United States of America

Manufacturing by Sheridan
Interior design by Beth Steidle
Frontispiece: *Ferns of Great Britain and Ireland: Polypodium Phegopteris* (ca. 1855–1856) by Henry Bradbury. Original from The Cleveland Museum of Art.
Spot art on chapter openers: Monsterverse/Creative Market/angelainthefields

Library of Congress Cataloging-in-Publication Data

Names: Alering, Alisa, author.
Title: Smothermoss : a novel / Alisa Alering.
Description: Portland, Oregon : Tin House, 2024.
Identifiers: LCCN 2024003600 | ISBN 9781959030584 (paperback) | ISBN 9781959030645 (ebook)
Subjects: LCGFT: Thrillers (Fiction) | Gothic fiction. | Novels.
Classification: LCC PS3601.L353558 S66 2024 | DDC 813/.6—dc23/eng/20240129
LC record available at https://lccn.loc.gov/2024003600

Tin House
2617 NW Thurman Street, Portland, OR 97210
www.tinhouse.com

DISTRIBUTED BY W. W. NORTON & COMPANY

1   2   3   4   5   6   7   8   9   0

For my mountain

IT IS HAPPENING AGAIN.

Snow melts, the crust of frost cracks and heaves. Water sinks belowground, swelling channels. Sap rises. Wild garlic sprouts, arbutus creeps, and bloodroot quickens. Curved shoots of spotted skunk cabbage thrust toward the light.

Beetle larvae wake and gorge. Red-tailed hawks wheel and shriek. Gusts sweep a fledgling from the nest, hard smack on the ground. The countless populations that call this mountain home are waking, but the seeds of decline are already sown. Eggshells soften, limbs fail to form, leaves wither and curdle, water roils brackish and sour.

Overhead, the stars, distant cold brothers who knew the world before the mountain was formed, revolve unmoved. Redness flares. Scabs multiply, membranes stretch thin.

That's the moment when unpredictable things seep in.

ONE

The Tangle of Rabbits

SHEILA KNOWS SHE IS SUPPOSED TO LOVE HER SISTER. But it's hard when Angie is snoring into her stinking bedclothes in the room they share under the uninsulated eaves. Sheila's side is threadbare and neat, the quilt on her bed stitched from scratchy pieces of men's suits: charcoal, slate pinstripe, and February sky.

Angie's side—but that's the problem, because Angie doesn't keep to her side. She sprawls like a dog flopped in the mud on a hot summer day. Like the poison ivy twining through the blackberry canes and spreading all over the shady side of the house. Cut down the tangle and in six weeks it will grow back twice as thick.

Sheila, though, likes to know where things are. That if she needs to, she can walk into the room with her eyes closed and put her hand on the thing she wants. There isn't much you can count on in life, but most of the time, things stay where you leave them. Things don't get into fights at the Skyline Inn and draw a knife on the bartender when he tells you to settle down or get out and then get taken away in handcuffs and sentenced to three years in the penitentiary upstate. They don't die in a motorcycle accident before you get to know them. They don't haul you off to live in town with some man who smells like smoke and sweat and gasoline and get pregnant with a sister you will never understand only to sneak you all out in the dark one night with only the clothes on your back and creep back in with the old woman on the mountain where you were born. No, things are reliable.

Angie doesn't have a quilt. Her clothes are mixed with her blankets and her shoes and the comic books she steals when she is sent to buy milk at the store in town. Her pillow is tumbled on the floor with the stuffing leaking across the tattered rug, the whole mess scattered with the dog-eared pack of index cards Angie keeps bundled in a rubber band and is always taking out and shuffling and drawing on.

It's no wonder the kids at school call Angie dirty and a liar and a thief. She is dirty. And she is a thief. She will stand there with something of yours tight in her fist and look you in the eye and tell you she didn't take it, you're crazy, she's never seen your locket, lunch money, felt-tip pen.

Sheila definitely doesn't love her sister when Angie takes the last pancake at breakfast, the one that is Sheila's by any standard of decency since Angie already ate four and Sheila only two. Sheila is eating slow so she can pretend they don't live like animals, so she can practice chewing one bite at a time, not like the dogs falling over themselves when she brings out the stew pot and dumps the last dregs on the ground behind the porch.

Sheila is eating like she imagines a person in the city might eat. It's almost working. Her stomach is warm now, and she isn't ravenous anymore. She has beaten her hunger, defied it, and takes every bite slower than the last. Maybe she isn't going to eat that last pancake, but she is going to enjoy sitting at the table and staring it down. Slowly but surely outlasting it, winning by being better and stronger. Then Angie grabs the pancake with the fingers she has just licked grape jelly off of, and folds it into her mouth.

Sheila can't do battle with an empty plate. She can't show the space where a pancake used to be that she is better than it. When she glares her hate across the table, Angie says, "What? You weren't going to eat it."

It's true; she wasn't. But that's not the point at all. That's what Angie will never understand.

❧

IN SPRING IT is mushroom time. The sisters go out into the woods where, only the week before, the rocks were glazed with frost and tiny fortresses of ice heaved up from the mud on the banks of the stream. They roam under the sycamores, carrying paper grocery bags and staring at the ground. Sheila tries hard, but she is distracted by everything—by snail shells and moth casings and thumbnails of green piercing through the dead leaves. Angie blunders, her big feet tripping. But at the end of the morning, it's her bag that is full.

Sheila wants to accuse Angie of cheating, but there's no way she could have. They are out here alone together. The gap where the Appalachian Trail crosses near the farthest edge of the property is empty today. There are no flashes of bright outdoor clothing, no conversations carried on the wind, no scrape of hiking poles on slippery rocks. No one else could have picked the mushrooms for her. Even if Angie had found them on a different day and stockpiled them behind a log to scoop into her sack today, it was still she herself who had sniffed them out from the leaves and twigs and the corncob fungus that looks the same as a morel but can't be eaten.

Angie drops onto a moss-furred rock with her full bag at her feet, waiting for Sheila to catch up.

"Why don't you ever have a boyfriend?" Angie asks, picking at a scab on her arm.

"Who says I don't?" Sheila thinks she sees a mushroom half buried under a lacy maple leaf, but it's only an old walnut gone black and mushy.

"Don't you want one?"

This isn't a question Sheila wants to answer. She feels cold. Or maybe she is hot. Whatever it is, it's not a nice feeling. It's raw, and she wants it to go away. She crouches and pretends she has spotted something extremely interesting near a rotting stump. But she doesn't have to worry, because Angie doesn't want to talk about Sheila. Angie wants to talk about Angie.

"I want a boyfriend," Angie says. "Like Troy."

"Mmm," Sheila says, like she doesn't know what Angie is talking about. But she knows perfectly well. Troy is three years older than Angie and two years younger than Sheila. He is on the baseball team. At lunch, he sits with the most popular boys in his class. He is loud. He talks back to teachers. He bullies younger boys and kids who wear glasses. He calls Angie "lesbo" and holds his nose when she trudges by, waving his hand at an invisible stink.

"He's not very nice to me," Angie says. "But that's just because he has to act that way. In front of the others."

So she does know, Sheila thinks. *Why would you do that to yourself? How could you want someone who so clearly despises you?*

"Sometimes I wonder what it would be like if he asked me to the prom. Or homecoming. When we showed up together, everything would be different."

Sheila used to imagine scenes like this too. Before she realized that nothing ever changes. Or if it does, things only get worse, not better. In her own dreams, when she tries to imagine other places, other futures, the picture won't come clear. Her view is blocked by a dense white fog. Beyond that thick smear is the place she wants to get to. She doesn't know where it is or what it looks like. Only that it's not here, and not this.

They go back to the house and dump the contents of their bags into a bucket, and Sheila pumps water over them. Angie runs into the house for salt and pours it in. The water is cold on Sheila's hands as she swishes the mushrooms around, the bugs crawling out to die. Leaf mold and dirt sinks to the bottom.

"They look like brains," Angie says, leaning over Sheila's shoulder.

Sheila watches her own hand, strangely blue in the water, and the bugs struggling to find a way out.

"If you eat enough of them, maybe you'll get smart," Sheila says, and whatever feeling had been between them in the woods is gone.

"You're not the only one who's smart. You're just good at following the rules. I know stuff you don't know. I know things you'll never know," Angie shouts and lopes away toward the rabbit hutches, stirring up mud behind her.

⁂

TAKING CARE OF the rabbits is Sheila's job. The rabbits live in a crooked hutch leaning against the western wall of the house. When Sheila brings an old bean can full of pellets to the cage and unlatches the wire door, they crowd into the gap, all soft whiskered noses and liquid brown eyes. Harmless, helpless.

Sheila hates the rabbits. Hates them for being so stupid and so trusting. For making her want to pet them and love them and hold them cradled against her cheek. Hates their whisper-soft fur that feels like love against her skin. She swats at them, and they skitter away. But they come back and crowd around her with their sleek necks and inquiring noses.

Sheila doesn't have to kill them. Her mother and the old woman do that. But she does have to feed them. To fool them. To keep them alive long enough to die. To make sure the possums haven't dug up the bottom of the hutch and carried them away. Other kids eat Lebanon bologna and Hamburger Helper. Sheila and her family eat rabbit and squirrel and deer.

In summer, the rabbits stretch out, feet splayed, panting in the heat, their long ears limp. In winter, they huddle together, crouched behind a wind block of old hay and newspaper in the farthest corner, trying to coax a few nonexistent degrees of stray warmth from the house wall.

Angie loves the rabbits, but that's because she doesn't know any better. The events of the real world seem to slide off her as if she's been greased. Angie's not dumb. She knows what happens to the rabbits, only it doesn't seem to affect her much. She squeals when she greets the rabbits. She squeezes them roughly and names them all. The one with the white spot above her nose is Sally. The one with the ear that falls crookedly to the side is Jack because he's a pirate. And when she stabs a fork into slices of them on her plate, she doesn't seem to know.

The sign fixed at the bottom of the lane is a weathered piece of plywood, nailed to a stake and driven into the ground next to the rusty mailbox. Strokes of red paint spell out "Rabbits $5." But no stranger ever comes up their long, rutted lane. They only ever trade with neighbors. The rest of the rabbits go into the pot. Into stew in the winter with a carrot and turnips, in summer sliced cold into sandwiches on potato rolls with margarine. Sheila's mother likes them with baked beans; the old woman prefers them with dandelion.

But there is one gray doe, Pearl, who knows better. She hunches in the far corner, chin resting on folds of fat at her neck. Her eyes are small and distrustful. If Sheila stretches out a hand, Pearl crouches even lower, flattening her ears against her back, and growls.

THERE IS A scar on Sheila's neck. On her throat, really. It is thick and pink and goes right around the front like a necklace. She doesn't try to hide it. Doesn't wear collared shirts buttoned to her chin. Doesn't pull her hair forward so the ends fall like cloaking ivy. Doesn't flutter her hands like birds to distract when she talks, saying *look over here not there*. She doesn't offer anything but a flat, challenging stare.

Sheila thinks she remembers the hospital, from somewhere in that mixed-up time after they fled Angie's father. The white lights and the voices of the doctors. The squeak of thick-soled shoes on tiled floors. Everywhere metal, gray and shining. A long hall with a blinking light at the end. Lukewarm pears in a cup dripping with syrup. Gripping the handrails in the bathroom, the hospital gown coarse against her skin. The cold shiver along her spine.

The doctor leaned over her, his nose hairs like winter briars in her close-up vision. The nurse had pimpled arms, and her breath smelled like coffee. In the daytime, they looked like a doctor and nurse, but at night by the light of the beeping machines, Sheila could see them for what they really were.

They told her to relax, and everything went blue and green, like opening her eyes underwater. She lifted her arms to fight them off—or thought she did—but her hands stayed at her sides. The doctor pulled up his mask and looked to the nurse, who nodded, her long ears flopping. They were the rabbits from the hutch, and they were wearing white coats. Their eyes gleamed red, and their tails stuck out the backs of their surgical gowns.

Sheila wanted to say, "Didn't I bring you dandelion? Didn't I smash the ice on your water when it froze?"

But the rabbits knew she hated them. They said, "Didn't you peel back our skins and hang us by our hind legs? Didn't you break our bones and put them in your pot? Didn't you season us with salt and pepper and mop us up with bread?"

Even as she tried to deny it, Sheila remembered the smell of the pot simmering on the stove, deliciously rich and meaty. Her stomach rumbled, and the rabbit doctor twitched his whiskers. "We know what you are. We're going to cut it out of you."

The nurse stroked Sheila's hair, her hand calm and soothing. Just like Sheila when she visited the hutch. The nurse had a dark spot on the back of her hand, just like Norma, the rabbit that pushed to the front to get the most dandelion. The one that would step on her brothers and sisters to grab a huge mouthful and lunge away to chew as fast as she could and come back for more.

Sheila always shoved Norma away, heaping the greens on the other side of the pen from her. She tried to make sure the other rabbits got their fair share. But now greedy Norma was in charge. Sheila was on her back and couldn't move. Greedy Norma laid a paw on Sheila's forehead.

"There, there," she said, and Sheila saw her teeth, long and square but still somehow sharp.

Norma pushed Sheila down into the bed on the trolley. What had seemed to be hard steel now gave way like spring mud. Sheila sank back as it oozed around her arms and legs, burying her strength to kick and fight. The rabbit doctor lifted the scalpel. His whiskers tickled Sheila's face as he leaned over her to make the cut.

The blade wavered in his unsteady paw, tufts of brown fur sprouting from his gloved hands. Sheila struggled and shrank, trying to squirm away as the scalpel drew closer. A scream clotted in her throat as Norma held her head with soft fur fingers.

The slice of the blade was ice and fire, a slippery unzipping of her throat. Air whistled against her opened skin.

Sheila fell down inside herself, plummeting into a dark well.

When she woke, it was late afternoon, and she reclined in a room that smelled like applesauce. Voices murmured in the background. She could hear someone breathing nearby, underneath the applause from *The Price Is Right* playing on the television mounted in the corner. Her head felt huge, and her throat was raw. Her tongue lolled thick and useless in her mouth.

No one came to visit her. That night, Sheila lay in the bed with rails, clutching the spoon from her supper tray that she'd concealed beneath the sheet. When the rabbits came again, she would be ready. But they never came. Every squeaking footstep turned out to be a nurse. A regular, real, human nurse, wearing lipstick and smelling like Aqua Net hairspray. Sheila never saw the rabbit nurse or doctor again. Never saw greedy Norma.

Ever since, Sheila's throat has been on fire. It burns and itches. She knows that it looks to everyone else like a scar. A remnant of something that once had been but now was gone. But Sheila knows different. The mark on her throat is not a reminder of the past but a clue to what is still there: a rope. A rope around her neck like she has been lassoed.

It started as a single thread that she hardly seemed to feel at all. But another thread soon appeared, winding around the first. Then another, and another, twisting together. By fifth grade, the twined threads were as thick as a shoelace. Now, in her senior year of high school, all those fine accumulating fibers have braided themselves into a rope strong enough to hang a man. Or woman.

No one else can see how the rope trails down her back, how it floats out behind her, how it catches on classroom chairs and other people's waving arms. How it snags on branches and slops in the mud. How sometimes, whoever or whatever holds the other end draws it taut and gives a vicious, reminding yank.

TWO

The Twins with Too Many Teeth

Angie thinks a lot about the end of the world. About globe-destroying mushroom clouds and how to survive when everything she knows has been blown away. About how much better that would be, to have the world erased and to be forced to rely only on her own wits.

She takes down her brother's hunting jacket from the hook on the back porch. When she puts it on, his dog Sue whines and thumps her tail at Angie's feet. The coat is too big, the sleeves too long, and Angie rolls back the cuffs at her wrists.

The boys in the movies always have a bandanna tied around their heads, but Angie doesn't have a bandanna. She finds a worn-out towel in the kitchen, washed almost to holes and the cloth thin enough to fold, and ties that around her forehead. She checks her reflection in a window. Her bangs are scrunched under the cloth. She pulls them over the top of the towel and finger-combs the strands until they drop over her brow. Better.

Then she is outside and on her guard against the roving gangs of survivors, the mutants, and the Russians. It's a dangerous world, and every day is a struggle for survival. First, she must find clean water. Angie takes off into the woods, jumping over logs, dodging from tree to tree, crouching behind boulders, heart hammering in her chest. When she reaches the spring, clear water trickling from the cleft in the hillside, vibrant green plants growing at its edges, she rejoices. She is saved. She will survive another day.

Angie cups her hands and slurps the cold water from her palms. Water achieved, food is her next mission. She zigzags commando-style back to the last house she passed, checks over her shoulder, and ducks into the root cellar. The people who live here are all dead. She has seen their decayed and blistered bodies in this abandoned house. They won't need these jars of fruits and vegetables lined up on shelves against the stone wall. They won't mind if she takes them.

She reaches for a jar and stops, hand in midair. What if the dead family have booby-trapped their supplies? She takes a deep breath to steady herself. Cocks her head and listens—but hears only her own breath rasping in her ears. That and the faint boom of guns and explosions in the next valley over. She doesn't have time to be careful. She closes her eyes, grabs a jar, and sprints for the exit.

Safe outside, she hunkers behind a boulder to shelter from the toxic wind. The cold of the half-frozen ground soaks all the way through her jeans and panties to numb her bottom. *Panties*: what an awful word. Angie cringes at the shape of it in her head. So childish, not the name for something worn by the brave survivor of a radioactive wasteland.

Angie doesn't know what the men and boys on the TV shows wear under their jeans and overalls, but it isn't panties. And what do those men have under that? Something on the outside. Something they stick inside you. She unscrews the jar of spiced pears. She can't get distracted. She has to eat to keep up her strength in case she has to run for her life. A gang of bandits could be over that hill, creeping silently in her direction, ready to overrun her. To take her supplies, strip her body, and kill her. Eat her, even. The world has gone crazy with cruelty, and anything is possible.

Angie tips the jar to her face, slurping the sweet juice and gulping the pear halves, their gelatinous weight slipping down her throat like oysters; sugar and clove instead of sand and brine.

She knows oysters from the before, from a late night when a cousin appeared with a glass jar of them and a sack of boiled shrimp, and the adults all sat around the table covered with newspaper, cracking shells and drinking beer after beer, their talk growing louder as smoke filled the kitchen and her mom wobbled to the stove to make coffee. When Angie looked into the milky jar and saw a colony of gray boogers and asked what they were, they gave her one. Her mom said it was wasted on her, but an uncle showed her how to dip the giant booger in peppered vinegar and toss it back into her mouth in one gulp.

The adults watched, holding in their laughter. She bit down on an explosion of warm mud, and she knows her eyes bulged, but she wasn't about to be their joke. She swallowed the oyster without crying or gagging or any of the things they were hoping she would do. After it was gone, she thought it wasn't so bad after all. She asked for a second, but her mom tossed her a loaf of store bread and told her to make a sandwich.

The clack of voices in the distance brings her back to the present. A flash of bright nylon flickering between the branches of the just-leafed trees, signaling the uneven bob of hostiles traveling along the old hiker's trail. Angie flattens herself against the ground, inching into cover behind a log.

In this blasted world, Angie is on her own. Her only advantage is that she knows this land. She doesn't fool herself that the rocks and trees are on her side, doesn't expect them to provide some hidden aid, smooth her passage, or stumble her pursuers. But she knows the flow of the water, the best places to hide, the tactical advantages. The others are city people, town folks, farmers. The mountain is not their place. This is her only advantage, and she must use it.

☙

SOME DAYS THE old woman in the back room doesn't talk, barely makes a sound, and Angie wonders if she is already dead.

The old woman is not her grandmother, though she is some sort of relation. Angie sometimes wonders how they got her, if she is a quirk of the house like the cupboard door that swings open when you walk by and the mildewed scraps of clothes in the attic and the rusty-toothed trap in the tractor shed.

"We had to go somewhere when we got away from your dad," Sheila says, scouring the burnt-on grease at the bottom of a pan. "Thena took us in."

"But who is she?"

"She's your granny's sister! Don't you ever pay attention?"

Angie slides a finger through the water slopped on the counter. Sheila always acts like she knows everything.

"You don't remember." Sheila tips the pan onto a towel to dry. "I used to tag along after her in the woods. She had a cane with a handle that opened into a seat, and she would sit on it when she got tired and tell stories."

Angie doesn't believe it. Not about the stories—Thena still tells those sometimes—but about her traipsing through the woods. The old woman is bent and hunched and drags one leg peevishly behind her when she comes to the supper table. She used to have a plate of startlingly pink-gummed teeth she kept in a cup beside her bed, but she doesn't bother with them anymore. Angie saw her once, sitting on the bed pulling on her stockings in the morning, and her legs were bald like a baby's, but her hair *there* was gray and wispy like an old man's beard.

The old woman complains about everything. She complains that it is too cold, and then she complains about the smoke when Sheila opens the stove door to put on more logs. She complains that the food doesn't taste like anything: Sheila can't cook, there isn't enough salt, the meat is tough. She complains that Sheila is too quiet and Angie is too loud.

"I still don't see why we're the ones who have to take care of her," Angie says.

"We're her family. We don't have a choice." Sheila says, stacking dry dishes in the cupboard. "I don't see why you're complaining. It's not like you do any of the work."

"She's so mean," Angie says.

"I guess you'd be mean too." Sheila spoons instant coffee into a mug and snips off the end of a bag of milk and pours it into a pan to heat on the stove. The old woman is the only one who drinks milk. Their mom brings it home just for her, the bags stacked like ghostly pillows in the sweating old icebox.

It is for Thena that they go out and cut dandelion shoots with a black-handled knife and bring them back in a crumpled paper bag. Then into a pot go the bacon ends, vinegar, an egg fresh from the chickens, the yolk as yellow as the school bus that ferries them an hour through hell every weekday at 7:30 and again at 3:00. The whole mess, sweet and bitter and sour, is poured over the wilted greens with their jagged leaves and offered to the old woman like she is a queen or the president.

She tastes it, and she blames them. What have they been feeding the chickens? Because the egg doesn't hardly taste at all. It's like it came from the store. What did they have to go and cut such tough leaves for? Didn't they know they were only supposed to collect the smallest ones, fresh and tender and new? If she had her good leg, if she had her health, she would show them the right way to do it.

But she doesn't have her good leg or her health. Both are gone into the past and are never coming back. Angie and even Sheila don't know what that kind of loss means. They are twelve and seventeen, and everything they see looks to them as if it has been fixed that way forever. Change, to them, is vague and abstract: The year before they were in that grade, and now they are in this one. The store in town used to be called Hartzell's, and now it's the IGA. Their brother used to live in the house, and now he doesn't. To them, people don't change who they essentially are. Imagining Thena as young and capable goes no further than putting a wig on her gray head and surrounding her hunched back with teenagers, where she looks preposterously out of place.

❧

ANGIE'S INDEX CARDS are slightly yellowed with faint blue lines, the pack held together with a rubber band. She draws monsters on the blank backs of the cards with felt-tip markers. She knows the creatures are monsters because they have too many eyes. Their necks are too long, and their legs are too short. She used all of her red marker and the orange one too, drawing the blood that drips from their fangs.

She writes their names thick and black across the tops of the cards, the letters squeezed against the edge where she runs out of room. She sits on her bed cross-legged and deals them out in front of her like she has seen her mom do late at night with the poker deck when she is off shift, drinking sassafras tea and listening to Loretta Lynn on the radio.

Angie deals the Dustman onto the quilt next to the bird thing with the black scribbles in its guts and twisted forks for legs. The Broken-Backed Turtle next to the Twins with Too Many Teeth. She says their names aloud when she lays them down. Saying the names is power, like knowing a secret.

Some monsters stay for weeks after they pour out of her pen onto a card, content to doze in the pack among their fellows. Others seem to kick the moment they arrive, demanding release into the wider world. When a card wants to be free, it weighs down the rest of the pack. Angie shuffles the cards through her fingers until she can feel the one that is heavier, slower, more real, more rounded.

She stops.

Yes, this one.

On the card, the Tangle of Rabbits are knotted together. Rabbits stand on rabbits, half devoured by other rabbits. Rabbit legs thrust in all directions—a foot into a face into a stomach into a tail. The rabbit made of rabbits crouches in the briars, hiding from its enemies, quivering and trying to survive without being seen. The briars weave around it, snaring its hind legs and tangling around its neck. Thorns tear its tender ears.

Angie barely remembers drawing this one, it was so long ago. Before their brother left, she thinks. Now it wants out. Sometimes finding the right place is quick, an impulse that calls the card from the pack to its destination in an instant.

Other times, like now, it's slow. Angie trails through the house, feeling the tangled rabbits in her hand, listening for their homing signal. In the kitchen, she pulls out a chair and climbs onto the table and slips the card into the shade of the light that hangs above them every night while she and her mother and the old woman and Sheila eat.

Angie is just putting her foot back down on the chair when Sheila's voice cracks out of the darkness.

"What do you think you're doing?"

Angie's foot slips off the edge and the chair topples, bringing her crashing to the floor.

"I turn my back on you for one minute and you break something." Sheila's voice is flat, accusing.

"It's not broken." Angie rights the chair and shoves it under the table before Sheila can notice that one of the legs is wobbly. "I'm not hurting anyone."

Angie stoops to pick up the other cards that have spilled in the fall. As Sheila watches her sister crawl across the scarred wooden floor, the rope cinches tight. She feels like someone has stuffed a sock down her throat. She wants out of here, somewhere there is more air, where she can breathe.

But where is she going to go? Out there is only the mountain, as familiar as the planks Angie scrabbles across, the battered table with its mismatched chairs, the faded curtains, the chipped plates drying beside the sink. As familiar as the finger marks on the walls, smooth and shiny from generations of hands touching the same places, year after year after year.

Angie collects the last card and gets to her feet. In the dim light, shadows shift across Angie's cheeks, uncovering the imprint of their family. Sheila can see their mother Bonnie's face in there, and Thena's too. The long line of women stretching endlessly back into the fog of time. And ahead. Forward, into the future.

Feeling Sheila's scrutiny, Angie rolls her shoulders defiantly. "What?" she demands.

"Nothing." Sheila turns away and climbs the stairs to their attic room, dragging the rope behind her.

THREE

The Diseased Fox

MANY FEET ROAM THE MOUNTAIN, AND THE MOUN-
tain knows them all as they track across her skin. The three
toes of turkeys, the split hooves of deer that gouge her mud,
the bear that turns over logs and scrapes the broken leaves for
grubs. The bare feet of Sheila and the heavy tread of hikers
passing through. Every step is a breath, a tickle, a pinch, a
sigh. The mountain sleeps through most of them, no more
than the twitch of a spider along her unconscious rib.

Two pairs of feet trip along a bare shale spine. Their thick-
soled boots dislodge shards that tumble down her slopes as
they climb. The creatures tread in tandem and pause often.
They breathe the mountain into their lungs and breathe

themselves back out. Their hearts beat against her. They are not of her; they smell of northern granite. Of cities and exhaust and a salt-tang whiff of the ocean far away east. Still, their pores are open, and they take her in. They nibble her leaves and pick her berries. Rub her moss between their fingertips and spin her quartz in the sunlight like jewels. They treat each other with the same careful wonder.

These creatures smell like humans, but they must be rabbits because they are stalked by a fox. Unlike real, watchful rabbits, they don't know how to protect themselves. Don't know to circle among the briars, white tails flashing, and scoot safely into an underground warren. They are too far from home.

They come to a stream and crouch to drink from the mountain's neck. They sip her water, and the mountain slides inside them, exploring their contours, knowing she will be back home to herself first thing in the morning, if not before. They stand and stretch and walk on.

The fox climbs behind the rabbit women, masking his breath, concealing the giveaway blaze of his eyes behind a shaggy hickory. The mountain doesn't like the way the fox smells. Not just starved for a meal but diseased, blighted, wrong. The fox pants not with hunger or need but with fury. It's in the acid of his sweat, the way he crawls and mumbles, the vile words that drip from his lips like tainted drool.

As shadows fall and the birds hush, the rabbits lie down and curl against the mountain's side, tucked into the crook of her elbow. They take off their heavy boots and cuddle and groom as rabbits do. They press their noses together and smooth each other's fur. They chatter under the stars in their temporary nylon shell. Warm and doing as rabbits do.

When the night is thick, the fox makes his move. The first rabbit screams, and he smashes a rock across her muzzle. She falls on her side, crunched and silent. He grabs the second by her scruff and shakes her. He beats and shatters and pounds. Blood sprays and her hind legs kick. He snarls and barks, but the mountain cares nothing for his noise. Feels only the vibrations, the twitches and pain, the hearts racing in desperate, rabbiting fear. The quick kill that should be over but is not.

The second woman is limp, dead, but the first clings to life. Her mind rings in and out of consciousness, a vibrating bell. She is face down against the mountain, wedged between rocks, broken mouth pressed to the dirt, cracked teeth scraping on roots.

A small tuft of breath escapes her swollen lips. Drops of saliva mix with her blood and fall to the mountain's soil.

Go, the rabbit woman thinks.

In her bleary, fading mind, this soft puff of life is her own self, her lover, her friend. It is all they have seen and felt and breathed since they arrived on the mountain's side, the rabbits they saw nibbling dandelion stems around the bathhouse earlier that day. A red wave rises in her eyes, she swims and flounders, but the puff hovers above the crest, seeking the exit to this squeezing, tightening burrow.

Yes, the woman thinks. *Even if I must stay here—die here*, she admits—*there is more to our life than this worthless end. I cannot save her. I must save something.*

The rabbit woman pulls on her frayed thoughts and concentrates for this one moment. She can feel all of herself, all the parts she had never noticed or known before. She can see how she is connected by threads and gusts and trails to *everything*, knitted loosely in some places and in others tight.

These threads have been all around her, binding her to the world, and now they are snapped, fraying, hardly any still connected. She grasps the ones that remain, pulling them to focus on the only thing that matters anymore, the thing that she has seen the clearest now of everything in her life, and she protects it with her breath and death.

She calls to that rabbit-shaped puff floating above the red tide, and with all her hope and anguish and love and dreams denied of the life they might have had, she gathers the puff into a bubble of safety and pushes it out. Out of her, out into the air, into the night, into the earth, into the mountain.

Go, go, go. Rise up, grow claws, shake the world. Tell them, tell someone, tell anyone. Don't let it be this and only this . . . as the rock falls on her again and she gulps out saliva blood breath, all her last will, and releases it into the dirt and embrace of the mountain. Her body a soft pelt, the woman is slack now, silent and empty.

The rabbit women's blood runs along the mountain's skin, trickles down through the rocks and pebbles, seeps along channels dug by roots to feed and paint the mountain's ancient bones with mourning. Their blood, their grief, their innocent rabbit spirit shakes something loose.

The mountain trembles.

☙

SHEILA STEPS OUT onto the log fallen across the rushing water. Its top is slick with spray and rot and growing soft shells of mushrooms as gray and smooth as snails. Her bare toes grip its slippery curves as she ducks under a swag of birch and edges out into the center, looking downstream as the water funnels over rounded limestone, jagged quartz, and green copper ore.

Gnats churn from the surface and buzz around her head. One dives straight for her eye, dodging the shield of her glasses. She blinks, but its body lodges tight, its wings scraping like a splinter. She pulls back her lower lid, rolling her eye in search of the invader.

Two jets from the air base scream overhead, skimming the tops of the trees, white serial numbers showing on their drab green bellies. The trees jerk, and the mountain shivers. Sheila lurches and the glasses slip from her nose. Her hand flies up, and she barely catches them. Her ankle bangs against the nub of a broken branch, and she lands hard, hugging the slimy log to keep from spilling into the creek below.

The water roars, and the smell of hot metal, rust, and pennies fills her nose. Red water pours toward her, chips of white quartz tumbling in the waves. The sudden flood is so high that the water crests the log and washes over Sheila's back, pulling the rope with it. She tucks her dangling feet against the log's underside and hangs on, feeling unknown shapes bang against her shins in the froth.

Clinging tight, Sheila strains to look upstream. A tide of naked, eviscerated rabbits is riding the creek's sudden fury. They are a jumble of bones with swollen cotton tails, their fur fraying into froth. They tumble and tread one another under as they struggle to rise to the top of the wave. Their whiskers stretch back in a scream, their claws grown badger-sized, fierce and honed.

Then the roar subsides. The flood passes, and the water drops. The pressure on Sheila's neck lightens. She heaves herself back upright, her thighs slimed with rot, the soft skin inside her arms scraped and bruised. Her glasses dangle from her fingers, dripping wet, snagged with debris. She picks fur from the hinges, shakes water from the lenses, and puts them back on.

She squints through the smeary drops. The jets are long gone. Her ankle throbs. But the forest is the same. Birds call and scold as they flit among the branches. A chipmunk squeaks and races into its hole. Only the plants pressed flat against the banks of the creek and the rust-red foam dissolving in the moss that hangs from the log reveal that any torrent has passed this way. That, and the smell in Sheila's nostrils, the strong taste of pennies as her tongue presses on the fish-ribbed roof of her mouth.

FOUR

The Nest That Writhes

SHEILA LETS ANGIE HOVER BESIDE HER AS THEY wait for the bus in front of the school. But when it stops and the doors open, Sheila hurries to the back where the older kids sit and drops into a seat against the window. Angie dithers in the aisle. The seats in front are half filled, and the kids in them glare warnings at her. They spread book bags and extra sweaters across the green vinyl.

"Taken," they say, as the bus jolts into gear and Angie lurches forward. "This seat's taken."

Angie looks back at Sheila, but her sister won't meet her eyes.

Sheila wonders why Angie can't see that invisibility is the way. You tuck yourself into a ball and let their words splatter against you. After the first hundred or so insults land, you're coated in their spit and venom—and though it stings, it numbs your skin and protects you from more.

It's like when the dogs get bitten by a copperhead. The first time, their eyes swell shut, and they slobber and crawl into the shade under the porch and whine and shake like they are about to die. If you leave a dish of milk out for them, they barely touch it, and it's two days before you can coax them out with a bit of chicken skin, by which time their heads have shrunk back down to almost normal size.

By the time they've had their fifth or sixth bite, they barely seem to notice. They go a bit puffy and don't finish their supper. But after a nap under a tree and some angry scratching at their face, you'd think it was nothing more than a beesting that troubled them.

Sheila figures that's what's happened to her. She's been bitten so many times she barely feels it anymore. But Angie fights back like she's being chased by a nest of yellow jackets, snapping at the air and missing every time. On rare occasions she does bite down on one—and instead of victory and relief, she gets stung inside her mouth.

Which is why Angie is frozen in the middle of the aisle like she doesn't understand why no one will share their seat. Greg Falcone—eighth grade, blue FFA jacket, half-grown mustache—wallops her in the small of her back.

Angie catches herself on a seat back and makes the quick choice to slide in next to Lori Harbaugh, a town kid with brown pigtails and a velvet dress, of all things. But the third grader's face bunches up, and she shoves Angie, who is twice her size and in the seventh grade. "Get off! You're not sitting here."

Angie tries to use her extra three inches and her thick muscles to ignore the command. But Lori knows that everyone is watching *her* now. If she lets Angie sit with her, it means she doesn't hate Angie. And if she doesn't hate her, it might mean she likes her. Then Lori will be known forever as Angie's friend.

Lori is medium smart and medium pretty and lives in a split-level ranch on the ridge above the Buchers' farm. Her mom drives a station wagon and does the shopping at the Wise market in Laurelsburg instead of the IGA in town. But if Angie sits with Lori, the third grader will catch whatever Angie's got. She doesn't know exactly what it is, but she knows she doesn't want it.

Sheila leans against the window, the rope coiled on the seat beside her like a sleeping snake. She pretends not to see. She tunes out their laughter. In the seat behind her, Dougie Weichert is chomping through a bag of sour cream and onion chips and trying to impress Karen Shank.

"It's the truth!" Dougie says between crunches. "I'm telling you, there was blood everywhere. My dad saw it."

Dougie's dad is on the ambulance crew, and he's always bragging about the emergency calls his dad goes on. There must have been a bad accident last night—a logging truck or a motorcycle skidding past the guardrail on a hairpin turn. Sheila pictures broken branches, twisted limbs, blood sprayed across jagged rocks.

Lori Harbaugh yells, "You smell! You can't sit here because you smell!"

All the kids are laughing at Angie now. Not just because it's embarrassing, but because it's true. Angie does smell. Sheila keeps herself as clean as she can, takes powder from the old woman's room and sprinkles it in the underarms of her shirts. Plucks the hairs that grow under her arms one by one with a pair of tweezers. Each hair she extracts has a slim black bulb on the end like a stem of wild garlic. In the last year, she has seen that Angie is growing her own tufts, but, in typical Angie fashion, seems not to have noticed that she's any different than she's ever been.

Sheila doesn't want to say anything. Doesn't want to get involved. Talking back never does any good. But her mouth opens on its own. It must have something to do with Lori's ridiculous velvet dress that would be ruined the first time a dog jumped on it with muddy paws. And the girl's neat white teeth and clean little pink fingernails. Or the way the rope is digging into Sheila's neck, even though she hasn't touched it.

"It's easy for you because you've got plenty of money," Sheila says.

Just like that, she's in and she's done. Because this is not an argument she can win.

The other kids shout back that a bar of soap costs fifty cents.

"You try washing in cold water. You try breaking the ice in the basin first thing and see how clean you are." But the other kids aren't listening. Sheila knows she is being ugly and screaming. But she is so mad. Now Angie is looking at her sister like Sheila is the one embarrassing *her*. Somebody balls up a page of notebook paper and throws it at Sheila. Dougie stands and empties the chip bag over her head. Salty, funky, sweet onion crumbs engulf her, cascading over her hair and down the neck of her shirt.

The bus driver, who all the kids call by his first name— some of them even go to the same church he does, where his college-bound daughter is the star of the choir—is watching the goings-on in his overhead mirror, but only with curiosity. He's not going to do anything about it. He's not going to get out of his seat.

The argument goes on—useless, stupid—until the bus arrives at the bottom of their lane.

∞

THE TAUNTS ECHO among the hushed pines even after the bus has rolled away. Angie grabs a stick and charges up their lane, slashing at weeds and beheading flowers as she climbs. Sheila scrapes the spitballs from her hair, and as her arm bumps the rope, the spring sunlight catches the glint of a bright new thread woven among the familiar fibers.

Another one. Already.

For one split instant, Sheila almost succeeds in wishing she could rip the whole thing off her neck and be done with it. But like always, her mind flinches from the thought before she can complete it. It's like she can't even think the words *cut* or *tear* or even *unravel* in the same sentence as *rope*—her brain won't let her. Like touching a raw wound, just the least intention to be rid of the rope drenches her with sweating terror. She can never stand to think about it long enough to figure out exactly what the horrible fate is that she's afraid of. But deep down in her gut she knows—she *knows* with a terrible, dreadful, paralyzing certainty—that if she ever tries to take the rope off, it will be the worst thing that has ever happened to her.

And so she doesn't think about it.

Angie is already almost to the top of the lane, like she has been energized by the fight on the bus. Sheila, on the other hand, is drained. She stares up the long, steep drive. Why does everything, always, have to be so hard?

When Sheila finally reaches the top and enters the dark house, she finds her mother kneeling in the kitchen, obliterating a long line of shiny black ants that have marched across the peeling linoleum and up the legs of the cabinet into a bag of dried apples that will have to be thrown out.

Bonnie looks up as she scrubs with a rag soaked in borax, crushing bodies that release a bitter smell.

"Can you get Thena's hair washed? I was going to do it, but I've got to take care of these ants." Bonnie nods at another bucket sitting in the sun. "The water's already warm."

Sheila drops her books on the table and gets ready to wash the old woman's hair. She sets Thena in a chair out on the porch and takes down the pins and untangles the brittle plait, pulling her fingers through the three stiff tails. The old woman closes her eyes as Sheila's fingers press into her scalp.

Angie turns on the TV.

Their mother yells at her to turn it off.

"But *Hee Haw* is on."

Sheila doesn't understand how Angie can want to watch a show that makes fun of people like them. Makes fun but also gets it wrong. Like it is funny to be poor. Like it is a barrel of laughs for everyone to think that you are ignorant and backward.

Hee Haw is not on. Instead, the reporter from WBAL is propped at his desk looking serious in a dark suit and tie. He holds a sheaf of papers in both hands.

Angie is breathless. Maybe this is it. Maybe the next scene will be President Reagan standing in front of the American flag and telling everyone the war with Russia has begun. She gets ready to hide her excitement.

But it's not a war. Just a murder. Two women from out of state were camping in Cononish Forest, three miles northwest of the Bark Camp Day Use Area.

The mother's hand stills, rag dripping, segmented bodies clambering over one another to escape the bucket. Bark Camp is twenty miles away by car, on the way to Iron Mountain. But it's only a forty-five-minute walk from their house along the Appalachian Trail, two low mountain ridges and one shallow valley away.

So this was what Dougie had been talking about, Sheila thinks.

The old woman asks what is happening. Thena can't hear what the man is saying on the TV, but she can feel the effect traveling down Sheila's arms and shooting through her fingers into Thena's scalp. But no one answers her—they are all listening. The shampoo runs into her eyes, and she cries out.

Sheila presses the towel to Thena's face.

The women were brutally attacked at their campsite, the WBAL reporter says. They had traveled from Rhode Island and were hiking the Appalachian Trail. The killer may still be in the area.

A tall man in a state police uniform appears on-screen in a gravel parking lot. Behind him, a wooden sign spells out "Bark Camp" in carved white letters. The camera pans to a blue hatchback with a Mondale/Ferraro bumper sticker and out-of-state plates. Another reporter asks the trooper about the campsite's proximity to a state asylum for the criminally insane. Could one of the inmates have escaped?

"We have confirmed with the Iron Mountain Rehabilitative Facility that all patients are accounted for." The trooper goes on to say that witnesses have reported seeing a man in the area at the relevant time. "He is described as between eighteen to twenty-five years of age, Caucasian with shoulder-length dark hair. He was last seen wearing a blue plaid shirt or jacket over a dark T-shirt. If you see a person who fits this description, do not approach him. Call the Pennsylvania State Police Hotline immediately. Backpackers are advised to hike in small groups and avoid confrontations with strangers."

Bonnie wrings out the rag and carries the bucket of dirty water and floating ant bodies outside to dump at the edge of the woods. Sheila rinses the soap from Thena's hair with water from the bucket her mother set out in the sun to warm, then pours cider vinegar over the thin strands. It smells like a sour orchard as Sheila bundles the old woman's hair into a towel.

Angie grabs the tail of a passing dog and wrestles it to the ground. They can say what they want on TV, but she knows better. It *is* the Russians. This one man is the advance guard. He got caught and had to kill to save himself, to get away without blowing his cover. Men don't go around killing people in the woods for no reason. There's got to be more to the story than what's on the news.

FIVE

The Creased Girl

IN THE SCHOOL LIBRARY, OLD MRS. STEMWEDEL IS
at the counter, in her green smock with the school button
pinned to the front. Her big glasses magnify her eyes so they
bulge like a praying mantis's.

It's first-period lunch, and the murders are all anyone can
talk about. Even the teachers are doing it. But here in this
book-lined refuge, Sheila might be able to escape. She signs
her name on the card, printing the letters small and tight, and
takes the borrowed magazine to a table in the corner, as far
out of the way as she can. She coils the tail of the rope under
her feet and settles down with her back to the wall. Turning
the pages is soothing, like eating a bowl of hot beans at the

kitchen table with warm socks on after spending a November day outside, chopping and stacking wood.

The girls in the magazines are smooth and perfect. When Sheila looks at them, it's not like the rope goes away, but she feels it less—its drag and scratch is muffled, numbed. There are blonde girls and brunettes. One with hair as black as Sheila's own but long and straight like a horse's tail, swinging heavily across her tanned, satin shoulders. She is wearing a green one-piece bathing suit with a hole cut out to show the inviting dip of her navel. She holds a cone of mint-chip ice cream in one hand, and sand clings to the soft dimple of her knee. In the background, the ocean's blue waves ripple onto the shore under the shadow of a palm tree.

Sheila has never seen the sea, though at the beginning of school in September, some girls come back with tans as dark as caramel corn, wearing T-shirts dripping with fringe that show the curve of their waists above their jeans. Scribbled across their chests, careless script reads "Rehoboth Beach" or "Atlantic City."

You can get from this town in the mountains to the edge of the world, where there are bumper cars and saltwater taffy and boys boys boys. If your dad works at the army base or is a supervisor at the shoe factory, you can pile into the family car with a cooler full of sodas and lunch meat and your little brother making faces at you from across the back seat and drive all the way. But if your dad is dead and your brother is in prison and your mom comes home from the Iron Mountain asylum at eight in the morning in a wrinkled uniform with dark circles under her eyes, the roller coasters and taffy and fried clams are as far away as the moon.

The girls in the magazine are brighter than real people, with sharper outlines and a stronger flavor. They are like the bottom of a jar of home-canned peaches, where the last drops of syrup taste like melted sun.

It's this thought of peaches that gets Sheila. That snares her and trips her up. Because if the girls are concentrated like the last spoonful of summer peaches, what would the girls themselves taste like? She doesn't stop to consider what a stupid thing that is to think. She just imagines.

Imagines that she is close enough—to the strawberry blonde in the faded jean jacket with the golden honey skin—to lay her cheek against her neck, where the girl's skin would be as warm and smooth as an apricot, Sheila's nose slipped inside the collar of her flowered shirt.

That girl would not smell of sweat or chicken feathers or onions or woodsmoke or cheap, cherry-scented shampoo. She wouldn't smell of wet dogs and musty blankets and underarms and itchy feet.

No, she would smell of sand, salt, and escape. Her hair would whisk smooth as silk against Sheila's cheek, tangling against her lips. Her arm would snake around Sheila, inviting her close, their angles bumping together, her thigh pressed against Sheila's. Tracing the terrain of the girl's body, her topography and heat, would feel like holding the baby rabbits, fragile but so alive.

The paper tears easily, with a faint *krrr*. Sheila darts a look over at the counter, but Mrs. Stemwedel is back in the office. After she has eased the girl free from the magazine, Sheila tucks her inside the cover of her math book and waits for the bell.

When she unfolds the page at home, Sheila half believes that the girl won't be there, will have vanished. That the world of the girl in the magazine and Sheila's world at home could not possibly exist in the same time and place. And yet, as she stares at the page in her room, the girl in the magazine is—unbelievably, amazingly—still there. She is still blonde and smiling. There is a crease across her middle, but her face shines.

Sheila lies down on the bed and presses the page against her chest. The girl with her smile and her golden glow and her bare velvet skin nestles against Sheila's ribs, close enough to smell taste touch. Sheila closes her eyes and the golden light flares, a tiny candle flame right under her ribs, next to her heart.

Sheila lifts the bottom of her shirt and slides the paper underneath. It catches on her bra, which she unhooks carefully so the page can slip under without tearing. The paper is cool at first, both slippery and rough. After a moment against her skin, it softens. She holds it in place, letting the glow stretch down to her stomach and up to her neck and out to her fingers. If anyone comes in, Angie or her mom, they won't ask what she's holding. They can't see it. The girl is her secret. The perfection is hers alone.

ANGIE LIES FACE down on the braided rug that smells like creosote and wet dog. She has their brother's old Boy Scout handbook open on the floor and a bag of circus peanuts at her elbow. A fiery mushroom cloud blooms on the television in front of her face.

When Sheila comes into the room and rests in the doorway, the picture on-screen wavers. Angie sticks her hand in the bag of orange marshmallows and carries one to her mouth. "Move," she says, chewing open-mouthed. "You're messing up the picture."

Sheila rolls her eyes but shrugs away from the wall. The picture clears for a moment, then wavy lines cut across the

Russian tanks rolling into the small town surrounded by cornfields. Static cuts in, and the voice of the guy announcing the Orioles game on the next channel over breaks through. Ghosts of ball players waver behind the machine guns.

"You can't stand there," Angie says. She stomps over to the set and steers the rabbit ears around with her eyes fixed on the screen. The baseball players fade. An American flag waving over a schoolyard comes into view.

"I can't believe you're watching this stuff," Sheila says and folds into a chair.

"I want to be prepared." Making sure the antennae stay in place, Angie drops back down onto the rug. "That man. He's a Russian."

"What man?" Sheila picks at the skin on her index finger. She has a hangnail, rough and dry, that snags on her clothes. She could go and find the clippers and snip it off. Or she could keep chewing at it until it starts to bleed.

"The one who killed those women."

Sheila bites down hard and tears away a strip of skin. "You're like everyone at school. Can't you talk about anything else?"

Angie squishes a candy peanut between her fingers. She tears it into smaller pieces, then mashes the bits together, sticks the gob in her mouth, and licks the stickiness off her palms. She scoots the bag of candy toward Sheila's foot. "Is there really going to be a nuclear war?"

"That's up to the president," Sheila says. "To Russia."

"Yeah, but what about after the bomb goes off?" Angie asks.

Sheila sucks the blood from her finger and takes a peanut. She knows how they will taste. Chalky, orange, disgusting. "Why do you eat these things?"

"I'm hungry."

"Yeah, but—" Sheila wonders why she bothers. The distance between her and Angie feels so big. It's not just that they shouldn't be related—they don't even seem to be the same species. Could having a different father really explain so much?

Sheila pushes the candy between her lips.

"If we could survive, it might be kind of cool," Angie says.

"Undrinkable water, poisoned food, radioactive storms, our hair and teeth falling out—that would be cool?"

"Yeah, but there'd be, like, zombies. And mutant bugs and stuff. Besides, we'd be fine. We've got our own food, and we know how to survive. It's only city people who are going to die. Nobody even knows we're out here in the mountains. We'll be, like, the saviors of the human race. The people who get to go on."

Sheila seizes Angie's wrist and drags her to the window. "You see that?"

"What? Earl's tree stand?"

"No, that." Sheila points. "That mountain. The one with the black thing sticking up on top like an antenna?"

Angie squints. "I guess. So?"

"That's where they take the president. It's all hollow inside and full of food and water and medicine underground. So that he can stay safe while everyone else dies."

"The president comes all the way out here? But that means we'll be extra safe. They'll send the air force and everything and—"

"No, dummy. It means it's the first place the missiles will hit. Or at least the second. That mountain is less than ten miles from here. The president might be safe, but we're not going to be invited inside. We're dead. We're nothing. We're obliterated."

Plastic crinkles, and Sheila sees that Angie has squeezed the bag of marshmallow peanuts into a tight ball.

"Jesus, I'm sorry," Sheila says. "Forget what I said. It's not going to happen. Even the president wouldn't be that dumb, to start a war that no one can survive. There wouldn't be any point."

Even as she says it, Sheila knows some people don't need a point. They just need weakness. They don't care what they do to themselves as long as they get the other guy first.

That night, in Sheila's dreams, the mushroom clouds keep exploding. She trudges through a cold wind that scrapes like sandpaper. She wraps a shirt around her face and mouth to keep from choking. She walks what feels like a thousand years, pushing one foot in front of the other. She doesn't know what she is trying to reach, only that it is ahead of her.

☙❧

EARL'S TREE STAND looks over a ridge to the west of the house, resting in the fork of two crooked oaks. Below it, blueberry bushes grow knee-high, and laurels rise to head height, their twisted trunks crowned with waxy green leaves.

Angie crosses the slope, dodging rocks coated in a thick sponge of moss. When she reaches the oaks, she climbs hand over hand up the slats nailed between the trunks. She pokes her head through the hole cut in the plywood floor and pulls herself inside. From here, she should be able to get a better look at the hollow mountain.

That bunker must be why the Russian scout was sniffing around. Then he had to kill those women, and his cover was blown. That's how you knew he was a bad guy: According to the movies, good guys only kill civilians if they can't help it, and they feel bad about it afterward. If he felt bad about it, he wouldn't have gone on the run.

Someone has been in the tree stand recently. Their evidence is everywhere: an empty can of Old Milwaukee and plastic cartridge shells. A crumpled packet of Skoal with a few flakes of dried tobacco left inside. A black sleeping bag that smells of mold and wintergreen, the flannel liner patterned with mallards in flight. It can't have been Earl, who hasn't been able to climb since his diabetic foot was amputated last year.

Angie discovers a discarded magazine, its shiny pages displaying women naked and pink, all of their insides showing out. The girls all look the same, just different shoes and different hair and their breast balloons inflated more or less. Boring.

Instead, Angie imagines that she's been caught by the Russian soldiers. The head Russki has the face of Troy Eckheart, star of the baseball team, who sucks face with Tara McDonnell against her locker between classes and has summer pool parties at his parents' house below the ski slope where everyone gets drunk and swims naked and Angie and Sheila will never be invited in a million years.

Russian Troy lowers his machine gun. Under his black leather hat with the fur trim, his gaze is stern and communist. He says Angie's name with his husky Russian accent, and something in Angie turns to red-hot liquid, like she has stuffed chemical hand warmers down the front of her pants.

She's burning and itching at the same time. But she mustn't move. She must be quiet, stoic, strong—give nothing away. The survival of the human race depends on her. She squirms back against the rough boards. Her thighs brush together, and the sensation thrills. Goose bumps trill up her arm. So she does it again, crossing her knees and grinding everything together.

All the while, Russian Troy is glaring and threatening, and now he is taking down his pants like the men in the magazine.

Or is he? Does she want him to do that?

Angie rewinds the tape a little, goes back to his face inches from hers, full of attention and menace.

How much menace?

She adjusts and fine-tunes, like angling the arms of the TV antenna to get the picture back in place. A sneer on his lips, but kindness in his eyes. No, not kindness. Determination. Brutality but not contempt. There, like that.

If he is going to take off his pants, it only makes sense that she should take hers off too. She reaches under her sweat-shirt and undoes the button on her jeans. Pushes them down, and her panties too. Thinks that rebel fighters probably don't wear cotton panties with daisies printed on them, but thrusts that aside before it interferes too much.

The wild, fresh air hits that part of her, and that alone is exciting. The sun shines, the trees ripple, everything is normal, and yet she is up here in the sky with her pants down around her knees, feeling so full like she might burst. Russian Troy is there too, but she doesn't know what to do with him now. Doesn't know how to use him to fix this. The movies don't go any further.

Just as she's trying to figure it out, a voice shouts in the distance. Angie turns her head and squints through a gap in the railing. Two dogs hunt across the slope with their noses to the ground, trailed by men in trooper's uniforms.

The police will want to know that someone has been here, using the tree stand. It might be a valuable clue. She buttons her pants and scrambles down the ladder, but when she gets to the bottom, the men and dogs are almost over the crest of the ridge.

Angie chases after them, waving her hands. "Wait, stop!"

An officer at the back of the group motions her away. "Stay back," he calls.

"I've got information. Over there." She points toward Earl's tree stand. "Somebody's been up there."

The officer looks at her from under his wide-brimmed hat. It is not the look of one comrade to another. It is not a look between equals.

"I mean it." Angie tucks her chin against her chest, trying to keep her voice low and gruff, man-to-man. "The murderer might have been using it for a hideout. There's a beer and some—" she can't mention the magazine "—and a sleeping bag and stuff."

"Is that so?" All of the men are looking at her now, and the dogs too, their long pink tongues drooping from their open mouths like they are laughing.

"I just saw it." They'd take her seriously if she were bigger, if she had a uniform too.

"You don't think your mystery man in that deer stand might have been—" he draws out the silence "—a hunter?"

"It's not deer season!" Angie thought the police were supposed to be smart. But this one doesn't seem to know anything.

The officer puts his hands on his hips, like he's talking to an audience at the school assembly. "This isn't a game, little girl. Catching criminals is a job for grown-ups." He glances around the otherwise empty forest stretching in all directions. "What are you doing out here on your own? Where are your parents?"

"I live here," Angie says. "I know what I'm talking about!"

The man nods. "Sure." He seems like he might be about to say something else, but a voice crackles over the walkie-talkie clipped to his belt, and he turns away.

"Ten-four," he says into the box. He circles his finger in the air and calls to the men. "Wrap it up! HQ is bringing us in."

"You should go home," he says over his shoulder to Angie as the pack of them leave, carving a path through the forest as stealthy as a freight train, sounding the alarm to every bird and squirrel and deer and fugitive for miles around.

SIX

The Gobbling Beak

USUALLY WHEN THEIR MOM COMES HOME IN HER uniform with her swollen feet in orthopedic shoes and her face sagging with fatigue, she brings with her the uniquely depressing smell of the asylum: Pine-Sol, wet paper, boiled beans and cabbage. But tonight she has a paper bag that she drops onto the table alongside her purse and car keys.

Angie skids into the room on bare feet and peers into the bag, which is stuffed with barbecued chicken—whole legs and thighs wrapped in foil sticky with grease and smoky with pepper and charred paprika. The smell brings all the dogs into the house to whine around the legs of the table.

"We can't afford this," Sheila says.

"The fire company's raising money to give a reward for information about that murderer. We're not so poor we can't help out," says Bonnie. They are that poor, of course, but she feels like she owes it to the girls to go through the show of pretending otherwise. Things will be better when Sam comes home. That's what she keeps telling herself.

"I could work," Sheila says. "I could come with you to Iron Mountain."

"You're going to stay in school."

"I will. But in the summer."

"That asylum is no place for a girl," the old woman says, leaning on her cane as she limps into the room and pulls out her chair.

Maybe it isn't, Sheila thinks as she passes out plates and fills a pitcher with water, *but at least it wouldn't be* here. *In this house, with these people, where nothing ever changes.*

Hunger leaps in her stomach. Sheila can already taste the salty, greasy meat. Her wanting is so strong she feels dizzy while she sets out bread and margarine and a crock of last season's pickles.

They all sit at the table, and Bonnie tells them that another nurse at the asylum is going on maternity leave so it might mean more shifts for her. The old woman has her own knife with a worn antler handle. She works the curved blade into a chicken thigh and scrapes off the meat.

Angie picks the meat off the bones and piles it on the side of her plate. Then she grabs a fistful of bread slices and assembles one-handed sandwiches crammed with slabs of margarine and pickles heaped on top of the chicken.

"What?" she demands, when she catches Sheila looking at her. "I've got to keep my strength up if I'm going to catch that murderer."

Sheila pretends to have a stomachache, that she ate something bad at school and isn't feeling well. She fixes herself a piece of plain bread and margarine and washes it down with water. It would be easier if she could carry her plate to her room or out onto the porch, but she stays at the table with the others, with the gut-twisting smell of the chicken, and watches them tear into it. She knows that if you want something too badly, you get hurt. But if you can deny yourself, you're protected.

Later, after the feast is finished and the table is cleared, and Bonnie has gone to remove her uniform and the old woman is back in her room, and Angie is chasing the dogs around the house pretending to capture them and take them prisoner, Sheila slips away to the trash. She unrolls the greasy foil and smashes her face into it, licking with a frenzy, pressing it closer and closer, the smell filling the whole cavity of her head. Licking until the foil cracks and she can taste the metal and still she can't stop.

Sheila knows she is dangerous inside, and this is the proof. This is why she has to hold herself back. She doesn't know what would happen if she didn't, but she can sense the terrible force when it leaps at the cage bars like this. She never wants to look this monster in the eye, but she knows it lives inside her, a prisoner in the cellar who she must never let break free.

When she finishes, the foil is in shreds, and the smell of chicken engulfs her. There is grease in her hair, her bangs wet and sticky with it, and paprika on her eyebrows. Sheila plunges the foil back into the trash barrel, crushed into the tightest ball. She wipes her face on the inside of her shirt, holds her hands out for a dog to lick, and dries her palms on the back of her pants.

LAST YEAR, A new girl joined Sheila's class at school. Her name is Juanita Herman.

The new girl wears clothes that pass but don't brag. At lunch, where Sheila drops her free lunch ticket into the trash and every day props the same crumpled paper bag and empty milk carton in front of her to evade the watchful scrutiny of Mrs. Richardson, the lunchroom monitor, Juanita sits at the end of the table, on the fringe of a middling group of girls who are slightly studious and slightly pretty. Juanita is not too smart and not too poor, and she fits in with them well. She is okay, normal. No one dumps milk over her head or shoots spitballs into her hair. When the other girls talk, Juanita swivels her head to follow, as if she is trying to learn from them. But Sheila never sees Juanita join in. Teachers never call on her in class. Sometimes Sheila wonders if she is the only one who can see Juanita.

In the one class they share, Juanita keeps her head down and writes carefully in her composition book, recording the dates of presidents and battles in the Civil War. She is left-handed, and the crook of her arm shields her words from Sheila's view. Sheila wants to talk to her, but she has no idea what she would say.

Besides, Sheila isn't sure what she wants to happen after she talks to the new girl. Sheila has seen what passes for friendship among the other girls at school and isn't sure that she's not better off without it. Once, when she was in third grade, before who was a real person and who was not had been fully established, Sheila had an almost-friend. She invited this almost-friend for a sleepover, and the girl agreed.

But the next day, the girl came to school and said her mother had the flu, and so she wouldn't be able to come. Couldn't ever come.

After that, Sheila and the girl didn't talk, didn't turn cartwheels together on the playground anymore. They pretended the invitation and its cancellation never happened. As they got older, the girl never said the awful things the others did, but she didn't defend Sheila either. That's how Sheila knew she didn't have anything Juanita Herman would want. But she couldn't stop noticing her, watching her.

Today, when the seniors are looking forward to graduation and everybody is talking about summer jobs at the Tastee Treat and trips to the amusement park in Hershey, and how Crissy Martin swears she saw the murderer watching outside her window when she was getting undressed last night, Juanita looks up as she passes Sheila in the hall between Vocational Agriculture and Problems of Democracy. It's just the smallest glance from under her short lashes, but Sheila feels like she has been seen.

Sheila is hot with alarm, sweat prickling under her arms. Juanita was probably looking over Sheila's shoulder at some boy or teacher behind her.

But what if she wasn't?

SEVEN

The Starved Woman

IT RAINS FOR THREE NIGHTS AND THREE DAYS. THE rain beats on the tin roof so close and so loud that it pierces Sheila's thoughts. Everything drips. The dogs huddle on the porch, whining to be let inside. Sheila pulls a plastic poncho over her head and splashes out to feed the rabbits and the chickens. The chickens squawk angrily, restless. The rabbits don't care. They are safe and dry and warm together, piled in straw.

Angie is impossible. She races up and down the stairs and tries to bring the muddy dogs into the house to play. She practices surveillance, stalking after Sheila, leaping out at her from around doorways and behind furniture, until Sheila threatens to kick her into next week if she doesn't stop it right now this instant.

Angie flops in front of the TV, but the rain and clouds mess with the reception and all the faces are red and blue shadows of themselves, the voices garbled by a static hiss that echoes the rain outside. Angie lies on her stomach and draws and draws.

The old woman complains of her aches—her legs and her hips and her fingers all gnarled by arthritis. The damp seeps into every part of the house. A tin pan catches the leak dripping into the kitchen. Angie has only knocked it over twice. The mother drives to the asylum for her shifts and reports on the flood stages at the bridges she crosses. Their own lane is so washed out that she parks the car at the bottom for fear of scraping a hole in the oil pan—it's their only transportation and the link to her job and income and can't be risked.

At last the rain stops, but water slops everywhere. The cellar is flooded. Half the spring seedlings and all of the new-sown seeds in the garden have been swept away. Once-neat rows are now a tumbled field of muck and leaf and gravel washed down from higher on the mountain. Spontaneous springs gush from the slope behind the house, carving fresh channels across the garden and yard to join the creek roaring in the valley below.

Sheila takes charge, locating shovels, rakes, and hoes. First they must fix the garden, and then the lane. She can't trust Angie near the delicate plants so sends her instead to carve a channel around the chicken pen and drain the lagoon that laps beneath their perch.

Angie scrapes her hoe through the mud. She can't believe she has ended up in a prison camp, forced to labor for the enemy. When she catches the murderer, he's the one who's going to be sweating on a chain gang.

But for now she keeps her head down. It's better if she pretends to be obedient until she sees the perfect chance to make a run for it. She can't outwit the enemy just by being stronger. She has to be smarter.

Angie runs through escape strategies in her head until the blade of her hoe snags on a root. She hacks at it, but it won't budge. She flings the hoe aside and crouches down. She reaches into the cold mud and tugs at the thing, but it stretches down for miles. *Wires,* she thinks. Telegraph wires and secret communication lines.

Her fingers cramp with the sudden urge to draw. She abandons her hoe and heads into the house, tracking sludge behind her. Angie sits down at the kitchen table and uncaps a marker with her filthy hands.

☙

THE WATER SLOPPING around Sheila's ankles is flowing downhill as fast as it can, but the soil has absorbed as much as it can hold, and there's nowhere for it to go. Sheila rolls up her pant legs and works barefoot to save a pair of shoes. Stepping in the icy muck makes her flinch, but she bites down on those feelings and plods on, gripping the hoe until she can't feel it anymore.

She digs deep channels to route the water around the garden. Picks out rocks and branches, clumps of moss, and the matted carcass of a squirrel that didn't survive the winter and has been washed out by the flood. She shores up the earth around the bean trellis and rights the toppling poles. The stand of rhubarb is fine. Some of the onions and most of the peas—while buried and filthy—were strong enough to survive. But the carrots, the spinach, and the beets are a total loss.

Sheila's hands are red from hoeing. She is used to the work, but her skin is wet, and the wooden handle is rough and swollen from the days of damp. A splinter slides under the soft skin of her finger. She drops the hoe and brings the finger to her mouth to suck, getting a tongueful of fresh mountain dirt.

When she goes inside, she finds Angie, head bent, scribbling away at one of her drawings. Sheila opens the cabinet over the stove for a box of matches and a fat needle. It's a good thing the splinter is in her left hand. She steadies her wrist against the table and flicks the needle's point over her skin, feeling for the wooden tip. She sucks her breath when she hits it.

Angie is drawing so hard the table shakes. Sheila glares. "Can you stop that? Just for a minute?"

"I gotta finish." Angie's hand keeps moving. The table keeps shaking.

Sheila shoves the table so the edge rams into Angie's chest. "I told you to stop! I can't get this splinter out if you keep moving the table. Which you'd know if you were out there helping me like you're supposed to instead of hiding in here and drawing your stupid cards."

"She wants to get out. I'll get back to it when I finish this," Angie says, her marker suspended above the card.

Sheila digs with the needle until the splinter releases, along with a bead of red blood. She squeezes to make sure she's got it all, then pours peroxide over the hole, watching as it bubbles and stings.

Angie comes over beside her, peering at Sheila's hand. She smells of spearmint gum and dank things growing underground. "Does it hurt?"

"A little. But there's nothing to see. It's gone now." Sheila dries her hand. "What do you want?"

"Here." Angie holds out the card she has been drawing. "It's for you."

Sheila glances down without interest. Angie's cards are some private game, and they have nothing to do with her. But when she sees this one, Sheila feels like a tree limb has snapped under her and she is already flat on her back with twigs in her hair and blood on her chin before she has figured out what is happening.

The woman on the card kneels on broken crockery, her face smeared with grease and blood. She has a mouth as big as the sun and black sinkhole eyes. Her clothes are torn to rags, showing her naked ribs and flat, bare breasts. A gouge in the center of her chest is a vortex that swirls endlessly down into the earth. Her intestines are a tangle of worms and roots that end in fists of claws. Her long black tongue unfurls all the way to the ground, where its pointed tip probes a pile of jagged chicken bones.

Black spots hit Sheila's eyes, and the rope tightens around her neck. She can't find her breath anywhere. The cornbread and drippings she ate for breakfast are halfway back up her throat. She swallows hard and clenches her teeth. She will *not*.

"You little shit. What do you mean by this?"

Angie flinches in surprise. "I thought you would know. She wouldn't tell me her name."

"How did you—" Sheila stops herself. It's just Angie and her stupid cards. She draws them all the time. They don't mean anything, no more than her fantasies about Russian invasions and zombie hordes. It's all part of her refusal to confront reality, the way she gets out of and around everything.

Sheila turns her back on Angie and the hideous card and returns to the garden and picks up her hoe. Angie chases after her, calling out, "It's for you. You have to take it."

That disgusting woman, that distorted mirror of Sheila's own insides is grinning there in Angie's hand, and the water is rushing in her ears. Sheila snatches the card from Angie and rips the awful woman in half, right through her terrifying, voracious middle.

"You can't do that!" Angie yells, looking like she is about to cry.

"No?" Something is building inside Sheila, encouraging her to take satisfaction in her sister's distress. It's ballooning inside her, and she's not inclined to block it.

"You said it was mine, so I can do whatever I want with it. And I'm going to do this." Sheila tears the card's halves into strips and stacks them and tears those into bits. Then she opens her hand and lets the pieces fall into the silted water rushing from the garden.

Angie jerks forward, trying to stop the pieces from falling, to save and collect them. But they are tumbling into the muddy water, carried down the mountain and into the creek and forever away.

EIGHT

The Man of Stone

ANGIE CIRCLES THE HOUSE, CROUCHED LOW AND ducking whenever she passes a window. She talks about booby traps and fishing line and the best places to lay a trip wire.

"He's not going to come here," Sheila says, pushing past her with a basket of wet laundry. She carries it out to the line strung between the house and a straight young poplar, draping shirts and socks and graying underwear over the cord and clipping them fast.

Despite what she says to Angie, Sheila lay awake in her bed last night, listening to every sound from the woods, each snapped branch and tumbled rock, trying to imagine what she would do if the killer burst into their room while they were asleep, their mom out at the asylum and the old woman helpless downstairs.

"You don't know that." Angie weaves between the flapping clothes.

"Even if he does, do you think he's going to be scared off by a twelve-year-old girl with a dish towel wrapped around her head pretending to be Rambo?" Sheila flicks a wet pillowcase at her. Angie squeals and twists away.

"If you knock anything down, you're washing the whole mess again, and I'm not helping you," Sheila says.

Angie picks up a stick and aims it at Sheila like a gun. "Rambo could take down that murderer single-handed."

Sheila hangs a last sock and heads for the house with the empty basket. "Probably. But what's that got to do with you?"

Angie chases after her. "It's not like the police are going to catch him. They're not even trying."

"You two are like a pair of cats," Thena says as they pass her drowsing on the porch, her dress pulled up to her knees to catch the sun's warmth. "You make my head hurt."

"She started it," Angie says.

"You're the one who's getting in my way while I try to make sure you have some clean clothes to wear so you don't stink. Least not any more than you usually do."

Thena pats Angie's leg with a twisted hand. "Angie, you come sit by me and let your sister get on with her work."

Angie plops down beside Thena, and the old woman taps Angie's shoulder. "Did I ever tell you about the time I met the man made of stone?"

The old woman *has* told them. Many times. Sheila used to like sitting like Angie is now, listening to Thena's stories, back when the rope was only a few threads thick, barely a tickle against her throat. Before she ever imagined the binding snare it would grow into. In those days, the stories had seemed to hold some essential information that she needed to know. But after she heard them over and over and nothing changed, she knew she had been wrong.

Lately it felt to Sheila like the stories were vines spooling out of Thena's mouth and seeking across the floor, stretching their tendrils into her ears, crawling into her body and twining around her heart, wrapping every bone and tendon and sinew. The stories tethered her to Thena, the family, the house, the mountain, forming links that were impossible to break.

"Weren't you worried he was a ghost?" Angie asks.

"I've seen plenty of dead men in my life. He weren't no haint." The old woman talks as if she is telling the story to Angie, but above Angie's head her milky cataract eyes drift over to Sheila.

"How can you be sure?" Sheila asks, hovering in the doorway. "How many ghosts have you seen?"

"Well, now." The old woman tilts her head and shuffles through her memories. "There was little Edith after the fire. That old man who drowned in Cooper's Creek and hung around the bridge near the sugar camp and spooked everybody's horses. And that bunch of Rebel soldiers up at Blue Ridge where they had that skirmish."

"Stop interrupting," Angie says. "I want to hear about the monster."

"I didn't call him a monster. What makes you say that?" Thena seems offended, like Angie has said a bad word in church. Not that they go to church all that much, unless somebody gets married or dies.

"Because he's not a ghost, and he's not a man, and he's made of stone," Angie ticks the points off on her fingers. "What else could he be?"

Thena laughs. "There's more kinds of things in this world than men and ghosts."

Sheila's fingers tighten along the basket's rim. She is too old to be listening to this nonsense.

"I was just a girl like you two, and it was my job to carry water to my brothers at the mine," Thena continues. "This was right at the height of the copper boom—they were digging the guts out of the mountain like nobody's business." She stops, remembering. "In fact, a few days earlier, they blasted so hard they about blew the top of Bear Ridge clean away. Effie and I felt the ground shake all the way over here."

"I wish I could have seen that!" Angie says.

"I was just minding my business, carrying my buckets, and when I got halfway there, this man stepped right out in front of me, blocking my path. He came from nowhere, like he'd stepped straight out of the mountain's side."

"There must have been a cave," Sheila says. The stories have snared her again. She's still listening, still standing there, the empty clothes basket dangling from the end of her hand.

Thena waves this away. "No cave. I half spilled that water, I was so surprised. His clothes were gray, like the feathers on a dove. His skin was gray, and his hair was gray, but he was a young man—tall and handsome and strong. He asked me for a drink of the water I was carrying."

"Did you give it to him?" Angie asks.

"I couldn't rightly refuse. But I watched him close to see what would happen. If he wasn't a man, might be he would choke on the water. But he swallowed it down and wiped his lip afterwards, smiling at me."

Sheila scratches her neck, the rope feeling suddenly tight.

Thena folds her hands in her lap. "I wasn't too worried. I had salt in my pocket—I figured that would fix him if he tried anything. But he caught my wrist before I could reach for it and nodded at me like we were playing a game and I had handed him the next move. He said he had seen me walking here before and he liked the look of me, if you can believe it. He said he wanted my help."

"What did you do?" Angie asks.

"The same thing she does every time," Sheila says. "You know how this story goes."

"Come on, I'm not a little kid anymore," Angie says. "You can tell the truth this time. Did you fight him off? Did you fake a sprained ankle and then bash him in the head with the water bucket so you could get away?"

"Don't be a baby." Sheila is getting a nasty satisfaction from spoiling Angie's fun. It swells inside her like licking the chicken grease from the wrappers in the trash, both delicious and wrong. She recites the end of the story: "One of the miners came by and asked if the man was bothering her. She said yes, and he told the man to go away, and then the miner walked her all the way home."

"No, your sister's right," Thena says. "It's about time you heard the truth. There was no miner."

Both girls swing their heads to stare at the old woman.

"I knew it!" Angie jumps to her feet. "I always knew there was something else. I bet you had a knife hidden in your sock and you fought him off!" She slashes the air with an imaginary blade.

"He held out his hand, and I took it."

"You *what*?" Angie's disgust is as thick as the scum on a puddle at the end of August. How could the old woman be so pathetic? How could she have been such a girl?

A laugh barks out of the old woman's throat. "There isn't always going to be someone there to save you. If some handsome miner had come along to walk me home, I reckon I'd have married him and moved away like all the other girls did."

Sheila runs her finger along the edge of the rope, trying to lift it away from her skin. "Where did this gray man take you? Who was he?"

"Now that I don't know. The last thing I remember is setting down my bucket. They say I was gone for three days." Thena slides her palms over her thighs. Maybe Sheila is imagining it, but it feels like the old woman's half-seeing eyes are again turned toward her, like there is something she wants Sheila to understand.

"Effie found me at the edge of the cow pasture, stretched out under the mayapples and covered in fine gray sand. All over, like I had been rolled in it. On my eyelashes and under my fingernails and even my toenails. Inside my ears, under my tongue, and all through my hair. It took three washes and twice as many rinses to get all that dust out. For weeks, I kept finding more in my shoes and pockets." Thena rubs her fingers together, like she is still feeling the grit. "Seemed like I was never going to be rid of it."

Angie sinks back to the floor and lands on Sheila's feet. Sometime during the telling, Sheila has dropped her basket without even noticing and glided onto the porch, standing right beside the old woman. Her ears are buzzing.

Thena looks up and says, "Angie, go and fetch my keepsake box."

"I'll get it," Sheila says. She wants to get away from whatever just happened. She wants to pull her face back to normal before anyone else sees it. She wants time to think.

THE OLD WOMAN'S room smells of camphor and cotton. Dog-eared paperbacks of cowboy adventures in the Old West, bought five cents apiece at the Christian Mission charity store, are stacked on the table beside the bed, next to a magnifying glass and a milk-green candy jar in the shape of a rabbit. A cut-paper silhouette of the old woman when she was young hangs on the wall, a long pigtail trailing down her back, her profile sharp and tight. An enamel pitcher and basin sit on a carved wooden dresser pushed against the wall.

Sheila squeezes into the gap and lifts the lid on the cedar blanket chest at the foot of the bed and finds the dented tin the old woman asked for, its black-and-gold design faded to a rusty charcoal. She's tempted to open it and see what's inside this secret box that holds odds and ends of memories. What did the old woman save from her encounter with the man of stone?

But it's not hers to dig through. Sheila closes the lid on the chest, and as she turns to go, the rope snags on the corner and jerks her off-balance. She tumbles onto the bed, her arm flailing against the wobbly table. The candy jar tips over and rolls to the edge, then thumps on the floor, breaking open. The sweet, medicinal scent of clove fills the air.

Sheila tugs the rope free and slides off the bed onto her hands and knees. Thena has had that candy jar since she was a girl. If Sheila has broken it, she can't replace it. The milk glass rabbit is split in half, its feet and body rocking near the bed, the head and ears rolled under the dresser. Sheila rights the bottom half and puts it back on the table. She gropes after the head, afraid of what she will find. But it's fine. She runs her hands over it, feeling for chips and cracks, but the glass is smooth under her fingers, the rabbit's ears whole, its face undamaged. She lets out the breath she was holding.

As she restores the jar to the table, something crunches underfoot. The candy. She still has to clean up the candy. The sweets that were once in the jar have rolled into every crevice, even under the bed. She clambers back onto her knees and scrabbles across the floor, scooping them into her palm. The impulse to stuff one in her mouth and clamp down, sucking until the sharp edges cut her gums and blood mixes with the sugar, washing down the back of her throat, is overpowering.

She shuts her eyes against the feeling, but she knows she's going to eat one, and then another and another. Once the sweetness engulfs her, she will keep eating them, crusted with grit, spider legs and all. But then freezing air gusts over her bare arm. It's like a fan blowing over ice cubes, and it's coming straight from under the old woman's bed.

The voices of Angie and Thena still thrum from the porch. Sheila regains her control and dumps the candy into the rabbit's neck, folds the quilt covering the bed so it won't drag on the floor, and as quietly as she can, heaves Thena's bed away from the wall. There, in the middle of the dusty floor, a few inches from the curled body of a long-dead mouse, is a trapdoor with a small handle of twisted iron.

Sheila pulls the handle and the door swings back on invisible hinges. Beneath it, wooden stairs lead down into the dark. The first two steps are dusted with a layer of fine gray sand. She can't see beyond the third step. A faint whistling comes from the darkness below, drifting on a current of cold, mineral air.

Sheila kneels at the edge and sticks her head a little way into the opening. But it's as black as black, and she can't see. She settles on the edge and lets a foot hang over. She is easing her weight—slowly, slowly—onto the first step when footsteps pound in the hall outside.

She scrambles to her feet, drops the trapdoor shut, and begins moving the bed to cover it.

"Can't you find it? She's bugging out." Angie sticks her head into the room as Sheila is smoothing the quilt back into place.

"I got it now." Sheila picks up the dented tin and hands it to Angie. "What does she want it for anyways? Did she say?"

"I think she's got a picture of Effie in there. She keeps talking about her, wishing she could see her again." Angie turns the tin in her hands. "Do you know when Effie died?"

Sheila lets a puff of air escape from her lips. "I think it's been a long time. All of her stories about Effie are from when they were kids."

"She must really miss her," Angie says.

"Yeah. Hey, do you want these?" Sheila holds out a handful of the spilled candy, lightly fuzzed with dust.

NINE

The Ragged Membrane

UNDER THE HOUSE, BENEATH THE FLOOR, UNDER the cellar, below the roots and beetles, beneath the limestone aquifers, the rabbit women's blood-cry works it slow way into the mountain's core. Their lament trickles and creeps, slides and drips, journeying deep inside.

What is days to humans and generations to mayflies is a mere flash of lightning to the mountain. As the rabbit women's grief is borne along, the force of it corrodes barriers and stretches membranes that keep apart things not meant to be together. Chambers buck and spasm. Old routes close. New routes open.

The mountain tries to tend to this splinter of grief, but it has penetrated far inside. So much else demands attention.

It's spring, and there is much to do: rockslides and moss carpets and new shoots. Baby turkeys and hungry weasels and lusting box turtles. Creeks running over banks and washing gluttonous holes in blacktopped roads. Foundations to erode, bones to dissolve, bacteria to incubate, toxic fungus to propagate.

So the mountain doesn't notice when those ragged membranes let leak something that has been sealed for a long time, when some shard of natural chaos combusts into being. Doesn't notice when, on her other side, some volatile, neglected aspect, both new and old, breaks free of its underground bonds and pops out into the daylight world.

TEN

The Bloody Red Eye

ONE OF THE THINGS SHEILA LIKES BEST ABOUT WORK-
ing at the Iron Mountain Rehabilitative Facility is that she is
surrounded by women. Many of the inmates are men, of course,
but they are locked behind doors on wards she will never visit.
The doctors and orderlies are all men, but except when the
orderlies pick up supper carts or return empty trays, she rarely
sees them. Even better, there are no boys her own age.

Sheila washes dishes in the asylum's basement kitchen.
Extractor fans roar, hoses spray, cart wheels roll and creak.
She drips with sweat, and gravy-flavored steam runs into her
eyes and down her neck, trickling under the stiff fibers of
the rope where it chafes her damp skin. Food here is never

a temptation. After spending hours in the kitchen with the revolting dregs swilling in the dishwater, the colors and flavors all mixed up, Sheila would be happy to never eat again. Just the thought of putting that pre-rotted stuff inside her body is impossible.

In the distance, a bell rings. Sheila hears it, but she is deep in the rhythm of her own interior space, and the sound seems far away. Then Martha the cook is by her side, shaking her arm and telling her they have to go out. Sheila releases the hose, and the water stops spraying and flows down the sink's drain.

She follows Martha out the side door into a blast of predawn chill. A fine drizzle falls on the pines and rhododendrons. Sheila hears its faint patter on the leaves, though she barely feels it on her skin. The smell of wet earth releases into the air, the decay of leaf and bug rising like steam.

The women who peel potatoes and mop the floors are waiting on the gravel by the dumpsters. Sheila's been done with school for less than a week and has only had this job for two days—she recognizes some faces but doesn't know their names. She doesn't see her mother among them. Doesn't hear or sense her in the sighs breathed out, the cigarettes retrieved from the pockets of dark blue smocks.

"They could have at least waited until my shift was over to start this foolishness again," says a dark-haired woman with painted pink nails.

"Why complain about a break?" asks an older woman tying a plastic rain bonnet over her gray curls. "I don't mind setting my mop down for a spell."

"Well, I have rolls in the oven," Martha says. "If I don't get back inside in ten minutes, they're going to burn to a crisp.

Then we'll have a real fire on our hands. This is the third time this month that the alarm has gone off. Do you see any smoke?" She wipes her hands on her apron. "I didn't think so. It's all that funny business on G Ward that keeps setting the system off."

All the women flick their eyes at the barred windows of the third floor. Sheila wonders why the patients haven't been evacuated too, but then she spots the untidy human rows lined up on the lawn under the spotlights, ringed by scowling orderlies with arms crossed over their white-uniformed chests. Behind them, the tall, loose-limbed figure of a teenage boy slouches across the lawn. He wears jeans and a black sweatshirt, and no one is paying him any attention.

"You need to stop worrying about G Ward," says the woman with pink nails. "Those loonies are locked up. It's that one still running around free in the woods that worries me."

"Ah, Jesus, what is the world coming to?" asks another cleaner, tapping ash from the end of her cigarette. "That was just terrible. Those poor girls."

"I told my daughters they're not to go anywhere alone until that lunatic is caught," Martha says.

A short young woman in an aide's uniform says, "My cousin Jimmy is on the ambulance service. He says the police don't have a clue. Not a single, solitary idea about who did it or where that maniac is now. That is not at all the kind of thing I like to think about when I'm driving myself over here in the middle of the night."

"I made Dean give me his shotgun," says the woman in the rain bonnet. "I keep it in the passenger's seat, loaded and ready to go. If that pervert tries to hijack me, it'll be the worst decision he's ever made."

The women laugh, chasing away their fears. Away from the heat of the kitchen, Sheila's temperature has dropped, and she pulls her arms to her chest and hunches her shoulders, wishing they could all go back inside. She rubs the tips of her fingers, which are bloodless and faintly blue. No matter what she does, she can't seem to get warm.

"What do you think?" asks a voice in Sheila's ear.

Her muscles want to flinch, but she clamps down on them and turns to see who is talking to her. It's the boy in the black sweatshirt she saw sloping across the lawn earlier, only now he is here, right beside her. His lank hair straggles over his forehead, and she can't quite see his face.

A little squirt of acid trickles through Sheila's veins. Someone like him is not supposed to be here. Here is supposed to be safe. She's supposed to spend her shift bent over the sink washing dishes and then go home. That's it.

"Don't you know it's rude not to answer a question?" His teasing tone signals greater danger.

Is he a worker? A patient? His rumpled sweatshirt doesn't look like any kind of uniform. Sheila glances at the other women, but they aren't paying attention. Martha is talking to a woman in cat-eye glasses that Sheila thinks works upstairs in the office, but Sheila is definitely in her line of sight. Martha's not waving her arms or shouting at Sheila to step away, be careful. So this boy must be known to them, must not be any real threat.

He follows her gaze and waves a dismissive hand. "Oh, they don't mind about me."

She's going to reply when he brushes his hair out of his face. This time she does flinch. Just below the pupil of the boy's right eye, a bloody red spot blooms in the white. Sheila wobbles. Something about that red spot in the white eye is firing a warning that cuts the strings in the backs of her knees and makes her vision swim.

"What's the matter? Are you afraid of something?"

"In case you haven't heard, there's a murderer on the loose," she snaps.

"Seems like you ought to be safe enough here."

Conversations like this are a maze with no right answers. Whatever she says will be turned against her. If she were closer to the woods, she could slip behind the cover of the deep-green leaves and disappear. But the distance is too far. The fire drill will be over soon, and she will be expected back at her station at the sink.

"I don't have to talk to you." Sheila carefully slides her gaze back toward him, avoiding the red spot in his eye. She needs to keep this as neutral as she can and get away as soon as possible. "I'm just here to do my job."

"That's no reason we can't talk," he says. "I don't see many people like you around here."

She wonders what he means by that: Young people? Teenagers like him? Or ugly, weak people he can torment, people who make good victims?

The back door to the asylum opens. Sheila can't hear what the night superintendent says, but by the movement of the other women, stubbing out their cigarettes and peeling away from the wall, she knows they are cleared to go back inside.

Sheila turns to follow them, but she has taken only two steps when she jerks to a halt, the rope yanked tight against her neck, cutting into her flesh and choking off her breath.

She whips around. The boy is where she left him, one leg outstretched. The toe of his high-top sneaker presses into the ground as if trapping something underneath.

He lifts his foot and the pressure on her neck releases, the rope slackens. She stares at him as she rubs her neck and coughs. No one can see the rope. No one has ever seen the rope. Not the kids at school, not the teachers, not the women here at the asylum; not Angie, her mom, or the old woman.

"How did you—"

"It's this." The boy points to his damaged eye. "It lets me see things."

Sheila swallows her disgust. She can't look at that red spot. She can hardly get the words out over her shock and fear. "I can't believe you did that."

He bunches his hands in his sweatshirt pockets, and his shoulders sag a little. "I just wanted you to stay. To talk to me some more."

"That's not the way to do it." Sheila wrenches the rope, twitching the end out of his reach. She runs after the other women, desperate for the sanctuary of the kitchen. As soon as she gets inside, she slumps against the wall and shuts her eyes, heart slamming against her ribs.

When she gets her breath back, she cracks the door and peeks outside, but the gravel space is empty and the boy is gone. His black sweatshirt is nowhere to be seen. She catches a movement in the woods among the crowded laurels, but it's only a rabbit behind the dumpster, hopping cautiously into cover.

☙

WHEN SHEILA GETS to the car in the parking lot at the end of her shift, the rain has ended. A thick fog has rolled through the valley, shrouding the trees up to their knees and blocking the rays of the rising sun.

Anyone could be out there, Sheila thinks as she approaches the passenger side. She is so tired. Her feet ache, and the tips of her fingers are as wrinkled as the old woman's face. She left her blotched apron behind in the big canvas hamper, but her clothes underneath are limp. Her armpits are sticky, and she can't escape the smell of gravy.

The women talking during the fire drill must have got to her more than she realized. And then that encounter with the boy. The whole rest of her shift all she could think about was being hunted. How it would feel to be stalked and killed. To believe you were alone and safe in the shelter of the forest—and to be so very wrong.

Sheila's mother's footsteps crunch across the gravel, and she gets in on the driver's side, dropping her pocketbook onto the seat and sliding across to unlock Sheila's door. Sheila waits a moment longer, looking into the thick, uncertain woods. On this misty morning, they could hold any secret.

Sheila gets into the car, pulling the afghan down so it covers the rip in the seat where the stuffing shows through. She twists around and looks in the back seat. There's a folded shopping bag, some bottles to be returned, and a pair of pliers. The armrest ashtray is flipped up, but there's nothing in it except a petrified lump of Angie's chewing gum.

"What are you looking for?" Her mom turns the key, starting a conversation with the car's reluctant engine.

"Nothing." Sheila settles back into her seat. She flips the end of the rope so that it thumps against Bonnie's leg in the driver's seat, almost brushing her uniform. It occurs to Sheila that maybe her mom and everybody have been able to see the rope all this time and just not said anything, haven't done a thing to help her.

But Bonnie only smooths the wrinkle in her skirt without looking down. She turns the key again and pumps the gas pedal while she adjusts the radio dial. Her station—every station—is harder to pick up when the fog comes down. "There's no one back there."

"You don't know that." Sheila picks at the fringe of the afghan.

"Well, why would he be?"

"Because he killed two women twenty minutes from here. It's been two weeks and they aren't even close to catching him. He's still out there."

"There's people in there"—Bonnie tips her chin at the looming bulk of the asylum—"who've killed a lot more than two. Worse than killed."

"They're locked up! They're not going to hurt anyone." Sheila hopes this is true.

"It's halfway their own fault," her mother says. "What were two city girls doing out here anyhow?"

Sheila has wondered that much herself. She doesn't know what people from a city are like, what they want.

"People like that think a place like this is something you can read about in a book or watch on TV." Bonnie taps her fingers on the steering wheel. "They think you can just make a big list and take it to some fancy store, and then load your car with bags of stuff and you'll be prepared."

What she doesn't tell Sheila is that she, too, had once dreamed of exploring somewhere new, escaping these cramped green hollows, spilling out into the wide plains and on to the big, big mountains of the West, the Pacific coast shining beyond. She and Sheila's father, Rodney, were going to get on his motorcycle and go, her arms wrapped around his waist, her cheek pressed against his leather jacket, the road spooling away beneath them, the future laid out like a buffet for them to pick and choose from everything in the whole wide world on offer.

"You're talking about things like snakes and bears or getting lost and breaking your leg," Sheila says. "It wasn't the mountain that killed those two; it was a man. You heard the news: *brutally attacked*. He beat them to death with a rock."

Her mother sighs. "I'm not saying they deserved that. But they had no business being out here. They should have stayed where they belong."

Late at night, she and Rodney had lain in bed holding hands, pulling crackling drags on their cigarettes in the dark, orange ends glowing, dreaming together of what the world held for them, too young and stupid to know that they only had one more year together, that Sheila was already growing inside her, paddling like a tadpole in the warm murk of Bonnie's middle, swift and amphibious.

Bonnie twists the ignition again, and the engine splutters to life. The seat beneath Sheila's thighs trembles.

"That man will be a million miles from here. He's not going to stick around to be caught," Bonnie says as she steers them down the winding drive. A white convertible breezes past from the other direction, the director of the asylum behind the wheel.

Then they are out on the lonely roads, climbing the crest of the mountain to home. Ferns grow knee-deep along the shoulder, laced with briars and unripe raspberries, so thick they could hide a bear. Could hide anything, really.

ELEVEN

The Edge That Bites

WHEN SHEILA GOES OUT TO CHECK ON THE RAB-
bits' new litter she finds the latch dangling loose and the
door breached. Though the gap's only as wide as her finger,
Sheila is already picturing an empty pen as she pushes the
door open and checks inside. But everyone's still there, the
does and the five newcomers the size of large biscuits. Two
weeks old, their eyes open and their fur plush. They hop and
explore the hutch. All seems well enough.

The mother rabbit tramples over the kits when Sheila
brings handfuls of fresh dandelion and clover. Sue the dog
stands guard underfoot, her brown eyes following Sheila's
every move. Sue's fur is as black as the poured midnight
of the kind of dress Sheila imagines on Juanita when she

fantasizes about inviting her to a candlelit dinner, the kind where she pulls out the chair and pours wine without spilling a drop—though she has never seen anyone drink anything but beer from the can and moonshine out of jelly jars. But she knows about romance: it needs pearls and high heels and floaty music on the record player.

Sheila rinses the rabbits' bowls and refills the water from the pump. Before she closes the door, she snatches the nearest kit and brings it against the skin of her face. It is softer than anything.

Angie appears. She wasn't there a minute ago, but now she is wrenching open the hutch door. The baby rabbit squirms in Sheila's hand. Angie is wearing the dish towel around her head again, and streaks of orange marker decorate her cheeks.

"How many times have I told you?" Sheila says over her shoulder. "You've got to keep the latch closed. They'll get out."

"It wasn't me!"

"You expect me to believe that? I guess it was Thena's Man of Stone then?"

Angie pokes around with a stick under the hutch. "Look! Someone's been here."

"Quit your lying." Sheila says it tiredly, absently. It's only what she expects from Angie.

"It was him! The murderer!" Angie taps the stick on the ground. "He must have been here last night!"

Sheila looks where Angie points. There's some torn moss near the leg of the hutch, and the mud is disturbed in a way that could be a footprint. Or could just as easily be an animal scratching or the random patterns of water runoff.

Sheila checks to see if Sue is showing any interest in the spot of the alleged footprint. But the dog isn't paying any attention.

She's just looking longingly at the rabbits, captive in their pen.

"Don't be stupid," Sheila says, smoothing the mud over the so-called tread. If she can't see it, it was never there.

"What are you doing that for? You're erasing the evidence!"

"Evidence of what?" Still, Sheila does now remember the dogs setting off an awful racket in the middle of the night. She had yelled out the window at them to be quiet and then stuck her head under the pillow and gone back to sleep.

She picks up the rabbits one by one and counts them again, just to be sure. "They're all still here. None of the rabbits is missing."

"I thought you didn't believe me," Angie says.

"I don't. Run and get the food."

"Only if I can hold one first," Angie says.

Sheila bodychecks her sister and pushes the door shut again. "They're too little. Maybe next week."

"You're holding one."

"That's because I know how to hold them," Sheila says. "I'm responsible."

"Stop treating me like a baby. I know what I'm doing."

Sheila isn't going to stay here all day arguing with her. "Fine. But you have to promise to hold tight in case it kicks or jumps. It won't be trying to get away, but it's brand new and doesn't know any better."

"I know that."

Sheila holds the rabbit away from Angie's grabbing hands. "Good. So promise."

"I promise."

The kit's feet dangle as Sheila transfers it to Angie. As soon as Sheila releases her grip, Angie seems to open her fingers on purpose and let the rabbit drop. It falls to the ground, stunned and frozen. But it recovers quickly and hops for safety under the hutch. Sue, who has been watching with avid eyes, is after it in a flash.

"Sue! No!" Even as Sheila yells for her to stop, the dog snatches the tiny rabbit between her jaws.

Angie stares, arms slack at her sides. She looks to Sheila to do something to fix this, as if it hasn't all been her own fault. But it's Sheila who will have to pry the limp body from between Sue's teeth. Sheila who will hold its cooling weight, feel the deflated cage of its ribs, empty and flat.

"Drop it!" Sheila commands.

Sue wags her tail. She has caught the escaping thing. She has been swift and bold and accurate. She is a good girl.

"Come on, give it back," Sheila coaxes. She lunges for the rabbit, but Sue shies away. The rabbit's legs bounce as the dog parries.

Sheila snaps her fingers and points at the ground in front of her. "Come. Here." Her voice is low, serious.

Sue hangs her head and slinks forward. She allows Sheila to wedge a finger into the back of her mouth and pry her jaws wide enough to retrieve the baby rabbit, the fur on its neck sticky with saliva.

Angie has tugged the dish towel off her head and is twisting it in her hands. "Is it okay? Did she kill it?"

The rabbit blinks, and its hind legs spasm. It's alive. Sheila holds it to the light, inspects it for punctures. She feels the gallop of its heart against her hand, its chest ballooning in and out. She dries its fur on the front of her shirt and returns the terrified rabbit to the hutch where it buries itself among its siblings.

"It's fine," Sheila says, shoving Sue out of the way and scolding her again. But there's no anger in it, and the dog knows it. Later that night, Sheila will throw her the green end of a boiled potato and a scrap of cheese.

She makes sure the latch on the hutch is secure, gathers the empty food cans, and heads back to the house.

Angie calls after her. "It was an accident. I didn't mean to."

Sheila whirls around. "Yeah? I wonder why so many accidents happen when you're around."

☙

ONE MILE NORTH of the rabbit hutches, the garden, and the house, an unmarked footpath splits from the Appalachian Trail. It leads through an outcropping of milky quartz and purple shale where nothing much grows except stunted blueberries and thick pads of moss.

Farther along, trees crowd in, ferns sprout, and the temperature drops. At the end of the path, a spring trickles out of the mountain's side into a shallow pool cleared of leaves. A tin cup rests upside down on a flat rock at the water's edge.

Just beyond, a one-room shack of weathered boards and corrugated tin hugs the slope. The shack has no windows, only a door propped open with a slab of plywood on which has been painted: "BEER $1." Scraggly chickens scratch in the dirt outside as Angie jogs into the clearing and heads into the shack. She threads between crates of soda and beer with labels twenty years out of date stacked on the floor. The crooked wooden shelves are stocked with candy, peanut butter, matches, and powdered milk.

The index cards are burning a hole in Angie's pocket. Now that she knows the murderer is so close, she asked them for help. But like always, they didn't give a straight answer. The card she pulled was the Blood Double. Two rabbits stand back-to-back on their hind legs, spines fused. They stare out at opposite sides of the card, holding identical blades in their forepaws as blood drips from the tips of their ears. A snare loops around their hind feet, binding them together.

She couldn't find a place in the house that fit them, so she came here in case this is where they wanted to be. She rubs the stack between her fingers. While she's trying to figure out what they want her to do, a curtain hanging in the far corner of the makeshift store flickers, and Angie shoves the card back into her pocket.

The man that emerges wears suspenders over a button-down work shirt with the sleeves rolled up over tanned and tattooed forearms. His weather-beaten face is half covered with a grizzled beard and topped with a grease-stained trucker's cap.

Angie salutes, and Butch raises two fingers in return.

"Your momma still letting you run around out here on your own?" he asks. "You know they haven't caught that fella."

"I ain't afraid of him."

"No, I don't guess you would be," he says.

"Besides," Angie says, worrying the edges of the card in her pocket, "what's she going to do about it? She's always at Iron Mountain. Now Sheila's there too. I'm not going to stay home by myself all day."

Butch scratches his beard. "I don't like that place."

"Because of the crazies?"

"Because of the doctors. They think their fancy educations mean they know better than you do about what's inside your own head. I tangled with their kind in the army. You wouldn't believe the stories I could tell you."

"Like what?"

He shakes his head. "Docs are some of the meanest critters on earth. Snakes got nothing on them. Let's leave it at that."

Angie takes two dimes out of her pocket. "Can I get a Hershey bar for this?"

"Might do." He lifts a misshapen Hershey bar and a bag of broken cherry drops from under the counter. "Not getting many hikers right now. That murderer has scared them off. Can't say as I blame them, but my stock is going to waste."

"You're a good man, Butch." Angie stuffs the candy in her other pocket. "Do you know of any caves near where that old copper mine used to be?"

"Why do you want to know?"

"Old Thena was telling us some story about when she was a girl. She says a man walked straight out from the rocks around there and kidnapped her. Says he kept her underground with him for three days."

"That must be . . . what? Seventy, eighty years ago? If you think the same man is the one hurt those camping girls . . . why, he'd be nothing but dust by now."

"I know. But I want to find it. I mean, if there's a space under the mountain that big, think how many Russians it could hold." Angie picks up a flashlight and shines it around the store. "Or murderers."

"Only place I know of is nothing to do with magic men. It belongs to Uncle Sam." Butch pushes a plug of tobacco into his cheek and gets busy stacking franks-and-beans C rations on the counter.

"Come on, Butch," Angie says. A chicken wanders in the open door, and Angie tracks it with the flashlight beam.

"You could keep someone underground for years in that big hideout for the president—that's what they built it for.

But that wasn't around when your Thena was a girl. They hadn't built it yet."

Angie clicks off the flashlight. "I guess the Russians are hardly going to hide out there."

"Probably not," he agrees. The trespassing hen flaps onto a shelf by the door and pecks at a box of soda crackers. "Get her out of here, will you?"

Angie lifts the protesting chicken off the shelf and is about to put her down when she sees why the cards wanted her to come here. A six-inch survival knife rests in solitary glory in a shoebox lid. Its gleaming blade ends in a curved tip. Serrated teeth notch the opposite side. A compass is embedded in the end of a grooved black composite handle. A leather sheath and sharpening stone lay beside it. The sign taped next to it says "$50."

"Where'd you get that?" Angie says, squeezing the chicken tight to her chest.

"A hiker traded it," he says. "Don't go getting any ideas. I didn't want to take it, but I felt sorry for the guy and let him pack up a lot of stuff in exchange. Which was right stupid— no one out here's going to pay me fifty dollars for that thing. I guess that'll teach me to listen to a sob story."

"At least let me hold it."

Butch looks at her and sighs. "Go on, then."

Angie tosses the chicken out the door and lifts the knife from the box lid. It feels amazing in her hand. It's heavier than she thought, the handle resting in her palm like it was made for her. This is no pocketknife—this is a real weapon. If she had a knife like this, she could make booby traps and fletch arrows. She could skin and gut the food she caught in snares and carve it up. She could strike flints to make fires to roast the meat. She could defend herself against the Russians and the zombies. She could protect her mom and the dogs and the rabbits and even Sheila if that murderer comes snooping around in the middle of the night again. With a knife like this tucked in a leather holster on her belt, she could sit on the bus anywhere she wanted. If she had a knife like this, no one would dare call her a *little girl*.

She turns the knife in her hand. "Fifty dollars, huh?"

"Yep."

Fifty dollars is an impossible amount. Angie has never had more than five dollars in her pocket at one time in all her life. And this knife is ten times that. She curls her fingers around the handle. She has to have it.

"I don't suppose—"

"Nope." Butch keeps right on stacking the little brown boxes.

"No. Right." Angie rests the knife back in the box lid. "I could do some work for you. Sweep up? Feed the chickens?"

"Sorry, partner. No can do. Fifty dollars is already a lot less than it's worth. I gave that guy a whole sack of provisions for it. I can't let that go for nothing. I'm no millionaire."

Angie scuffs her boot against the boards. "Sure. I know."

She heads for the door, but not before she slips the Blood Double card safely onto a shelf between a couple boxes of crackers.

"You take care of yourself, hear?" Butch calls after her.

Angie picks past the chickens scratching in the dirt outside, shoving them out of the way with her foot. She doesn't have fifty dollars. She doesn't know how to get fifty dollars. But there has to be a way. That knife was meant for her. Why else would it turn up at Butch's store, right under her nose?

TWELVE

The Seen Unseen

THE NEXT TIME SHEILA MEETS THE BOY, SHE IS AT THE
end of her shift, just before dawn. Her face is bloated with the
need for sleep. As she gets more tired and steamed and clammy,
the rope chafes her neck. She tugs at it with her swollen fingers.

A truck arrives at the loading dock, delivering pallets of
flour, soybean oil, canned corn, and other staples. It's not
Sheila's job to shuttle them into storage, but Martha and the
other kitchen workers are decades older than her and have
bad backs, bum knees, bunions, and arthritis. The man who
drives the truck brings the goods as far as the door and no
farther. Not his job, he says, climbing back into the cab and
reversing away from the dock.

Sheila stacks three cases of instant potato flakes and heaves, but she can't get them off the floor. She doesn't understand what's been happening to her lately. She carried stacks of wood all winter and shoveled paths out to the rabbit hutch, and now she can't even lift a few cases of potato flakes. She takes one off the stack and struggles the other two into her arms. When she returns from the storeroom, the boy is lifting sacks of oatmeal onto his shoulders, seemingly without effort.

"Where do you want these?" he asks.

At the sight of him, Sheila's neck itches and she feels the fear again, that awful joke when he choked her with that casual twitch of his foot. She looks around for Martha—for protection, for backup, for safety in numbers. But the cook is frying something in a giant pan on the stove, oil splatting and fans blasting.

"Come on," he says. He juts his chin at the crates of goods yet to be carried into the back and put away. "It'll go faster if I help."

Experience has taught Sheila that nothing is to be feared more than an appearance of kindness, especially from boys. She prefers them to wear their nastiness where she can see it, like the felt letters stitched on their jackets in proud school colors: *B* for basketball, *A* for asshole, *S* for sadist. But she is so tired. Her eyes itch, her feet ache, and fire burns between her shoulder blades, licking toward her skull.

"Fine," she says, drawing the tail of her rope closer to her body. "But watch where you put those feet of yours."

He carries the oatmeal into the storeroom and puts it where she indicates, then goes back for more. She monitors him out of the corner of her eye as she carries boxes of dry milk and instant grits. He looks normal. Well, mostly normal. But she can't figure out what he's doing here. Not just in the kitchen but in the asylum at all. He's too young to be a doctor. His hooded sweatshirt and white high-tops are the opposite of the orderly's uniform of white pants, white shirt, and black shoes. Maybe groundskeepers can wear their own clothes. Except she's never seen him pushing a lawn mower or raking leaves.

When the dry goods are finished, he points to the rest: gallons of milk, blocks of cheese, flats of eggs. "Where do these go?"

"In the cold store."

The boy fills his arms and follows Sheila. She feels his breath at her ear as she pulls the lever on the giant walk-in refrigerator. Inside, the cold nips the bare skin of her arms. But it's nothing to the chill that seems to come from inside her, like her bones and organs have been stored in an ice-house overnight.

Sheila doesn't want to talk to him, but she can't help it. She has never in her whole life met someone who can see the rope that trails behind her. So why him? Why this strange, dangerous boy with the wound in his eye?

If he can see the rope, maybe he can help her get rid of it. But she's only just met him. She needs to know more about him first.

"So what is it you do here?" she asks.

"I live here."

"But you're not a patient?" It comes out like a question, but she's pretty sure he's not. The other women wouldn't have reacted so calmly to him during the fire drill if he were an escaped patient.

"You know Dr. Sachs, right?"

"Sure," she says. "He's the head doctor. Do you mean he's your—"

The crate of eggs the boy is holding tumbles to the floor. Eggs roll and split, oozing sloppy whites and gelatinous yolks.

"Dammit," Sheila says. "I better go get the mop."

"I'll get it," he says.

Sheila picks out the biggest fragments of broken shell from the mess and is wiping down the eggs that have survived when the boy comes back wheeling the mop and bucket.

"So what about you?" He sloshes soapy water over the tiles. "What's your story?"

"I needed a job." She rinses the salvaged eggs in the sink and rests them on a folded towel to dry. "I hope Martha doesn't notice that we're short a few."

"Doubt it. She must break some too." He leans on the mop handle. "But why here? Why wash dishes in a place like this?"

"My mom works here, so I can get a ride with her. And . . ." Sheila's mouth wants to keep going, though an inner voice is telling her to shut up before she gives something important away. "It's not so bad. I mean, it's awful. It's hard work, and I'm tired all the time, and my feet are killing me, but it's better than most places. Nobody notices me unless they're handing me a tray to rinse."

"Why don't you want anyone to notice you?"

Because I'm ugly, Sheila thinks. *And a freak. When people notice me, that's when bad things happen. I get spit on and elbowed in the ribs and shoved in the back, and my books are stolen, my hair pulled, and my locker jammed.*

"I just don't," she says. "Look, it's nice of you to help out and all, but this doesn't mean we're friends."

"What would it take to be friends?"

She must be losing her mind, because she actually considers the question. Working beside him has given her a false sense of normalcy, and she has let down her well-trained guard. But he won't get her that easily.

Sheila pushes away from the sink. "What do you want from me?"

He holds out his hands. "I'm not your enemy." The red spot in his eye gleams like the laser sight of an assassin in one of Angie's movies. "Don't you want to know why I can see you so well?"

Sheila doesn't trust him, but she can't deny that there is some weird connection between them. So, fine. If he's going to be here, she may as well get some use out of him.

"You said it was your eye. But there has to be more to it than that. Can you see the rope right now?"

"Sure," he says. "It's right—" He shifts toward the spot on the floor where the end of the rope trails under the wheels of the mop bucket.

"Don't!" Sheila snaps. "Let's get this straight: I don't know what this rope is, but it's attached to my body. You don't have any right to touch it or come anywhere near it, no matter what you can see. If you want to talk to me again, you are never, *ever* to touch that rope. Do you understand?"

"If that's what you want."

"It is."

Martha appears, her face pink and shiny, grease spotting her apron. "Thank you so much for putting away that truck-load, hon. I was coming to help you as soon as I finished those fritters. I can't quit when I've got hot oil on the burner like that. But I see you're done already! How did you do it so fast? I heard you singing to yourself back here—"

Sheila opens her mouth to protest, but Martha waves it away with a laugh.

"Nothing to be embarrassed about. I like to sing a bit of Carter Family myself when I chop vegetables or knead dough. A tune makes the work go lighter. But next time, I won't leave you to do it all by yourself."

Sheila looks from Martha to the boy and back again. He is sitting there on an upturned milk crate, his hand on the handle of the mop, plain as day. How can Martha say that Sheila has been working alone?

When Martha returns to her pots and pans, Sheila glares at the boy. "She can't see you."

"It seems not," he agrees. He flips his hair over his face and saunters away, the wheels on the mop bucket squeaking behind him.

THIRTEEN

The Prisoner in the Cellar

ANGIE SPRAWLS ON HER BED IN THE SISTERS' SHARED room. From the hidden space behind the dresser where she keeps her treasures—turkey feathers and turtle shells, stolen erasers, an earring with the stone missing that she found in the crack of the school bus seat—stored in a motley collection of cracked canning jars and Little Debbie boxes, she takes out the porn mag she found in the tree stand.

She doesn't know why she brought the thing home. It's dog-eared and waterlogged. The women on the sun-faded pages are foreign to her, their bodies nothing like her own or the others she has seen without clothes—her bony sister, her tired mom, the slack and shriveled old woman in the room downstairs.

The magazine women are also nothing like the goose-fleshed girls in her class on the first week of school each year, when the gym teacher makes them all undress and shower together after running wind sprints to remind them who has the authority. For the rest of the year, the rule is skipping showers and dressing hastily at your locker before slinking back to class. Keeping your eyes down and peeking through your lashes and wondering where you stand and tracking who is showing off a new lace bra and who is still wearing white cotton panties bought by their mom in a three-pack at King's.

Angie must never look up, never let them see that she is watching. Because that's when they shout, "What are you looking at, lesbo?" And she *is* looking. Looking and comparing and rating and judging. But desiring? No. Only comparing. And they must be doing the same. Otherwise, how would they know she is looking?

But this magazine, with splats of pine sap sticking the pages together, with dried beetle shells and pieces of wing falling out of the crease at the center as she turns through the stories, is meant for looking.

The women are the same each time: the smiles fixed on their faces, their legs splayed, their manicured hands darting toward their privates. They remain static, but each time Angie goes back to the magazine, she expects to find something. It feels like there is information hidden within, if only she can figure it out.

Angie likes how the layouts are simple and easy to understand. Here are two girls, and they are friends. You know this because they look alike. Girls who are friends wear the same brands of clothes and fix their hair in the same styles and wear the same kind of makeup. The girls are bored because they don't have a boyfriend. That's also easy to understand because girls who are pretty and wear makeup want boyfriends.

Then a boy shows up. He has big muscles, so he will be the boyfriend. The girls take off their clothes, and the boy takes off his clothes. The girls squeeze their breasts and hold them out to the boy.

"Where did you get that?" Angie hasn't noticed that Sheila has come upstairs and is looming over her, her face angry and unreadable.

"I found it." Angie draws the magazine closer, wishing she was on a page of all letters and words and not so much pink flesh, so many open mouths. "In the woods."

Sheila's mouth twists. "Gross. Why did you bring it back here?"

Angie hates it when Sheila acts like she is so grown-up. She's only five years older but seems to think this gives her the right to make all the rules. "I can do what I want."

"Why are you even looking at that? Don't you know it's for guys?"

"Duh. Of course I know that."

"Everybody calls you a lesbo, you know. Maybe they're right." As she says it, Sheila half hopes that it's true. Then at least she and Angie would have *something* in common. But at the same time, she hopes it's not so. She doesn't want to have to share her secret with her sister, tangle Angie's public stain with her own private truth.

Sheila grabs the magazine out of Angie's hands. Angie doesn't let go and the back cover rips, but Sheila comes away with most of the pages. She holds it above her head, out of Angie's reach. "I should show this to mom," she says. "I bet you'd catch it big time."

"That's not fair! I'm not hurting anyone."

Sheila wonders if that's true. When she came into their room and realized what Angie was looking at, she felt like she had been stabbed. Surely that counted as hurting someone.

She turns her back to Angie and pretends to flip through the pages. "Oh man, this is worse than I thought. Mom is going to be so mad. I bet you won't be able to go into town for weeks. I bet she won't even let you go to Butch's to beg him for candy."

"Don't you dare!" Angie throws her arms around Sheila, snatching at the magazine. Sheila fights her off.

"Please!"

Sheila spins back to face her sister, hugging the battered pages to her chest. "If I don't tell, what will you give me?"

"I'll pick beans," Angie offers. "And go down the lane to get the mail."

"No deal. That's your job anyways."

"What do you want then?"

Sheila has to think about this. Most of the things she would want Angie to do for her—straighten her side of the room, make their mom's breakfast when she gets off shift, take over feeding the rabbits for a while—she doesn't trust Angie to do right. She's so unreliable that having a threat to hold over her isn't much of a bargaining chip.

Sheila relents. "You can not talk about that stupid murder anymore. And stop wearing that ridiculous dish towel around your head."

"I guess." Angie thinks this is going pretty well, especially since in a day or two, she'll go back to doing whatever she wants.

"Not so fast. You can clear out that stand of poison ivy near the rabbit hutches."

"Fine." Angie holds out her hand. "Can I have it back now?"

"I said I wouldn't tell mom. I didn't say anything about giving it back."

Sheila is downstairs and out the door before realizing what she's decided to do. She runs straight for the woods, for the cover of leaves and the shelter of trees, the rope bumping on the rocks behind her. She drops to her knees and twists the magazine between her hands, trying to pull it apart. It slides and squeaks but remains stubbornly whole.

Like lifting the boxes of potato flakes, Sheila is finding it harder than she expected. She's breathing hard, using all her strength, and still the blasted thing won't give. She resorts to tearing out individual pages and ripping them across the middle. One by one, she shreds and mangles and destroys, her fingers frantic. Her eyes are thick and puffy, her nose swollen and dripping. She claws her way through those awful, exposed, glassy-eyed women. She has to get rid of them. Has to make them not exist. Tear them into nothingness and make them go away.

Sheila drops back onto her heels, exhausted. Her hands are red and sore. But the job is done. The women are gone. She digs in the soft spring dirt with the edge of a stone and crams the shreds of naked women into the hole. She piles the earth back on top and stamps it firm. Long after the ground is well and truly packed over the paper's grave, Sheila is still pressing her foot into the soil with all her weight.

❧

SHEILA'S FIRST PAY packet comes in an envelope with her name and the amount, $85.15, written on the outside in black pen. She can feel the outline of the dime and nickel through the tan paper. Inside, she finds four twenty-dollar bills crisp from the bank and a softer, more worn five.

When she had gone upstairs to the office to collect it at the end of her shift, banging erupted behind the locked doors that lead to G Ward. An orderly rushed past her, unlocked the doors with the keys at his waist, and slipped inside. The banging stopped, then started again, louder and more violent. Someone yelled and was abruptly cut off. Sheila continued down the hall, her steps echoing against the high ceiling and the mint-green walls.

Later, in the car, Sheila sees the corner of a similar tan envelope sticking out of her mother's unzipped pocketbook on the seat between them. Sheila isn't sure how much she should give her mother from hers, so she hands over the whole thing. Bonnie takes it, checking the bills against the number written on the outside.

"Mmm," she says. Sheila doesn't know if this means she is pleased or disappointed. Bonnie plucks out two of the twenties and the five. She hesitates, returns the five to the envelope and hands it back to Sheila.

As they pull out onto Horsekiller Road, the announcer on the radio tells them what they already know: the murderer still hasn't been caught.

"How hard can it be?" Bonnie says. "He's only one man."

Sheila doesn't answer. Her mom's not talking to her, not really.

They are halfway through a Patsy Cline song when Bonnie says, "You want to get something special for yourself when we go to the IGA later? Some Little Debbie cakes or some ice cream?"

"Mom!"

"I know your sister's the one with the sweet tooth. But I got to use most of this"—she pats the pocketbook—"to pay Bud back for helping out with the car last month. I promised I'd pay him for those parts as soon as I got the cash together. I don't want to be in nobody's debt for long. But that doesn't mean you can't get yourself something."

Bonnie knew that Bud was willing to help out in other ways too. He had let her know that loud and clear when he fixed the carburetor, but she shut him down fast. Men pretend to be worthwhile at first; they buy you a drink and hold the door and help you into your coat, and a little bit of dark honey runs through you at all the attention, but then quick as a flash, the whisperer of sweet words turns into a thing that sits on the couch and farts and picks his teeth and ignores you unless he's shouting for a beer.

Ferns whip by out the window, and Sheila listens to the roll of the tires on the blacktop as they pass the railroad bridge and the state forest entrance signs.

"A girl needs to have money of her own. You won't always have someone to take care of you." The road curves sharply downhill, and Bonnie taps the brakes in a half-hearted way. "I wish somebody had told me that when I was your age."

Sure, Bonnie got lonely, but mostly she was too tired to care all that much about it. And while sometimes she wished she had someone she could set her cares down on for a spell, the problem with that was it only made picking them up again that much harder after she had felt the world without that weight grinding her down. It was better to just keep on going on her own, no matter how hard.

When they are at the store, Sheila stutters in front of the bakery case, where a woman in a hairnet is packing trays of fresh doughnuts into boxes, cinnamon and hot sugar filling the air. Sheila sees herself ducking into the corridor behind the pay phone, shoving one after another into her mouth, biting into their pillowy softness, the sugar coating melting against her tongue. And then choking on them, all the mashed dough backing into her throat, gagging her like the wadding in the lumpy cushion Thena sits on at dinner to rest her brittle bones against the hard oak chair.

Sheila forces herself to walk away. She picks up an orange soda for Angie, a flavor she herself can't stand, the flat sweet taste and artificial smell like cleaning fluid. She gets Thena a paperback western. Sheila doesn't know if she's read this one or not, but it doesn't matter. The old woman's cataracts are so bad she can hardly make out the words anymore, but she will be pleased to get it all the same.

Sheila wanders through the aisles, keeping the rope tucked under her elbow, away from the wheels of shopping carts, and looks at all the things she could buy for herself—the rows of glossy magazines shining with pretty, glossy girls, and the little plastic cases of colored powder and lipstick tubes that promise to make her glossy too. She doesn't want any of them as badly as she wants to keep the remaining money in the envelope intact.

At home, they dump the shopping bags on the table, and Bonnie heads back to check on Thena. Angie is sprawled in front of the television, drawing on her index cards. She chews one end of her marker and glances up occasionally at the staticky screen of cartoons. Sheila puts everything away, but she is conscious the whole time, as she reaches into a cabinet or stoops to a low drawer, of the pay envelope in her pocket.

As soon as she can, Sheila escapes to her room and contemplates the cash. This is her money, but where is she going to keep it? No place in this room, in the whole house, or anywhere on the mountain is hers alone. She shoves the envelope of bills back into her pocket, feeling their gravity and potential, and waits.

She finds the answer later that night when she is fetching potatoes for supper, to be fried with onions and greens from the garden and a hunk of just-got-paid ham. In the cellar, opposite the vegetable bins, is a shelf of rusting tools and a can of forgotten paint, a dried spill of red draped over its lip, left over from when her brother painted the motorcycle he rebuilt years ago.

Sheila pops off the lid with a screwdriver. Inside, the remaining paint is dry and cracked. She runs a finger inside and scratches at the bottom. Nothing comes away but flakes. Perfect. She withdraws the crumpled envelope from her pocket and smooths the sweaty bills. Then she tucks the flap securely closed, folds the envelope in half, and nestles it in the can. She presses the lid shut and returns the can to the shelf beside the tools.

No one has touched that can for years. Angie doesn't do any of the cooking and won't collect potatoes unless you make her. Knowing that she has found a good hiding spot feels to Sheila like having a magic spell.

Every pay packet she receives after that, Sheila hides her share in the can. She's going to continue until she gets over one hundred dollars. When she lies in bed at night and the old woman's snores rattle through the floor and the screech owl shrieks in the trees outside, Sheila thinks of the money folded together so neatly, safe underground beneath her. She is not sure what she could buy with one hundred dollars, but she likes saying the words—*one hundred dollars*—in her mind.

FOURTEEN

The Sealed Gap

SAPLINGS SPROUT FROM THE MIDDLE OF THE OLD logging road, and the ruts are filled with dead leaves, but it still cuts a track through the forest that's easy enough to follow. Angie hurries along it so fast she's almost running, every third step a little hop of excitement that propels her forward. No matter what Butch says, she knows the copper mine holds secrets just waiting for her to discover. After all, Thena told them that story about the Man of Stone for a reason.

At first, Angie scoots right past the entrance because she's looking for something out of an Old West prospector cartoon: a man-sized shaft cut into the ground, braced with timbers. But in reality, the mine is just a slump in the mountain's side that could as easily be a gully washed out by centuries of rain as it could a tunnel dug by men with picks and shovels and the occasional stick of dynamite.

Judging by the thick curtain of vines matted across the entrance, no one has been inside for years. Still, maybe the murderer is a master of camouflage and has just made it look untouched. He has fooled the police all this time—maybe this is how he's been able to hide out for so long.

Angie creeps closer, alert for any sound. He could be right there, right on the other side of that tangled cloak of leaves, a rock gripped in his hands, ready to smash down on her head. Her fingers clench the flashlight she brought with her, wishing it was the knife from Butch's store.

The longer she listens, the more she hears nothing but her own breath, the more electric shivers of anticipation travel up the backs of her legs. It's now or never. She rips aside the vines and leaps into the mine with her best battle cry, sweeping the flashlight wildly in front of her.

She strikes and blocks, fighting off the shadows of hostile defenders. She bashes the first man in the head and the next in the ribs, taking them all down in a symphony of gasps and grunts. When the last one is vanquished, her adrenaline subsides, and the bodies of her fallen enemies fade and disappear. The smell of blood and cordite reverts to stone and mineral. She stands, slightly out of breath, in the empty dark space, the echoes of her shouts lingering against the bare rock walls.

The space around her is about the size of the room she shares with Sheila, capped by a ceiling so low she can barely stand up. The rock walls are slick with moisture, the surfaces closest to the entrance furred with moss. Water dribbles somewhere back in the gloom, splashing into an unseen pool.

She steps forward, keeping a sharp eye out for snakes waiting to sink their fangs into her unprotected calves. Her toe kicks something that clatters and tumbles, but when she gets a better look, she sees it's only an old can of 7 Up with an outdated design, crushed and rusted. She moves farther into the mine, the sallow beam of the flashlight revealing more forgotten junk—the coiled springs of a flayed mattress, a heap of sodden paper, broken glass that glitters, even what could have been a small fire ring, but it's all old. Ancient and useless.

The cards bundled in her pocket are dull and quiet, like they're sleeping. Something in this place doesn't want them, so she must carry out this mission alone. The darkness back here is so thick it seems to eat the flashlight's beam. But the splashing water is louder, its echo promising more chambers and greater depths to explore.

The walls narrow around her as Angie splashes through deepening water so cold it must be flowing straight from the mountain's heart. Her excitement pulses, and she hopes the cards in her pocket will now begin to wake. She's getting close to something.

She's so sure of success that when she stumbles against the cave-in, she can't quite believe it. A boulder the size of a cow is wedged in the middle of the shaft, its sharp point jabbed into the solid rock floor like a railroad spike pounded by a giant. Smaller rocks pack the gaps around it, blocking the tunnel completely.

Angie digs at the rocks, but they don't budge. She can't squeeze past, and there's no way a full-grown man could. No one bigger than a rabbit could get through those gaps. She gets down on her knees in the slimy water and peers underneath, trying to see if there is any route farther back where a murderer could hide or a tunnel could lead to the underground kingdom of the Man of Stone.

There's nothing back there, just animal bones and old mining equipment, unused for decades. She backtracks to the main chamber and runs her hands over the stone surfaces, looking for the secret catch she has missed, the lever that will roll back a section of wall, raise the fallen rocks in a single motion like a gate to reveal the secret camp where the murderer is hiding out, shivering and whimpering, terrified that he has been found at last.

But there is no murderer, no Man of Stone, no entrance to a secret Russian camp. Just solid rock.

Angie knocks the flashlight against the wall. "Stupid mountain. I don't see why you can't just show me where he is."

She jumps as a slab breaks loose from the ceiling and splashes into the water near her feet.

Angie picks it up and looks at the thousands of tons of dirt and stone and tree suspended above her head.

"See? You could help if you wanted to."

Angie waits, but no more rocks fall. The mountain is still, the mine is silent.

She drops the rock back in the water and crawls out through the vines. The air outside the cave lands on her like a weight, hot and smothering, so much hotter than when she went inside. She squints through the treetops and checks the sun in the sky. How long was she in there anyway?

The forest is the same as it ever was—trees arching overhead, creek rushing in the valley below. The distant hum of tires on Fern Ridge Road, gnats and deerflies darting at her eyes and ears, out for her blood. She breaks off a birch twig to swat them away and starts back home, no longer running or hopping, most of the steam gone out of her.

Retracing her steps along the logging road, she walks and swats, walks and swats, shaking the branch in front of her face, tearing the leaves ragged, thinking about her dinner, about how unfair it was that the roller derby lady got away with her crime on the last episode of *CHiPs*, about how Sheila thinks she doesn't know about the secret in the cellar, about the money her sister is stashing down there in an old paint can.

As she passes through an area of high grass, the distinct smell of fox pee drifts into the air, skunky and herbal. Through the waving leaves, Angie spots a heap of something in the road ahead. It wasn't there before, on her way here—she'd have noticed. The humped shape looks like an animal, but it's not running away. It could be a rabbit caught by the fox, dropped and left behind when she approached.

But coming closer, she sees that it's only cloth, a bundle of old rags, stinking and clumped. She grabs a stick and pokes at the heap, ready to jump back and run. She doesn't know why she feels so spooked; it's just some dirty old clothes. It's not like they're going to leap up and attack her.

The poking stick disturbs only a few fat flies, so Angie feels brave enough to bend down and pinch the corner of the cloth with the tips of her fingers, holding her other hand over her mouth. This clue was left here for her to find, and she's not going to be a girl about it. She shakes it out, but the fabric clumps stubbornly, something dark and viscous binding it together.

Using her foot to hold down one edge, she stretches it out, almost gagging at the smell released from its folds. It's a man's shirt, the collar and one sleeve ragged with tooth holes and sticky with drool—no doubt thanks to the fox. Yellow lines crisscross the blue plaid fabric, or what she can see of it under the crunchy black stains. Bloodstains.

FIFTEEN

The Blistered Laurel

THE FAMILIES OF THE MURDERED WOMEN HAVE driven in from the coast to take their bodies home and bury them behind marble stones in green graveyards that are shown in brief glimpses on TV. But the murderer is still on the loose.

The state police remain in the county, patrolling the back roads instead of the highways, and people look at strangers a little differently if they are waiting beside them at the IGA. They ask themselves just who is that man pumping gas into a rusted pickup at the Phillips 66 on the Skyline Trail.

The women who work at the asylum say that the murderer must be clever, to dodge the police for so long. But others say he doesn't need to be all that smart—there's a lot of woods out there and plenty of places to hide. Still, the police have helicopters, bloodhounds, know-how. They're sure to catch him soon.

"Now you tell me why two women would come all the way out here—all the way from where was it? Rhode Island?—to pitch a tent and sleep in the woods. Don't they have their own trees out there?" says Martha.

"It would make more sense if one of them was a man," says Tammy, a cleaner who smokes like a chimney. "Men always want to go somewhere dumb."

"If I was going to travel all that way for a vacation, I'd want to go someplace nice," says Alice, picking at her nail polish. "Somewhere without any bugs and no rocks poking me in the back every time I roll over."

"Somewhere with a toilet," Barb declares, pressing both hands into the small of her back and stretching.

"Duane got me to go camping with him right after we got married," says Tammy. "He made it sound romantic, like we were going to lie on our backs and gaze at the stars. That we'd be like Adam and Eve alone in the garden."

"Did he bring his snake?"

"You've got a filthy mind, Barb." Tammy exhales a long stream of smoke. "I tell you what he did bring: a couple of six-packs of Rolling Rock. He called it camping, but I call it sitting in the woods getting drunk and watching his beard grow."

They all laugh.

"What about you, Sheila? You ever been camping?" asks Alice.

"I guess I don't see the point," Sheila says. But she wonders what would happen if she and Juanita were the women in the tent. Zipped inside the nylon shell, snuggled under the taut fabric roof. In the dark, every movement, every breath, every scent would be closely exchanged.

Would they unroll their sleeping bags side by side? Or squeeze into a single one? Sheila's never seen a sleeping bag before. Wouldn't it be uncomfortable to have your arms and legs pinned down like that—like being bound with a rope? Maybe that's why the killer was able to sneak up on them, why he found them as helpless as rabbits asleep in their hutch.

Would Sheila have grabbed Juanita's hand when she heard the footsteps approach? Squeezed tight and whispered for Juanita to be quiet, keep still. Her ears straining for the next snap of a branch that could so easily be a deer or a bear. But one that didn't move on. One that smelled of tobacco and old sweat.

When the first blow came, would she have screamed? Rolled out of the way? Curled into a ball and covered her head with her hands? Wrapped her body like a protective shell around Juanita's? Sheila wasn't sure. In that messy, hot, dark night, she knew there was no telling what she would really do.

Tammy drops her cigarette and crushes it underfoot. "Guess we'd better get back."

As the women file inside, the boy appears at Sheila's elbow, falling into step beside her.

Sheila pulls the rope closer to her body and checks to see if the others have noticed him, but most are inside already, heading back to their stations. Only Martha pauses, holding the door for Sheila.

"I'll be just another minute," Sheila says, and when the door shuts, she turns to the boy. "Have you been here all the time? Were you listening?"

"I'm always here," he says.

"If anyone sees me talking to someone who isn't there, they're going to think I need to be locked up on one of the wards." She hurries toward the woods and hears the boy following behind her. "I'm not sure they'd be wrong."

Once they reach the cover of the drooping pines, Sheila shoves her hands in her apron pockets and studies the boy. Examines him through one eye, then the other. Either way, he seems real enough, in his jeans and high-tops, his hair hanging in his face, mercifully cloaking the red spot in his eye.

His mouth twitches. "I'm real." He stretches a hand toward her, his sweatshirt pulling back at the cuff to show his skinny wrist. "Go on."

He's offering his hand for her to touch, Sheila realizes. So she can confirm his reality. She doesn't think she wants to, but she has to know. She's not going to take his word for it.

The boy's hand hangs in the air, and Sheila extends her own finger. She inches toward him, waiting for him to smell of sweat or cigarettes or shampoo or anything that a teenage boy might smell like, but she detects only the high, clean scent of pine.

Just as she's about to make contact, she imagines her fingertip slipping right through his skin, dipping into his hand and dissolving. The world around her tilts, but she forces herself to close the space between them.

His hand is firm against her finger. He feels like flesh and muscle and bone. If maybe a few degrees cooler than normal, like the difference you feel when passing from a sunny field into a shady hollow.

"Satisfied?" he asks.

Sheila breaks contact and swings her hand like she's trying to shake something off. A slight wind rustles through the tops of the trees, but the air at ground level remains calm. The leaves of the laurels stand out dark green against an impossibly blue sky.

"What are you?" Sheila's heartbeat drums inside her chest. The thick pines screen them from watching eyes, which was good when she didn't want to be seen talking to someone who isn't there. But she also knows how much harm can come to you in a few seconds out of sight. When the teacher's back is turned, while the bus driver is opening the door, in the girls' bathroom, under the bleachers.

Sheila pictures the boy bending over the broken bodies of the women, the rock raised above his head, slamming it down again and again, raining vicious blows. The women's blood spraying back, splattering him: on his shirt, face, hair, in his eyes.

The boy crouched low beside a stream like an animal, splashing himself clean, sluicing the blood away, getting it all out except for that little telltale speck in his eye.

"What do you know about what happened to those women?" The bottoms of Sheila's feet itch, like they're trying to tell her how much they want to be moving, getting the hell out of here, out into the open, away from him.

"I didn't kill them," he says.

Sheila scrunches her toes inside her shoes. She knows it's ridiculous to think that the red spot in his eye is a fleck of blood from the murdered women's veins. Blood doesn't stay red when it's not fresh. It doesn't last for weeks, and it can't stain someone else's eye. But it's also ridiculous to think that a six-foot someone in a faded sweatshirt and high-top sneakers is invisible.

"But you know something." It's not a question.

"What are you so afraid of?"

"*Someone* around here beat two women to death in their tent with a rock. A man the police can't seem to find."

"So? Are you like those women?" The boy's laser eye seems to shine a red beam right through her, turning her secrets inside out.

Heat spreads across Sheila's back like a swarm of devouring ants. The rope tightens around her neck and beads of sweat pop out on her chest.

"I've never even been to Rhode Island," she manages to say.

"You know that's not what I mean."

Quick images of Juanita flash through Sheila's mind. The girls in the magazines, pressing their pages against her skin. This boy can see the rope that chokes her and drags her down. What else does he see?

The boy makes a circle with his thumb and forefinger and holds it to his damaged eye like he's peering through a telescope.

"My turn," he says.

"What are you talking about?" Sheila backs away, folding her body in around itself. If she had a shell, she would shrink back into it and close the trap.

"It's only fair." The boy looks like he's enjoying himself. "You got to check me out. But what if I have doubts about you? What if you're not what you appear to be?"

Sheila imagines his hand on hers, the cool contact of his skin. "I don't want you to touch me."

The boy holds his hands up, palms out, as if showing how harmless he is. "I won't."

He backs up for six long strides and then stretches his arms wide and wiggles his fingers in the empty air. "See? I'll stay all the way over here."

Sheila knows, logically, that if he comes toward her, she can run and be back in the safety of the asylum parking lot in moments. So why does she feel like her toes are slipping over the edge of a steep ravine?

"Close your eyes," he says.

"I'm not sure—"

"Just do it." He indicates the wide space of forest between them. "You're safe."

She closes her eyes, and at first she feels nothing. Then the lightest whisper of sensation against her skin, like she is being brushed with the fine tuft of a rabbit's tail. She didn't hear him move, didn't sense him come closer, but he must be touching her. She should have known better than to trust his promise. She flutters an eyelid and peeks through her lashes.

She is alone. The boy is still all the way over there—still all that empty space between them.

"Eyes closed," he says, and embarrassed to be caught, she obeys.

Now she feels dizzy, lightheaded, like the whole-body buzz that follows a wasp sting. The tingle on her skin sinks deeper, like he is scanning below the surface, digging past her flesh and into her heart and shadows. Into the murk and darkness where she keeps her need and her shame.

When she can't stand it any longer, Sheila opens her eyes. The boy is across the clearing from her, his eye glittering like a flame fueled with fresh kindling. She feels naked, exposed. She's afraid to ask what he has seen.

"You're so scared of everyone," he says. "Of what they say, of what they might do. But you've got it all wrong. They should be scared of you."

SIXTEEN

The Unlatched Gate

THE FIRST SIGN OF COMPANY IS THE BARKING OF the dogs.

Two figures wander out of the woods, blinking in the bright light of the clearing around the house. The man is bearded and sunburnt, his straw-blond hair straggling from under a baseball cap. Sheila's first instinct is to run to the house and get the rifle. But then she sees the woman, shorter and also sunburnt, trudging a few paces behind in her hiking boots, and realizes they are both carrying heavy canvas packs.

Sue races toward them, growling and showing her teeth. Sheila hopes the hikers can't tell that she doesn't mean it. The man slows and raises his hand, but before he can speak,

Sheila hollers, "You're off the trail. You can pick it up a couple hundred yards that way." She points across the creek to the pines on the other side.

"We know. We came that way." The man is younger than Sheila first thought, only just out of his teens, the same as her brother Sam. Sue has stationed herself in front of the stranger, and though she barks once or twice to keep up appearances, her whole back end is now wagging.

The woman's gaze flits over the sagging house and dilapidated sheds, and she shoots a look at her companion as if to telegraph that she thought this was a bad idea all along. But she says to Sheila, "We lost all our food two days ago."

"Well, I don't know," Sheila says. "We don't—"

"We're not asking for a handout," the man says. He crouches and extends his hand, and Sue runs straight to him. "But we are hungry. Maybe I could do some work for you in exchange for something to eat?"

"We wouldn't ask," the woman says, "except the bears got all our food. You're supposed to hang it in a tree, but we didn't think bears were a problem this far south."

"They aren't," Sheila says.

"That's what Russell said. But something ate that food."

Before Sheila can ask why their stupidity should be her problem, she hears the old woman cough and spit. Thena is on the porch, leaning on her stick. "We don't have much, but we can spare a mite for visitors."

"That's decent of you. We appreciate it." The man sticks out his hand to Sheila. "I'm Russell, by the way." He sheds his pack, and the woman does too. Sheila notices they are too dumb to check in the gaps for a copperhead before they sit down on the stone wall in the shade.

Angie melts out of the woods behind them, her feet splashed with mud. She doesn't seem surprised by the hikers, and Sheila wonders if she has been following them.

"Did you come from the Trail?" Angie asks.

"Yep," says Russell. "We started in Virginia and are headed to New Hampshire. I wanted to do the whole thing, but Gayle has to be back at school by September."

Angie stares at Gayle. "Aren't you too old for school?"

Sheila slaps Angie's arm. "He means college, dummy."

"Did you see the murderer?" Angie asks.

"We heard there was some trouble," Russell says.

"He killed two people!" Angie mimes a violent stabbing. "Aren't you worried he's going to get you?"

Gayle shifts uneasily, but Russell shrugs. "He's not going to bother us."

"What makes you so sure? The police haven't caught him. He could be *anywhere*."

Normally Sheila might be embarrassed by Angie carrying on like this, but she didn't invite these two here, and she figures they deserve everything they get.

"Those two women were alone. But Gayle's got me." Russell pats Gayle's knee. "We don't have anything to worry about."

Angie's attention slides off him and onto their packs, an irresistible heap of canvas, buckles, straps, and drawstrings. "Do you really carry everything you need to survive?"

"Pretty much?"

"Can I see your canteen?"

Russell nods, and Angie slings the strap across her chest and unscrews the cap, peering inside. "It smells like pennies," she says.

"You got that work for me to do now?" Russell asks Sheila.

It's not like there's not enough work to be done; it's that Sheila's not sure she wants some stranger who just traipsed out of the woods doing it. And like as not doing it wrong so she'll just have to go back and do it over again herself. What are men good for? It's hard to remember. Strong things, she decides.

"I guess you could dig part of the garden for fall. We got to get the cabbages in soon." She takes him over and shows him which section to work on. "Start here by the beans, but don't go any farther than the potatoes." She hands him a digging fork and spade. "You got that?"

"Yes ma'am," he says. "Just one thing—which ones are the potatoes?"

When Sheila gets back to Gayle resting on the stone fence, Angie has hefted Russell's pack onto her back and is strutting back and forth in front of the house with her knees raised high.

"I'm sorry about my sister," Sheila says. "She's a bit—"

"No, it's fine," Gayle says. "I wish I enjoyed carrying that pack half as much as she seems to. Let her be."

Sheila doesn't want to like Gayle, not one little bit, but she finds that she sort of does. Tired and weather-beaten though she is, the young woman has a smile that lights her face. And she hasn't said one mean thing to Sheila since she appeared out of the woods. So when Gayle scrapes her broken nails over the mosquito bites that pepper her tanned legs, Sheila takes her to the spring and shows her how to crush the jewelweed that grows in the runoff and squeeze the slippery gel from the stalks. Gayle rubs the stuff on her legs, and Sheila watches her hands slide over the muscles of her calves.

"Oooh," says Gayle, closing her eyes. "That feels so good."

Gayle looks up then, and Sheila winces away, embarrassed that she was watching.

"Everybody on the trail is talking about that murder." Gayle crushes a stem and applies it to her other leg, smoothing the sap over her skin in slow, circular motions. "Aren't you scared living out here with somebody like that on the loose? I mean, there can't be another house around for miles. Who would you call for help?"

"Our mom says it was those girls' fault for coming here from the city." Sheila isn't sure she believes this, but her blood is rushing in her veins like a spring rain, and she wants Gayle to stop talking about that man and what he did.

Gayle drops the jewelweed and wipes her fingers. "That's ridiculous. That's like saying if you went to the city, you'd deserve to be murdered because you came from the country."

"I don't know anything about cities." Sheila slaps at a mosquito on her neck, surprised to realize she can barely feel the rope right now. It's still there—it's never *not* there— but it feels like she's had a shot of something that takes away the pain.

"Well, I don't know what type of snake not to step on or how to start a fire or what those screams are that sound like someone being killed in the dark outside our shelter when I'm about to fall asleep, but I'm here all the same."

"Screech owl," Sheila says.

"Seriously? Is that it? Just a bird? It sounds like a woman with a knife to her throat." Gayle starts to laugh, but her face quickly straightens. "Jeez, that's not funny, is it? Those poor women."

"Did he make you do it?" Sheila asks. "Come out here?"

"Russell? No, of course not. I wanted to come. I wanted to see if I could do it." Gayle's fingers worry the button on her shirt cuff. "I already know more than when I started. I know that touching the shiny plant with three leaves makes me itch like hell, that putting food at the bottom of the pack means I end up with sticky clothes and nothing to eat, and that the socks I paid ten dollars for at the outfitters in Damascus aren't worth five cents."

Sheila hides her shock at the idea of ten-dollar socks, but Gayle doesn't notice. "It's been a while since I talked to anyone but Russell. I thought I didn't have anything left to say, but I guess it's more that I don't have anything left to say to him."

That doesn't surprise Sheila too much. But she realizes she had better go check on Russell and make sure he isn't stepping on anything important.

When she comes back, Gayle says, "Okay, you're right. This trip was his idea. He's been talking about it ever since freshman year. I wasn't going to let him do it alone. But it's been great. Just terrific." She meets Sheila's eyes. "Honest. It's why I love him—he shows me who I really am."

Sheila nods like she understands, but she wonders how anyone could be confused about who they really are. You are exactly who you are forever and always. No matter how much you wish otherwise.

She doesn't know what to do with this young woman from the city with her bright eyes and open smile, her tanned collarbone peeking through the top buttons of her plaid shirt.

"Do you want to see the rabbits?"

Sheila doesn't wait for an answer, just turns away and leaves it to Gayle to follow or not.

When they approach the hutch, the most recent litter crowds against the wire.

"Oh, they're adorable!" Gayle says.

Sheila slides back the door and separates a single clump of fur from the wriggling pile. She hands the kit to Gayle, who cradles it against her chest and strokes its abbreviated ears.

"These guys are the cutest thing I've ever seen," says Gayle, nuzzling the kit. "Why do you keep so many?"

Sheila is saved from answering by Russell, who arrives from the garden drenched in sweat. Sheila yells for Angie and sends her to get some food together. Gayle hands the kit back to Sheila, who sticks it in with its siblings and locks the hutch.

Angie comes back with a plate stacked with sandwiches. Margarine is smeared on the edges of the bread, and wedges of pink meat peek out from between the slices. A couple of not-quite-clean radishes and green onions roll in the salt sprinkled at the plate's edge.

She skips back to the house and returns with two tumblers of cold tea with green leaves floating in it. "It's mint. From over there." Angie points to the wet ground near the spring. "If you drink that, you can eat as much as you want and you won't get a stomachache. It's good for your digestion."

Russell takes a tumbler and drains it in one gulp. Gayle selects a sandwich and looks at it doubtfully. But she closes her eyes and tries a bite. After a pause, she swallows and then finishes the sandwich in three more bites and reaches for another. Russell is chomping into his third. Sheila wonders what it would be like to eat so freely, so unselfconsciously, with your hunger and need all bare on the outside for anyone to witness. Like you didn't have to hide or disguise it: simply that you had walked miles and your body was depleted and so you filled it back up.

Sheila gives Angie a dirty look. She shouldn't have brought so much or cut the meat into such thick slices. They will be eating eggs for supper for the rest of the week.

Angie wanders off in the direction of the hikers' packs again. "I'm just going to fill your canteens for you."

"Seems like I haven't eaten anything that wasn't hard as a pebble in weeks. All those peanuts and raisins and granola mixed in the bag together until they start to taste the same," Gayle says, making a face. "But this is wonderful. I feel like I could go another twenty miles today."

Russell has something stuck in his teeth and is trying to fish it out with his tongue. He takes a break long enough to say, "That's good, because we've got at least another sixteen until the next shelter, and we've got to make it there before dark."

Gayle squints at the sun already moving into the west, and she seems to sag a little. Then she smiles and draws her shoulders back. "Four miles to spare, then."

Russell sets his empty glass on the stone wall and stands. Angie is back with the filled canteens, and she hands them to him.

"I know I was awfully hungry," Gayle says, easing into her pack and adjusting the straps across her chest. "But those sandwiches were so good. It wasn't chicken, was it? Did you put some special seasoning on it?"

"Just fresh country air," Sheila says. She points them back to the trail, and they head off, balancing carefully as they hop from rock to rock across the stream. On the other side, Gayle turns to look over her shoulder at them and waves. Then they are gone, swallowed by the forest.

When they are out of sight, Sheila whirls on Angie. "What did you take?"

"Nothing!"

"Liar." Sheila twists Angie's arm. "What was it?"

"I didn't *take* nothing," Angie says, wriggling free. "I gave it to them." She pulls the stack of monster cards from her pocket and waves it at Sheila. "I thought they could use some company."

"THEY WERE FROM New York City," Sheila says, passing hard-boiled eggs and green beans around the table that night while explaining to Bonnie why they have so little meat.

"That gal seemed nice enough." Thena slices a hunk of margarine from the stick and drops it on top of her beans. "Can't imagine why she'd want to live some place big and dirty like that. Cities aren't full of nothing but perverts and murderers."

From what Sheila can tell, there isn't a shortage of those anywhere. Plenty in the first category can be found down the road at the Skyline Inn every Saturday night, and you only have to turn on the radio for the latest news about the second.

"When Chernenko fires his missiles, New York will go up in flames. No one will survive. There won't be anything left except a big crater—full of cockroaches." Angie dumps vinegar over her beans and shakes on the black pepper. "Cities have lots of cockroaches because of all the garbage."

Bonnie taps an egg on her plate and pries at the shell with her thumbnail. "I went to New York City once."

Sheila chokes on a shred of dill. She didn't figure her mother had been any farther than the next county, Baltimore at the most.

"My friend Joyce was going steady with this boy—Ricky, his name was—from over by Cold Springs," Bonnie says. "But he took up with another gal, some friend of his sister's from church, and broke Joyce's heart. So she signed on with Pan Am to be a stewardess, and they sent her to New York to get trained. Before she finished, she had a weekend off, and she sent me a bus ticket so I could visit. I stayed in the dorm with her."

"What was it like?" Sheila asks. Sheila tries to imagine her mother striding along the streets of New York arm in arm with her glamorous friend. Was she stared at on the street? Or when she opened her mouth to talk? What did it feel like to be somewhere with so many people?

"We saw the Statue of Liberty and went to the top of the Empire State Building. We went with the other girls to a bar in Greenwich Village . . ." Her voice trails off, her gaze tied on the calendar from the dairy store hanging behind Thena's head.

It seems like a million years ago. The tall buildings, the roar of the city streets, the endless streams of men and women flowing from every direction. Until this moment, Bonnie had forgotten it ever happened, the memory lost and buried under ashes, like that old volcano that erupted in Italy. Back then she had still believed that something miraculous could happen, that her life could take a sudden sharp turn and she would find herself somewhere new. Somebody new.

"Foolishness," Thena says. "I worried the entire time that you'd run off with some sailor."

"What happened?" Angie asks. "In the bar?"

Their mother pats her pockets for a cigarette, but when she locates the pack, she lays it on the table beside her plate and doesn't take one out. Instead, she lifts her fork and spears some more beans.

Bonnie's wild dark hair and bright looks had attracted plenty of attention. Joyce said she should stay, sign on, and fly with her. But Bonnie couldn't stomach the thought of spending all day on her feet in the belly of a machine, catering to smug businessmen and having her ass pinched. Which was hilarious, really, now that she spends all night in the bowels of an asylum catering to men who spit in her face, shit their own pants, and still try to grab her ass.

Sheila asks, "Does your friend still live in New York?"

"New Jersey, I think. She sent a Christmas card a few years back. She met a man on one of her flights. Older than her, but nice enough, I guess."

"She never comes back here?"

Bonnie pushes back her plate and wipes her mouth. "She said she never wanted to see Ricky's ugly face again."

Angie slices a bean in half. "New Jersey's going to get it too. From the radiation. It will just take them longer to die."

☙❧

LATER THAT NIGHT, Sheila dreams about Russell and Gayle, about them curled in their bedrolls, on the bare boards of the shelter at Dead Doe Gap. About the murderer sneaking up on them while their eyes are closed and their breath whistles softly in and out. She can only see him from behind, but the knife he grips in his hand has a gleaming blade and a curved tip, like something you'd use to skin a deer.

Sleeping Sheila wants to warn them, but no sound comes out of her mouth as the murderer bends over their bodies. Her heart pounds, and the picture jumps. Now Russell is right in front of her, his eye swollen and his teeth missing and blood running from the cuts on his face. The murderer grabs him by the throat, and his eyes bulge. With his last breath he yells at Gayle to run for it, to go, to save herself.

SEVENTEEN

The Secret Keeper

"DO YOU THINK PEOPLE ARE THE SAME WHEREVER you go?" Sheila asks the boy.

They are in the woods, sheltering behind the screen of laurels. Through the gaps in the waxy leaves Sheila can make out a group of "good" patients from C Ward pulling weeds along the driveway under the supervision of burly orderlies.

It's deep summer, and their grove is bursting with honeysuckle vine. Sweet-smelling and buzzing with bees, the thick networks cover nearly every surface: trees, bushes, logs, and even rocks. Nowhere is safe from the ambitious climber.

Sheila is still not entirely sure she trusts this boy. She doesn't know who or what he is, or why only she can see him, but she does know that he will never be at school with her. He will never be at home with her. He exists only here. Talking to him is like pouring all her secrets into the trunk of a hollow tree.

"Are you asking if you would change if you went somewhere else? Or if different places grow different kinds of people?"

"Both? Neither? I don't know." Sheila sags against a vine-smothered trunk. Russell did all the heavy work in the garden, so why is she so exhausted? "These hikers came by the other day. They lost their food and wanted to work for lunch. They were from New York City."

"Yeah? What were they like?" The boy pinches a pale yellow blossom from the blanket of vines and pops it into his mouth.

"The guy was a doofus, but the girl with him . . ." Sheila plucks at the rope, which is growing tight and itchy. She's trying to figure out how to explain what she wants to say. How and whether to tell him all the complicated things Gayle made her feel. "She was nice, I guess."

"There are nice people everywhere." The boy parts the curtain of honeysuckle and crouches on the ground, peering into the undergrowth.

"That's not what I mean." Sheila tries to figure out how to explain, how to make him see why it's so complicated. He acts like he knows so much, but just when she needs him to understand, here he is pretending like he has no idea what she's talking about.

She works her jaw a few times, then gives in. The words leap out of her like they have been dammed behind her throat for weeks, and given even half the chance, they are going to burst through.

"There's this girl at school," Sheila says, adjusting the rope so she can breathe a little better. "Juanita. Juanita Herman."

Sheila can't believe she has just said Juanita's name out loud. She waits for something to happen: for her skin to spontaneously burst into flames or for her entire class to pop out from behind a tree to sneer and yell, for a plane to fly overhead skywriting *Sheila is a lezzie*.

She braces for the boy's reaction, but he's still poking around under the vines. Which is fine by her. It's easier to get the words out when she's not looking at his face, not pinned by the laser-red dot in his eye.

"I don't know what it is about her," Sheila says. "I guess most people would say she's pretty ordinary. She's not super popular, but nobody hates her either. She writes with those big bubble letters like all the other girls, and I don't even care."

Now that she has started talking about Juanita, she doesn't want to stop. Something inside her is unspooling, like once her words and feelings got a taste of freedom, they weren't going back in the dark cellar where she's been holding them.

"I think about her all the time," Sheila admits. "I just want to be around her."

"Have you ever talked to her?" The boy springs to his feet. He's cradling a wild rabbit against his chest, one of its eyes swiveled sideways to watch her.

Sheila feels a frantic stab of alarm at the way the rabbit is just *sitting there*, letting him hold it. It should be kicking, scratching, biting, struggling—anything to get away. Doesn't it know how vulnerable it is?

"I'm not going to hurt it," he says.

"It doesn't know that!" But Sheila seems to be the only one who's concerned. The rabbit nestles against the boy, as tame as if it has eaten clover from his hand every day of its life.

The boy holds the rabbit to his face, smoothing its fur against his cheek. "Why do you think you can't have what you want?"

"If I were the sort of person who gets what she wants, would I be spending the summer in a basement washing dishes for people who send their supper trays back smeared with shit?"

"You're asking the wrong question," he says.

A helicopter drums overhead, rattling the tops of the trees and drowning out the chatter of the forest. The rabbit finally shows some fear. It scrabbles against the boy and dives down the open neck of his sweatshirt to burrow against his ribs.

When the noise has passed and the bees buzz around the blossoms again, the boy points to Sheila's rope.

"What if we cut this?" he asks. "We'll get a knife from the kitchen, the big one Martha whacks through pork joints with. I'll help you. We could do it right now."

"No!" Sheila says. The familiar terror sweeps over her, crushing the air from her chest. She steadies herself against the trunk and waits for the dark spots to retreat from her eyes. "I can't."

The boy combs his fingers through the rabbit's long ears. His fingertips are dirty black crescents showing under short nails. "It's going to kill you, you know. You don't have long."

His words stab her with the bright point of their truth before she shoves them away. "Don't be stupid. This rope has been wrapped around my neck almost as long as I can remember. I'm used to it."

The boy points to a young wild cherry choked with honeysuckle. "This tree's used to it too. The vine's been wrapped around it for years. But now, when it should be growing stronger, the vine gets all the light from the sun and sucks all the water and food from the ground. The vine's getting stronger, but the tree is being smothered. It can't keep up."

The rabbit bumps the tree with its nose and several thin, pale leaves flutter to the ground. "It only has a couple of seasons left if somebody doesn't come along and chop that vine off at the root," he says.

"Vines don't have to kill things," Sheila argues. "There's green beans and peas, and Virginia creeper. None of them do any harm." But she's looking at the sickly tree, drooping under the weight of the vine. Maybe what he's saying is true, but she's too tired to think about it.

"It feels like something terrible will happen if I even try."

"Something terrible is going to happen if you don't."

SHEILA TAKES THE steps down into the cool darkness of the cellar, where the air smells like roots and stone. She likes to visit the money she has earned, both in her head and in person. She doesn't know yet what it is for, but she knows that each dollar she tucks into the paint can gets her closer to the prize.

It's like there's an empty space in her head, like a blank, black panel in one of Angie's comics. A square without a light on. Sheila's first paycheck—the money left in her hand after she made her purchases at the IGA and stored the rest down here—sparked a glow that lit one corner of that dark square.

Each dollar she adds to the can enlarges the radiance, pushing back the edges of darkness to reveal more of the picture. Each dollar gives her more room to explore and lessens the scratch of the rope around her neck.

Thinking of each week's new total is like scrying the next stroke of the pen. Fifteen dollars, and rough outlines form. Thirty-six dollars, and blurry smudges resolve into sharp lines. When she crosses one hundred dollars—$102.50 to be exact—the edges of the next frame come into view. Every dollar, every nickel, peels back a sliver of darkness and exposes more of the story.

Sheila holds the current total in her head when she leans into clouds of steam at the asylum sink, when she meets the boy behind the laurels, when she is half dozing to Tanya Tucker's lament as she leans against the window on the drive home. She cradles that number close at night when the moths fling themselves at the windows and gnats fry themselves under the shade of the lamp and fall crisp and lifeless to the floor.

How many dollars would it take to get to Baltimore? To take the bus, to buy a car. To go away for a few days. To see the ocean. To never come back. How much would it take to bring Juanita with her? Two hundred? Five hundred? How many dishes until that?

EIGHTEEN

The Thing in the Spring

AN ORDERLY PUSHES A CART LOADED WITH EMPTY supper trays down the long corridor and leaves it wordlessly beside Sheila's sink. She can always tell the trays that come from G Ward. For one, there are no knives or forks. The patients on G Ward get flat wooden scoops like the ones that come with miniature paper tubs of ice cream. Their liquids are served in Dixie cups.

But it's not just that. The trays from G Ward have their own distinct smell. Somewhere between the Aqua Net Martha uses to keep her beehive in good shape and the bottom of an August mud puddle on the verge of drying up, half-grown tadpoles and all.

Sheila lifts the trays off the cart, scrapes away the uneaten food, and drowns them in the gray, soapy water. She is nearing the bottom of the pile when her fingers catch on some kind of flap on the underside of a tray. It feels like paper.

She pushes her fogged glasses onto the top of her head and fumbles at the tray, peeling back the flap until it comes loose in her hand.

The paper is thick but softened by the steam. She holds it to her face and squints, trying to get a better look at what is drawn on it—and nearly drops it in the sink.

It is the same awful, starved woman with the black holes for eyes and spiraling maw at the center of her chest that Angie drew and gave to her after all the rain. The woman on the card is now thinner than ever, her knife-edge bones barely knit together by scraps of skin. Her black tongue stretches even longer from her bare skull, like it's going to lunge off the page and slap Sheila in her steaming face.

Sheila stares and stares, her head buzzing. This isn't possible. She remembers destroying the card, tearing it between her fingers. She remembers the scraps fluttering to the muddy ground, the white shreds swallowed by the fast-flowing water and whisked away down the mountain.

Now here it is in her hand again. Even in the steel room of chicken skins and lemon Dawn, the card smells of camphor and sassafras root. And it's stuck to her wet fingers like glue, like it will not let her go.

The ringing in her ears blocks out the running water, the industrial mixer, and Martha's radio reporting that a suspicious man was seen raiding the dumpster behind High's dairy store last night. Sheila's blood shrinks away from her edges, rushing back into the vital cavities of her heart and liver so fast that she loses her balance and has to catch at the slippery edge of the sink to keep from sliding to the wet tiled floor.

This card, this blackened, distorted mirror, should never have been drawn. Now it has roared back from destruction, resurrected and recombined itself, heaving its exposed bones through the mountain's unseen channels to force itself back into her hand.

Sheila pulls herself upright, and the noise of the water rushing from the faucet comes back to her. She is sweating all over, but she is so cold. The flesh on her arms prickles with bumps that spread across her neck and shoulders.

There has to be an explanation. Something that will make this make sense.

Sheila wants to blame Angie—after all, she drew the hideous thing in the first place. But Angie has never been to the asylum and certainly never set foot on G Ward.

Holding the corner with her fingertips, Sheila slides the card into the pocket of her smock. She thinks she can hear the woman's bones rattle and the cry of her hoarse voice. She squeezes more detergent into the sink and blasts it with scalding water from the sprayer hose. Artificially lemon-scented clouds of steam billow around her as she rinses the remaining trays, aiming the spraying water like a cannon.

☙☙

SHEILA TRACKS DOWN the boy on the asylum's west lawn. His white sneakers dangle from the branches of a towering hundred-year maple. She peers into the glossy leaves to find him draped over a limb like a bobcat, his back against the trunk, a book in his hands.

She swipes at his feet, but they're just beyond her reach. He's so absorbed in reading—or pretending to read—that he doesn't seem to notice her at all. A nurse pushing an inmate in a wheelchair is giving her a curious look, so instead of calling, Sheila tosses a pebble, bouncing it off the book in his hands.

He looks up, and she catches the glint of red in his eye.

The boy taps the book's mildew-spotted cover. "Did you know that the Iron Mountain facility was built on this spot because of the nearby springs? The water is supposed to have healing powers."

"Where did you get that?"

"There's a library on the second floor. They used to think reading was good for the patients."

He closes the book and hops to the ground. "Of course, that's out of fashion these days, same as thinking that magic water is going to fix what's wrong in people's heads. They keep that room locked now."

"If it's locked, how did you get in?" Sheila says. "Never mind, I don't want to know."

"I've noticed."

"You think you're funny, don't you?" Sheila checks over her shoulder to make sure no one can see her talking to him. "I don't have much time. If I'm not back in the kitchen in ten minutes, Martha will have a fit."

"You're the one that came looking for me."

"If you're such an expert on this place, what do you know about G Ward?" Sheila shakes the rope out of her way and circles the tree. "Everybody acts like it's so special, like something top secret is going on in there."

"You know what the people who work here are like. They like to have something to talk about. It makes their day more interesting."

Sheila knows that's true. Look at the way they go on about the murdered women and breathlessly follow any news about the hunt for the murderer. Still, she knows there's more to G Ward than he's letting on.

"Have you ever been in there?" she demands.

"It's locked," he says.

"Yeah, just like the library."

"Why is it so important all of a sudden? G Ward has always been locked, since the day you got here."

"Because *this* came from there." Sheila retrieves the starved woman from her pocket and shows it to him.

He takes the card and studies it. The front of his sweat-shirt twitches, and the rabbit from the other day pokes its head out of a pocket.

"Where did you get this?" He pats his shoulder, and the rabbit scampers along his arm to sit beside his head, as if it, too, is examining the card.

"That's what I'm asking you. It was stuck to the bottom of a tray I got back from G Ward."

"What does that have to do with me?"

"Who else around here is apparently completely invisible and can come and go through locked doors? I don't imagine you would have any trouble getting onto G Ward and putting this there."

The boy holds up his hands, and the rabbit wobbles to keep its balance. "Okay, okay, you're right. I probably could do something like that. But why would I? Why are you so upset?"

"My stupid sister drew it. She gave that"—she points at the card—"to me weeks ago, and I ripped it up. I tore it into pieces and dropped it in the mud. It was completely destroyed. And now it's back!"

The boy's head swivels between Sheila and the image on the paper. Like he can see exactly what it's saying. Like he knows what she really is.

Sheila fights the urge to snatch the card out of his hand and flee to some dark corner.

"You said your sister drew this?"

"Angie draws things like that all the time. She has this whole collection of weird monsters that she carries around with her. She sleeps with them under her pillow. Sometimes she gives them to people. She's a creep."

The boy scratches the rabbit's ears, and it rubs its face against him. "Whoever drew this knows more than they're letting on. They see more."

It's all Sheila can do not to roll her eyes. "You're joking. My sister runs around playing war games all day. She doesn't think about anything except candy and comic books."

"Maybe you underestimate her."

"Unlikely. Besides, she's *my* sister. What would you know about it?"

"Nothing, probably. But have you ever asked her why she does it? What these drawings mean?"

The cards do seem important to Angie. She takes them with her everywhere—it's like they're her imaginary friends. On the other hand, Angie also thinks the murderer is a Russian spy hiding in the woods and that she, a twelve-year-old girl, is going to capture him.

"Even if she is some genius artist," Sheila says, "that doesn't explain how the card got put back together again and ended up on a tray coming out of G Ward."

"You're right. It doesn't." The boy holds the card out to Sheila.

She backs away. "I don't want it. It's disgusting."

"You tried to get rid of it once before, and it didn't work. Keep it until you figure out what it means." He presses the card into her hand.

"Keep it," he repeats. "It belongs to you."

NINETEEN

The Green Tunnel

ANGIE SHAKES THE BLOODSTAINED SHIRT UNDER SUE'S nose. "C'mon, Sue. You're as smart as those police dogs, aren't you?"

Sue tips her head to one side and looks at Angie.

Angie brings out the bit of pork gristle she has saved and unwraps it. She lets Sue have a good sniff. Sue snaps for it, jumping and wagging her tail.

"That's right," Angie says, pulling the morsel away. "That's what you get if you do a good job. Now go on, Sue, get after him. Find me that murderer."

Sue whines and paws at Angie's hand, trying to lick the pork right out of the paper.

Angie passes the bloody rag in front of Sue's nose one more

time, then trots forward a few paces, dangling the stinking cloth. "Like this. Follow it. You can do it."

Sue chases after her a couple steps, but she has her silly face on. Angie drags her hands over her face, smelling the pork grease that clings to her fingers. This doesn't happen to real policemen. They have smart dogs that have gone through years of training. All she has is a dopey dog that her brother brought home in a cardboard box to stop his buddy up the road from drowning her. He said she was going to be his gun dog, but Sue was never any good at hunting. To be fair, neither was her brother.

Truth is, no one in this family seems to be any good at anything. Angie gives in and tosses Sue the rest of the pork. She's just turning back to the house when she hears a blood-curdling bay. Sue is frozen in position with her tail stiff and pointed like an arrow. She quivers there, then jams her nose to the ground and takes off down the mountain, yipping high and fast. Angie chases after, but she can't keep up.

Whatever Sue's on the trail of, it's taking her straight down the mountainside as fast as her four legs can scramble. If she doesn't stop or turn aside, she'll reach the hard road in a few seconds—long before Angie can reach her.

"No no no, Sue! Stop! Come back!"

In what seems like just a few seconds, Sue has reached the edge of the property and is breaking through the bushes at the sides of the road.

Angie sees the logging truck coming, but there's nothing she can do.

Angie yells and yells until her throat is raw, but Sue pays no mind, barking furiously as she bounds out of the trees, onto the blacktop, and right into the truck's path.

The driver blasts the horn, and Angie watches stock still as Sue's gleaming black body disappears under the crushing wheels.

The truck doesn't stop, only roars on in a cloud of stinking gray exhaust, flinging stones from its eighteen wheels.

Angie can't make herself look. She can't stand to see Sue's flattened body, lifeless eyes, smashed ribs—and all of it because of her. Her fault, hers hers hers. Her own body is like a jammed radio frequency, pinned between puking, screaming, and sobbing. She collapses onto the dirt of the mountain, the back of her hand wedged between her teeth, chewing miserably.

At last she steels herself to look up, to face what she has done, and there is Sue, dancing around on the other side of the road, pink tongue panting from her mouth, looking completely unfazed. The dog has somehow survived her journey under the truck's killing wheels without a scratch on her.

Angie's relief is instant. She's on her feet before she knows it, racing toward the dog to wrap her arms around Sue's warm, wriggling, living body. She pelts down the slope, hops over the ditch, so intent on Sue that she doesn't see the pickup barreling around the curve from the other direction.

Her screams mix with the tires' screech as the truck fishtails and finally judders to a stop, the front grille level with her head, the top of the hood grazing her mouth.

Angie's ears ring, and everything feels both incredibly clear and buzzing with static at the same time. She's taking in the fact that she's still on her feet, upright and whole, when the truck door swings open and heavy boots hit the ground. A voice shouts, "What the *hell* do you think you're doing?"

Angie's mind lags a few seconds behind, still trying to grasp what just happened, but her body reacts to the fury in the man's voice, cringing away.

But then she sees it's only Butch. Just Butch. Her friend.

Her relief doesn't last long. Butch is madder than she's ever seen him, face red behind his beard as he stalks toward her. "You want to tell me why I almost smeared you across the Cold Springs Road?"

"It was Sue. I was trying to save her."

Butch looks at the dog, who is sniffing happily in the bushes. "Looks fine to me."

"She ran out in front of a logging truck. I—"

"Can it. Get in the truck and get out of the damn road before we all get hit." Butch's face is still so red, so ferocious. Angie can barely look at him. Her eyes slide away to stare at a rat snake flattened on the blacktop, its scales flaking off, flies buzzing around.

Butch stomps to the back of the truck and drops the tailgate. Sue jumps happily into the bed, and Angie slinks over to the passenger door and climbs inside.

Butch's radio is busted, like just about everything else in the truck, and they ride in silence for the few minutes it takes to drive around by the hard road to the bottom of her lane. This isn't what it's supposed to be like with Butch— Angie feels like she's riding in the truck alongside her mom or Sheila.

When she can't take the silence anymore, Angie says, "What happens when you die?"

"I've never been dead so I can't say as I know."

"But you've seen someone dead before, haven't you?"

Butch's mouth tightens, and his fingers twitch on the steering wheel. Angie knows Butch doesn't like to talk about Vietnam. But as a soldier, he had to have seen dead bodies— maybe even made some that way.

She hurries on. "I was just thinking about those women that got themselves killed. They weren't from around here. But they died here. Does that matter?"

"How do you mean?" Butch says as the truck rattles off the hard road onto the gravel next to the rusted mailbox.

"Do they get mixed up? From being in the wrong place?" Angie reaches for the door handle but doesn't turn it.

Butch glances over, but he's already moving the gear shift into reverse. "A lot of people die away from home. Let's hope it's a long time before you have to find out more. Now get on with you."

Angie gets out and slams the door. Sue jumps out of the back and races ahead, eager to get back to the cool dirt under the porch. Angie wants to say something more to Butch, but she doesn't know what. So she just raises her hand and watches in silence as Butch's truck jolts down the road.

She's only partway up the lane when the shaking hits her, violent waves that crash through her body. Suddenly, she's exhausted, cold and weak all over. She drops down on her butt, nauseous and dizzy, everything rushing back to her now with vivid clarity, brighter and clearer than when it was actually happening.

Angie staggers to the edge of the lane and unspools her whole body into the dirt, not even feeling the gravel poking along her spine. It smells sweet here, where thick vines of honeysuckle, multiflora, and blackberry blooms close in from both sides of the lane, forming a green tunnel that insulates her from the rest of the world.

All the adrenaline of what just happened—the chase after Sue, the dog's body scraping under the wheels of the logging truck, the full-frontal view of the grille of Butch's pickup right against her own face, licking her with the impact that never came—is draining out of Angie now, leaching through her bones, her skin, and passing directly into the ground. She wonders what it would be like if all of her energy left, just kept going, spiraling out and down into the mountain forever.

The murderer's shirt is still in her pocket, and Angie takes it out, trying to imagine what it would be like to lose so much blood that it soaked the threads of a shirt until it turned black. She holds the cloth up to the sky, blotting out the sun. Then takes her hands away and lets the fabric fall onto her face. Her body heaves, and she closes her eyes. Everything is quiet and still as her breath rasps in and out through the ragged, bloody cloth.

TWENTY

The Truthteller

MAYBE THE OLD WOMAN HAS BEEN DYING FOR A long time, but she had the will to keep the secret inside her body, to sit with ruin in her bones and not let it out. Now her strength is failing, and she can't keep her death from showing through. She spends more time in the past, carrying water and chasing cows with her sisters, her mind roaming where her body cannot.

Sheila helps Thena climb out of bed and settle into a chair. The old woman lifts her arms, and Sheila pulls the soiled nightgown over her head and replaces it with a clean one from the dresser. She strips the bed of the damp sheets and checks the mattress beneath. It smells faintly of urine, but the rough wool cover is thankfully dry.

"Angie!" Sheila yells through the door. "Bring me a fresh set of sheets. And a pillowcase."

"Are you warm enough?" she asks Thena. The old woman's eyes are cloudy, but she nods like she understands. She raises her arm, hand grasping at empty air.

"It won't be a minute," Sheila says, bending over her. "And then we'll get you back in bed."

Sheila marches toward the door. "Angie, I told you—"

"I'm here," Angie says, appearing with an armful of linens. "Hold your horses."

Sheila takes the bundle and shakes out the bottom sheet. She smooths it across the mattress and tucks in the corners. She looks for Angie to give her a hand, but her sister is dancing around the room, stabbing and feinting at the rabbit candy jar with a big knife.

The first thing Sheila thinks is that while the boy at the asylum has been right about many things, his notion that Angie has some kind of hidden smarts couldn't be more wrong. The next thing she realizes is that she doesn't recognize the knife Angie is wielding with such enthusiasm—it has a molded red handle and an odd, curved blade.

"Where did you get that?" Sheila asks, giving up on the sheet corner, which snaps back into the middle of the bed.

"None of your business!" Angie shouts and runs out of the room.

Sheila has too much to do to waste time chasing after her. She finishes making the bed and gets Thena settled back on the pillows. She pulls a comb through her hair, divides it into three sections, and twists it strand over strand, her fingers moving without thought.

Sheila ties off the braid, checks to make sure Thena has a cup of water at hand, and turns to leave.

"Wait!" Thena cries out. "Effie!"

Sheila turns back. Thena's face is twisted in frustration. She kicks at the sheets and scrabbles a hand toward her feet. "Help me get this thing off my leg."

Sheila lifts the sheets and runs her hands down the old woman's bare leg. The skin is dry and a few hairs sprout along the blade of her shin, but Sheila feels nothing else, not even when she rakes lightly with her nails to be sure.

"There's nothing there."

Thena shakes her leg. "It must have got hold of me when I crossed the fence line. Get it off. It's slowing me down."

Sheila pulls back the sheets so Thena can see for herself. "I just checked. You're fine."

But the old woman's eyes scrunch like she's about to cry. "Get it off!" Her leg jerks and pinpricks of blood appear above her ankle, like the jagged tears from a blackberry vine.

❧

THAT NIGHT, THENA stays in her room and doesn't come out for supper. Sheila brings her bread and margarine, a soft egg, and a dish of watermelon pickle. When she returns to collect the plate—the yolk broken, the bread half eaten—she doesn't notice Angie lurking in the shadows at the end of the hall.

When Sheila is gone, Angie pokes a toe into the darkness of Thena's room, a scout feeling the way. Nothing happens, so she snaps the rest of her body to catch up, gliding across the floor until she feels the flat weave of the rag rug under her feet.

Now that she is close, Angie doesn't look at the old woman lying in the bed. Instead, she listens to her breathing, which labors in and out like someone working a pump. Whatever is going on, Angie wants it to stop. She wants it to go back to the way things were. She takes the cards from her pocket and shuffles, waiting for them to tell her what to do. The paper hums between her fingers, looping over and over until . . . *now!*

Angie splits the deck and extracts the hot card from the middle and turns it over.

Oh no. Not this one, please not this one. In the dim light, she can see the torn leaves in the Worm King's hair, the sinewy roots of his arms, and the red crawler wiggling in the corner of his eye. He stares back at her, daring her to disobey.

The Worm King is powerful enough to intervene—Angie knows that. But she doesn't trust him.

Thena snores. Sheila's feet shuffle overhead, creaking the floorboards of their room upstairs. Their mother is in the kitchen, clanking dishes, stacking pots and pans. The Worm King burns in Angie's hand, like a fox crouched over a rabbit hole, ready to spring.

Angie turns all the cards face up and races through them. They're all wrong. All of this is wrong. She's not doing it the right way. She keeps flicking the cards from hand to hand, licking her dry lips. Something else will come up. Something better will offer itself. It has to.

Then she sees it—a long face, blank and featureless. Two hands outstretched, fingers splayed. In the palm of the left hand, a mouth stretches wide in a scream or a laugh. In the right hand, lips twist behind thick stitches holding the mouth firmly closed. Nestled between the ribs in the center of the creature's chest is a wide, blinking eye.

The Truthteller. It's her only choice.

Holding her breath, Angie inches to the bed and slips the card under the mattress. A cold draft billows against her ankles, like a fan blowing over ice cubes, coming straight from under the bed. Thena mutters in her sleep, and Angie bites her lip to keep a shout locked inside. But the old woman is only turning onto her side under the blanket. It's time for Angie to go.

Folded in her hand, the Worm King scorches her palm. He's so angry. Angie hasn't played by the rules, and now she will have to figure out what to do with him. She knows he is not done with her.

☙

THE NEXT DAY, Thena wants to get out of bed. Sheila helps her make her way to the front room and settles her into the best chair, in front of the open window where mud wasps buzz in and out of their nest under the eaves and humming-birds sip from the scarlet blooms of the runner beans. The summer outside is thick and green, but Sheila pulls a thread-bare quilt over the old woman's knees just in case.

When Angie gallops past, chasing Sue in a game of tag, Sheila grabs her sleeve. "You stay and sit with her. Don't go wandering off somewhere."

Angie makes a face. "Why can't you do it?"

"Because I've got the washing to do this morning. Unless you want to trade?"

Angie rubs Sue's ears but doesn't say anything.

"I thought so. Just keep an eye on her, and if anything happens, holler for me."

That gets Angie's attention. "Happens? Like what?"

"If she has a funny turn or something," Sheila hisses. "Okay?"

"What are you two whispering about?" Thena asks, her voice sounding stronger than it has in weeks.

"We were just arguing over who's going to make supper tonight," Sheila lies.

"Effie always chopped while I cooked," Thena says. "It makes the work go easier."

"Must be nice to have a sister you can count on," Sheila says, cutting her eyes at Angie.

"I got to go to our room first," Angie says.

"Fine. Just don't take forever. And while you're there, you may as well bring the sheets from your bed too."

Sheila lugs the washtub out from the corner of the porch and has to stop to catch her breath. She rests her hands on her knees, fighting the wave of dizziness, then drags the tub onto a bare patch of grass and starts filling it with water she heated on the stove. She adds a spoonful of washing powder followed by the soiled sheets from Thena's bed. She's pressing them under the water when Angie returns with a pile of linen and a length of rope dangling from her pocket.

"You can dump them there," Sheila says. Angie drops the sheets beside the tub and heads inside. Over the sloshing of the fabric against the tub's sides, Sheila hears the voices of Angie and Thena through the open window.

"Here, tie my wrists," Angie says.

"What do you want to do that for?"

"So I can practice getting loose."

"You are a strange child," Thena says. But she must be tying the rope, because a moment later Angie says, "Tighter!"

Sheila kneads and sloshes, staring out over the collapsing stone fence, half listening to the rhythm of her hands and trying not to think about the hanks of her own dark hair she found left behind on her pillow this morning. When she shakes free of the memory, she realizes Thena is telling

Angie another one of her stories. Her voice is strong and clear and drifts easily through the open window.

"There once was a girl who lived on this mountain," Thena was saying. "The girl was so thin that her bones jutted out under her skin like birch branches in winter."

"Didn't she eat?" Angie asks.

"At first she did, but it seemed like it was hard for her. When a plate was set in front of her, she ground her way through the potatoes and meat, chewing with determination, like she was crawling through a swamp on her belly. But then she stopped taking the plates altogether, just stood and turned away. Even when she was smacked, she would sit down again, but she wouldn't eat."

Sheila's hands freeze in the wash water. She thought she knew all of Thena's stories, had listened to them all so many times she could have told them herself. But she has never heard this one before.

"The girl became secretive, flinching when anyone came near and ducking out of sight. She crouched at the edge of the porch, holding her stomach, and gagged and coughed, but nothing came out of her but air, no matter how hard she heaved or sweated or closed her eyes and wished it would go away."

"Gross!" Angie's voice says. "What was wrong with her?"

"Nobody knew. But something had to be done. Her grandmother said so, and her mother agreed. So one day the mother grabbed the girl as she crept along the house's walls. The girl tried to run, but the grandmother was faster because she wasn't old yet and her hands didn't shake and her eyes were clear for what she needed to do."

Sheila bunches and stretches the heavy cotton, scraping it against the slats of the washboard. Turn and slap. Turn and slap. She doesn't want to listen, but the old woman's words seem to be aimed straight at her ear.

"The women didn't know if the mountain had claimed this girl out of love or punishment. But whichever it was, the girl was suffering. If the girl died—as she would soon—she would belong to the mountain forever. The women wondered why, when the mountain had so much time, it couldn't wait another forty, sixty, even eighty years before nestling the girl against its stone ribs. But the mountain was ready now."

"Cool!" Angie says.

"The older woman fastened her fingers around the girl's thin wrist. The girl shook her off and tried to run, leapt like a rabbit with its tail in the mouth of a chasing dog. But together the two women brought her down face-first on the braided rug and dragged her back by the ankles, her cheek scraping over the strips cut from work shirts, flowered dresses, and a dead uncle's striped Sunday suit.

"The mother pinned the girl's arms, and together they rolled her in a blanket. The girl was wild but weak, and she fought between fury and fainting, her eyes twitching under her lids as she rolled in and out of consciousness. The mother sat astride the bundled girl, and the old woman gripped an antler-handled knife. The blade was worn thin from honing, straight in the center and pointed at the tip."

Sheila's hands go cold to the ends of her fingers. The sheets bunched between her hands have lost meaning.

"The old woman held the knife with the same determination as the girl chewing for hours through a boiled potato. 'Where is it?' she demanded. 'Where is it hiding?'"

"Is the girl haunted?" interrupts Angie. "Does she got a demon in her?"

Thena doesn't answer, only continues the story. "The woman cast her eyes over the girl—her defiant chin, her hunched shoulders, her bellowing ribs, her kicking feet. The girl bucked something fierce, struggling to escape.

"'Hold her still!' the woman shouted to the mother.

"Then she added a few words that might have been a prayer or might not and stabbed the knife into the girl's throat."

Angie lets out a hiss of excitement, but Sheila barely hears it. She's not here anymore. She is somewhere in the blue sky looking down on a girl kneeling beside an old washtub in a patch of white clover.

"The mother twisted her face away, but not before blood splashed across her cheek. The girl shook in her mother's arms, and she held her daughter tight. Something fell to the floor, solid and heavy.

"A piece of quartz the size of a walnut. Blood stained the floor where it fell, but the stone itself was clean, coated in pale mucus that the old woman peeled back with the tip of the knife. Underneath, the rock was milky white and veined with gold. But deep inside lurked an iron-red flaw, like a drop of blood under ice."

Sheila holds her breath, afraid to make a sound.

"The girl fainted dead away. Blood surged from her throat. The two women had to work fast. The older one flayed the girl's throat—she had to find the tail, the root that had tied the stone to the girl's body. She had to remove every last tendril. She grabbed and pulled, and the fine white worms came wriggling out."

Sheila's throat closes, and she doubles over, gagging. She can feel it, the choking tickle in the poor girl's throat. She clutches the sides of the tub, trying to make the air in her lungs flow in the right direction.

"Did the girl survive?" Angie asks.

"They sewed her back up with a needle and thread. You would have thought the mother was sewing lace on a christening gown, her stitches were so careful and small.

"The worms they burned. Lit them at one end and watched them sizzle into ash. Then the old woman scooped up the stone with her bloody hand. She wrapped it in a swatch of cotton with a yarrow blossom and two iron nails and tied the knot with a length of plastic she plaited out of an empty milk bag. She hid the bundle away where no one would find it."

Angie is disappointed. "So they saved her?"

"For a time," Thena says. "But you can't win against a mountain. The mountain always finds a way."

Sheila dumps the tub onto its side, and the dirty water flows across the grass. The old woman's mind is going, Sheila reminds herself. Only yesterday, Thena was calling for her long-dead sister, imagining they were together again.

Sheila wrings the sheets between her hands and twists them tight, squeezing out the water with all her fading strength. This is just another story, and it has nothing to do with her.

TWENTY-ONE

The Stinking Thief

THE COOL AIR OF THE CELLAR IS A RELIEF ON SHEILA'S skin. It smells of earth and stillness, and she welcomes the dim light after the glare of the sun in the world above. Thena's story has left her feeling like she has fallen into a swollen creek and can't get her head above the churning water.

The paint can rests on the tool shelf, right where she left it last payday when she added another nine dollars to the stash. She gave the rest to her mother to cover groceries because paying for the old woman's extra medicine has eaten every available dollar and then some. As they carried the bags and loaded them into the car in the IGA parking lot, Bonnie said that she would find a way to make it up to her, but Sheila turned her head and pretended not to hear.

But now she wants to touch the bills and reassure herself that here, at least, nothing has changed. She lifts the can from the shelf and pries off the lid. Her fingers graze the envelope inside, soft and creased from handling. Her breath slows. Her muscles release, and she feels like she is spooling out into a smooth stretch of water, lifted on the gentle current.

Sheila lifts the flap—and plunges over a waterfall. The envelope is empty, and the cash inside is gone.

A strange calm drapes over her like a blanket. Sheila replaces the envelope in the can and puts the can back on the shelf. She returns to the door where the sunlight from outside shines down the stairs. She leans against the frame and swallows hard. Closes her eyes, then opens them. She takes a firm hold on the panic rising in her throat and stuffs it down into her feet, where it leaves her toes curled with ice.

She retraces her steps back to the shelf. She reaches for the paint can and—looking straight ahead at a tangle of cobwebs against the damp stone wall—lifts the lid. Feeling carefully, she extracts the envelope and promises herself that this time the money will be there. The paper is flimsy and weightless, but she insists she can't be sure until she sees. It won't be true until she opens her eyes.

But she can't stay in the cellar for the rest of her life. Or even the rest of today. She has to feed the rabbits and the dogs, pinch bugs off the squash vines, chop the branches of the fallen hemlock for kindling, and find something to make for supper.

Sheila opens her eyes. The envelope is empty, and all her money is gone gone gone. She had over two hundred by now—$210.70. And now she is back to zero.

The can clatters against the stones as she sinks to the ground, crushing the empty envelope in her fist. The ceiling drops, the walls collapse, the floor sinks away, the light blinks out. Sheila is alone in the dark.

Finally she begins to recover. She picks herself up and collects the tumbled can from where it has rolled under the collapsing onion bins. When she sees the white paper stuck in the bottom, the flicker of hope is so dim it doesn't breach her despair. She reaches for it with the dullest curiosity, observing herself pull it out as if her hand belongs to someone else.

She is holding a small rectangular card. Blue lines are printed on one side, and the shadow of marker bleeds through from the other. She turns it over.

A bulging, hairy creature hunches in a maze of dark tunnels that snake from the edges of the card. At the exit to one of the tunnels, a hand sneaks out, its nimble fingers grasping for prizes beyond the card's edge. The monster's shadowed face bares its teeth with wicked glee. In the tunnel behind it, a heap of stolen treasures gleam.

SHEILA WAITS UNTIL evening, when she and Angie are alone in their room. Bonnie is downstairs listening to the radio. The news reports have stopped talking about the murderer so much. It's like they've given up.

Bonnie hums along to Tammy Wynette as she sets out her uniform and writes letters in her head to her jailbird son. A son is special because he can do all the things a man does: work hard, earn money, lift heavy things, make decisions, fix cars and roofs and leaky sinks. But he came from your body, and he always belongs to you.

She and Rodney were going to take little Sam with them when they fled west. Rodney had brushed her hair behind her ear, looked into her eyes so tenderly, and whispered, "We're going to do it, baby. I'm going to take you all the way to the Pacific. You and that boy are going to be swimming in the sea." They would raise their son on the road to be full of courage and adventure, bold and self-sufficient. What a glorious start he would have.

Sam was just a baby in his crib and shouldn't have been able to understand, but maybe he had. Maybe he blamed her for taking that glorious future away from him, wrenching off his trajectory like a sheared railroad track. After all, a boy needed his father, and Sam had his cruelly stolen away. He was wounded, injured, wronged, denied. Any missteps or wrong turns he made—she couldn't blame him. It had all happened before he could even walk. It wasn't his fault. As his mother, she is the only one who knows his tender secret, the little boy he once was. She still sees that in him and will always forgive him.

Upstairs, Angie has taken off her pants and is puttering beside her bed in her T-shirt and a pair of graying panties with a big hole on the hip. Her back is turned to Sheila, and as she pulls the shirt over her head, Sheila tackles her and slams her onto the bed.

Angie claws at the shirt stuck to her face, but Sheila holds the fabric tight, trapping her.

"Get off me!" Angie kicks and flails. Everything smells of kerosene. Angie got into a patch of chiggers when she was chasing after Sue, and their mother rubbed kerosene into the bites to drive them out. Angry red bumps circle Angie's ankles, wrists, and waist and scatter along her inner thighs to her crotch.

"Not until you tell me where it is." Sheila scrapes her fingernails over a thick ring of bites and Angie wails.

"Quit it! What are you talking about?"

Sheila leans close to Angie's covered face and hisses, "My money. What did you do with my money?"

Angie thrashes and her elbow connects with Sheila's chin. Sheila falls back, and Angie wriggles loose, sitting up and yanking the shirt over her head.

"I didn't take your stupid money."

"Don't lie to me. I know you took it. You left your card." Sheila slaps the thief card down on the bed in front of Angie. The creature hunches in the mouth of the tunnel, guarding its stolen treasure.

Angie's eyes go wide, and she reaches for the card. "But—"

"Are you going to tell me it's not yours? That you didn't draw it?"

"It *was* mine, but I gave it away." Angie hugs a pillow to her naked chest. "To those hikers. It's what I put in their pack when they left."

Sheila remembers Angie fiddling with their packs. If Angie's telling the truth, does that mean that Gayle and Russell were the ones who stole her money? She can't believe Gayle would do something like that. Now, Russell, she could easily believe it of him, but how could he have known that her money was hidden in a paint can in the root cellar?

Sheila scratches at her neck where the rope is rubbing painfully and she seems to be developing some sort of rash. She steps back from the bed, putting a little space between them. Could Angie be telling the truth?

"I saw them go," Sheila says, thinking out loud. "They crossed the creek and hiked back out to the trail. Surely they didn't come back all that way."

Sheila wonders if now is the time to ask Angie about the card she found on the tray from G Ward. She wants to blame

Angie for that too, except for that whole problem with Angie never having been to the asylum. Still, the boy said there was more to Angie than she could see.

Before Sheila can make up her mind, Angie asks, "What were you going to do with it? What were you saving that money for?"

Fractured images flash through Sheila's head so fast she can't make sense of them. Juanita, cities, strangers, dark tunnels, bright lights, the crash of waves on the sea. People, things, and places she doesn't recognize, that she can't describe or even imagine. Places with more space, more room, more everything.

"That's not the point," Sheila says.

"You must have been saving it for something." Angie's hair sticks up in tufts from the struggle with her T-shirt, and the bites on her skin stand out like red alarms, but she is looking at Sheila with something like sympathy, her chin resting on top of the crumpled pillow.

"I worked for it. It was mine." The loss Sheila feels is like someone blasting the asylum's sink nozzle of cold water right through her chest, greasy pea residue dripping down her ribs and splashing on the floor.

"How much did you have?" Angie scratches at the bites on her wrist.

Sheila swallows hard so she can get the words out. She is not going to let Angie see her cry. "Two hundred dollars."

Their eyes meet, and for a second, Sheila thinks that Angie understands how important this is to her. She almost feels bad for how she attacked Angie a few moments ago. Maybe they really are sisters. Maybe someday when Angie is older, when they are both grown up, it will be different between them. They will share things and help each other. They will understand.

"Maybe the Russians took it," Angie says.

Sheila shuts her eyes and lets a long breath fade from between her lips. This time, she's mad at herself. For ever thinking that she and Angie could be friends. That they had anything in common.

"I could help you get it back. And if we catch the murderer, we could even get that reward." Angie leans over the side of the bed and paws through the pile of dirty clothes. She pulls out the knife she was brandishing in Thena's room while Sheila was trying to change the sheets and waves it in triumph. The brand-new, expensive-looking knife with the red handle that Sheila has never seen before.

A fiery curtain descends on Sheila's vision. She should have known better than to ever trust a word Angie says. After all, she only has Angie's word for it that she put that card in the hikers' packs in the first place. Angie is a liar, has always been a liar, always will be.

Sheila hurls herself at Angie and twists her arm behind her back. The knife clatters to the floor.

"Liar! You shitting liar!" Sheila straddles Angie and shoves her face into the blankets.

Angie says something, but with her mouth pressed into the mattress, it comes out as "Maagh!"

"You took my money and you bought that fucking knife." Sheila punctuates every word with a vicious shake.

Angie gets her mouth free long enough to cry, "That's not what happened!"

Sheila pins her sister to the mattress, leaning on her with all her weight. A red flush spreads across Angie's face as Sheila presses down harder on her back. "Where did you get it then?"

"I didn't take your money." Angie tries to curl into a ball. Her words splutter through her hiccupping tears. "You're hurting me."

It takes Sheila a minute to register that Angie isn't fighting back anymore. That she isn't fake crying, but outright blubbering like a little kid. Like a kid that's scared.

Footsteps sound on the stairs, and Sheila freezes.

"Everything all right up there?" Bonnie calls.

"Fine," Sheila yells back. She nudges her sister with her knee until Angie gulps her tears down enough to echo, "Fine."

Sheila releases Angie and gets off the bed. She won't look at her sister. Angie stays collapsed on the mattress, crying into the sheets.

"Stop crying," Sheila says. "You're not hurt."

Sheila retrieves the knife from the floor.

Angie begins to squeak out a protest, but Sheila cuts her off. "Since my money paid for this knife, it's mine now."

SHEILA SCOOPS A can full of rabbit pellets from the bag on the porch and pumps fresh water into the bucket. She has today off from the asylum, and she is glad to get out of her room and away from the lingering stain of her fight with Angie yesterday. It will be hot later, but for now the sun is only just rising, and a thick fog congeals around the middle of the trees.

As she carries the bucket toward the hutch, Sheila thinks about how many shifts she will have to work just to make up for what she has lost. She's not looking where she is going, which wouldn't be a problem in the winter but is stupid in the summer because there's no rule that says a copperhead won't be lazing in the grass just because she's dwelling on her disappointments. So when her foot bumps something that shouldn't be there, her first reaction is *snake!*

Sheila jumps back so fast the water sloshes out of the bucket and right over the loose, unbraided hair of Thena, who is sprawled face down in the middle of the path in her nightgown, one arm outstretched toward the trees, her bare toes pointing back toward the house.

Sheila sets down the can and bucket and crouches over the old woman. One of the rabbits hears the rattle of feed and presses its face to the wire of the hutch. Sheila reaches for Thena to roll her over and see if she needs help. But when she touches the knob of her shoulder—when she makes contact with the flesh through the thin flannel—Sheila knows there is nothing left to do. She holds her hand under Thena's nose, but she has seen enough dead things to know that she's not going to feel any breath.

At first she thinks of violence, that the murderer got her. But there's not a mark on Thena except the scrape and bruise of falling on her face. Sheila rocks back on her heels. Lately, except for the day when she told the story, Thena has barely had the strength to sit up in bed and couldn't hold a spoon without shaking. And yet here she is, a few steps from the edge of the forest.

Thena's nightgown sleeve has fallen back, and her outstretched arm is bare and hairless. But that hand is curled into a fist, Sheila notices, as if holding onto something.

Sheila isn't sure she's going to do it until she is already peeling back the fingers of Thena's hand. There *is* something inside. The tail end of a white cloth is tucked in the wrinkled folds of the old woman's palm. Sheila tugs on it, and the object spills out, round and dense, bundled in a scrap of cotton and wrapped with a braided plastic cord.

Plastic that could have been cut from a milk bag, Sheila's mind volunteers before she stamps the thought down and shoves it away. She picks at the knot, but her fingernail pries back from the bed, flaking away from her finger like a fish scale. Sheila slams the nail back into place only to find that others are coming loose too. A shudder ripples through her body and a bulb of undigested egg rises in her throat. Sheila closes her eyes and breathes hard through her nose until the nausea passes. When she opens her eyes, Angie is suddenly beside her.

Sheila drops the cotton bundle in the can of rabbit food and shovels pellets on top.

Angie stares down at the old woman. Sheila wishes she hadn't spilled all that water on her head. It makes her look undignified, like she was caught in the middle of her bath. In the middle of something private.

"Is she sick?" Angie asks, hand hovering near her own mouth, like she's about to suck her thumb.

"I think it's a little bit more than sick." Sheila smooths the old woman's hair. "I didn't think she could walk by herself anymore, let alone come all the way out here. I wonder where she was trying to get to that was so important."

They hear the rumble of a car slowly climbing the rutted lane. Sheila squints at the sun burning through the fog above the trees. Their mother is coming home from her shift at the asylum.

"What makes you think she was going *to* somewhere?" Angie says. "Maybe she was trying to get away."

TWENTY-TWO

The Twisted Root

THE FUNERAL IS HELD IN THE SMALL WHITE church on Cold Springs Road. Sheila has been here once or twice before: on a freezing Easter in a skirt that bared her shivering knees, at a summer picnic where she ate too many popsicles and got sick on the seesaw out back, and when her mother married Angie's father and Sheila sat in the front row with a scratch in her throat and refused to look at his face.

Now she drifts at her mother's side, wearing her mother's dress, too big in the chest and too short in the skirt. The long sleeves hide the deep-purple bruises that have mushroomed across her flesh after the grapple with Angie, and pieces of tape wrap the tips of three fingers, masking the missing nails beneath. Relatives file past, laying bony hands on her mother's shoulder. Old ladies in beaded hairnets envelop her in powdery hugs. Men with thick, Elvis-like sideburns clasp her hands between their nicotine-stained fingers and tell her that it's a shame, a real shame.

The preacher stands at the front next to the casket that her mother signed away her next six paychecks to buy. Sheila takes her turn in the line. The lid is open, Thena arranged on her back with her arms folded, her hair brushed and fanned loose on her shoulders, the yellowed ends trimmed away. Apricot rouge brings a false blush to her slack cheeks.

Sheila thinks of Thena's story of the Man of Stone, tries to imagine the old woman as young. She supposes it was possible—if someone who was alive could be dead, then someone who was old could have been young. So where had Thena gone for those three missing days? And where was she going now?

The organ begins to play, and everyone takes their seats on the hard wooden pews. Halfway through the eulogy, Bonnie grips Sheila's hand. She doesn't look at Sheila or say a word. She stares straight ahead at the coffin and the preacher and the bunches of lilies tied with white ribbon and squeezes until Sheila feels like her finger bones will be crushed into sand, leaving just pouches of skin hanging limply at the ends of her hands.

When the preacher finishes and the coffin lid is closed, everyone clomps down the stairs to the basement. They line up at the folding tables and help themselves to macaroni salad and Jell-O molds. Great-Uncle Harold's son George has brought deer sausage, sliced into rounds by his wife. Sheila is helping an old man with shaky hands safely deliver a piece of shoofly pie onto his paper plate when she is engulfed in a cloud of gardenia.

"I hope you're going to have a slice of that yourself." Erma Jean is Sheila's cousin Glen's second wife. Her dress is not black but navy blue, and she wears a chunky gold necklace around her plump throat. She is well into her fifties but talks in a baby voice like a kindergarten teacher.

"I don't think I feel very hungry today," Sheila says.

For a moment, Erma Jean almost looks embarrassed, but she sweeps it aside with a pat of her shellacked hair. "Of course not, dear. I didn't mean that. It's just that it doesn't do to get too thin. You look like a haint. Has your momma not been taking care of you?"

Erma Jean pinches Sheila's arm. It's meant to be affectionate, but it feels like the claws of a crab. "Have some of my peach cobbler. With plenty of ice cream. That will fix you right up."

"I take care of myself just fine," Sheila says.

Erma Jean clucks her tongue. "I know all the diets these days tell you girls you have to be thin. But take it from someone who knows: a man likes a bit of meat on the bone." She glances down at her own fleshy arms and laughs.

Sheila thinks of the boy at the asylum. Did he like "meat on the bone"? She gets a flash, like someone changing the channel and then flipping it back. In that flash, she sees the boy, red-lit and savage, holding a rabbit to his mouth and tearing into it with his teeth. The blood spot in his eye matches the blood that drips from the rabbit's flopping ear.

Then Sheila is back in the church basement, and everything smells like gardenias and menthol cigarettes, and the ham on the table looks like slices of pale pink flesh. Which is exactly what it is.

Sheila sways and gropes behind her for a chair. Erma Jean rolls a slab of ham around a gherkin and pops the parcel into her mouth. She chews as she talks. "What are you? Fifteen now?"

"Seventeen." Sitting down, Sheila feels steadier. But she has to get away from Erma Jean. From this food and these smells. She wants to be outside in the forest, in a dark grove of pines with the needles thick on the ground, muffling everything, holding back time.

"That's plenty old for romance. You find yourself a fella yet?"

If only it were as simple as being found or not found. Sheila would build such a maze that no one would ever find her. She would travel to the center and live there in a neat square of green, to be known only by those she invited. She would give Juanita the map. The boy wouldn't need one.

If anyone else stumbled into her maze, she would lead them to the spring where fresh water bubbled clear and tempting, the only sound in the quilted silence of the pines. A single drop on the intruder's tongue and they would forget who they were and why they came. They would forget their names.

Erma Jean pats Sheila's shoulder. "It's not too early, you know. Who a girl marries is the most important decision of her life. You don't want to get left behind."

Angie rockets into the room and skids to a stop in front of Sheila. She refused to wear a dress, and after a couple of rounds of arguing, Bonnie gave in and told her she didn't care what she wore but she had better wash her face. Her outfit of brown pants, green shirt, and rubber boots looks more like a uniform for military school than respect for the dead.

"Cousin Billy says he's going to teach me how to shoot!" Angie takes imaginary aim at the framed picture of a gaunt

Jesus on the wall behind Erma Jean's bouffant, grabs a square of sheet cake, and races out of the room.

"That child," Erma Jean says. "I can't figure who she takes after."

☜☞

ON THE WAY home, Angie sprawls in the back seat with the window rolled down, complaining that her stomach hurts.

"Serves you right," Sheila says. "How many pieces of that cake did you eat?"

"Three," Angie mumbles, but her stomach knows the truth—it was six. She's just about to tell them she thinks she's going to be sick when they swing around a bend and see two police cruisers parked across the road ahead, rooftop lights throwing patches of red and blue across the trees.

Bonnie takes her foot off the gas and coasts to the gap between the cruisers. A tall trooper approaches, and Bonnie winds down the window. The trooper leans in, resting his big hands on the sill. She gives him the fake smile she keeps for doctors, policemen, and her boss at the asylum.

"Where you headed today?" His voice is deep and lazy with authority.

"Home," Bonnie says, staring straight ahead.

"And where is home?"

"Just up the road."

The car is hot now that they've stopped moving. Sweat slides down Sheila's breastbone, like bugs crawling under the cheap fabric of the dress. Angie is surprisingly quiet, not clambering for a better view of the gun holstered on the trooper's hip. Maybe she really is sick.

"Is that right?" he says, but the air seems to lighten, and Sheila thinks he's going to wave them through. Then one of the local police boys hustles over to the trooper and says something quietly that she can't hear.

Whatever whisper of goodwill had appeared on the trooper's face vanishes. "Step out of the car, ma'am."

"What?" Bonnie says. "We just buried a family member. We—"

"Out of the car," he says, as if he hasn't heard. He peers into the back seat. "Your girls too."

Sheila shoves the heavy door open and fights against her dress to stand up. She makes Angie get out of the back seat. Angie's forehead is damp, and dark circles stain the underarms of her khaki shirt. Her hands hover protectively over her gut.

The local cop darts toward them, holding up his hand. "Stay where you are."

Sheila thought she'd recognized him. He's one of the Colson brothers. She'd know that smirk anywhere. The Colson boys used to swagger through the school hallways, doling out favors and punishments according to their own law. Now here one of them has a badge pinned to his chest and a gun at his hip, and he is the *actual* law, the body and face of justice.

But whose justice? Sheila wants the murderer caught, of course she does. Those women deserve justice. But would Robbie Colson be so eager to catch the murderer if he knew the truth about the women from Rhode Island? Or does he just want to be the hunter, to catch someone and make them pay?

"Whose car is this?" the trooper asks Bonnie.

"Is that all?" Bonnie is worrying the inside of her cheek like she does when she needs a cigarette. "It belongs to my son. He can't use it right now."

"What's your son's name?"

Sheila can't hear any more as the trooper guides Bonnie to the back of the car and has her open the trunk while the other deputy digs around in their belongings.

Angie sways on her feet, then slides down the side of the car. She rests her back against the rear wheel, knees up and head down, dripping sweat onto the side of the road.

Deputy Colson looks at her with disgust and skitters back, his hand moving toward his belt. "What's wrong with her?"

He's acting like Angie is a live cottonmouth.

"She's just a kid," Sheila says. "We just been to a funeral, and she don't feel good. Can't you let her be?"

He doesn't answer. Instead, he lets his eyes roam all over Sheila, like he's sizing up a laying hen at the 4-H show. At first Sheila thinks he recognizes her too, but then she realizes she has pushed back her sleeves because of the heat and he is staring at the bruises on her wrists. They are even bigger and darker than they were when she got dressed, livid pools of black and green spreading over her arms like fungus.

"You fall in a box of rocks or something?" He sounds like he's joking, but his face gives away his revulsion.

She tries to hide her arms behind her, but what's the point? He's already seen them. She drops her gaze and that's when she sees that welts have bloomed all over her legs too. Those definitely weren't there this morning.

The trunk slams. The state trooper is finally done with Bonnie. He gives them permission to get back in the car and then leans down to give his final warning.

"We believe the murderer is still in the area. After all this time, somebody must be helping him." He gives the three of them a searching look. "He's a dangerous man."

☙☙

AS SOON AS the car stops at the top of their lane, Sheila wrenches open the passenger door and, still in her itchy dress and stiff shoes, escapes to the hutches. She says it's because she forgot to feed the rabbits that morning, but it's more that she wants to get away from the anger on her mom's face and Angie's sickness. Sheila hates the rabbits, but they don't make facial expressions, and they don't make noise.

Sheila shakes the can above their bowl, and as the rabbits hop forward, something hard rolls out from under their feet. It's the wrapped bundle she found clutched in Thena's hand the day she died. In the confusion, Sheila must have emptied it into their bowl along with the pellets. She had forgotten all about it.

Her dress has no pockets, so she drops it down the neck and tucks it into her bra. She runs her hands over the fabric to smooth it and thinks no one will notice, not today. She fills the rabbits' water, shoves their noses out of the way, and latches the door.

She hunches a little as she stumbles back into the house, worried that someone will ask what is that lump on her chest. But her mother is leaning back in a kitchen chair, her shoes kicked off under the table and her nylon-covered feet propped on Angie's stool. Angie, suddenly recovered, is belly down on the rug in front of the TV watching nurses in white uniforms make eyes at handsome doctors. Sheila slips past both of them and up the stairs to her room.

She pulls the bundle out of her bra and wrestles her arms around until she can reach the zip on the back of the dress and tug it down far enough that she can shimmy herself free. She puts on a pair of cutoff shorts and a baggy shirt. Her whole body seems to breathe again, to pleat back into its normal shape.

Sheila hangs the dress over the back of a chair and picks up the bundle. The wrapped object is the size of a snake's egg and feels heavier than it ought to. As she tumbles it across her palm, sweat flares on her forehead, flashing back to the moment beside Thena's body when her nails sloughed away. She knows that damage wasn't caused by the bundle—whatever brought that on must have been seeded days before. Still, Sheila almost expects the lump to start wriggling from the inside. To split where there is no seam and for something long and gray and wet to writhe onto her palm.

But the white cotton bundle stays as still as the old woman's body lying in her casket. Sheila is sure she has never seen it before, never come across it in Thena's room. Yet she feels a nagging familiarity, like she once knew what it was but has since forgotten. She plunges her nose against it and sniffs. The wrapped object smells of earth and iron, and bitterness like cabbage leaves after frost.

Voices from Angie's TV show hum through the floorboards. A door thuds, and her mother's footsteps tap toward the bottom of the stairs. Sheila holds her breath, but the footsteps pass on. Still, Sheila doesn't have all day. Her mother will call for her, or Angie will come bounding up the stairs and burst through the door. If Sheila wants to find out more, she needs to do it now.

Sheila wraps a sock around her hand to protect her fingertips and feels under her mattress and removes the knife she took from Angie. She hasn't hidden it particularly well because she doubts there is anywhere in their room that Angie couldn't find. But even Angie knows better than to take it back now.

Sheila balances the bundle on the scarred wooden floor and grips the knife by its molded red handle. She hesitates, then drags the sharp tip across the plastic cord. It springs apart, and Sheila sets down the knife. She folds back the white cloth of a worn handkerchief.

Inside is the dried head of a yarrow blossom, two iron nails, and a lump of quartz the color of milk. The yarrow crumbles as Sheila picks out the nails and turns the rock over in her hand. It is smooth and round, marbled with gold veins that converge onto a deep red core like a drop of blood under ice.

Her throat constricts as the rope pulls tight. Black spots sprinkle the edge of her vision. Sheila slams one hand to the floor to steady herself. Tells herself that this rock she's holding in her hand doesn't make the old woman's story true. No one could have survived having their neck split open with a hunting knife and stitched back together with a needle and thread.

Probably, Sheila thinks, Thena was thinking about this rock for some reason. It meant something to her and was on her mind. That's why she told the story about it a few days ago, and that's why she was holding it when she died. None of this means it has anything to do with Sheila.

Sheila scratches at the red spot on the rock. It's not paint or some other stain on the surface, but a bloody wound that reaches into the heart of the stone. A lump rises in Sheila's throat, making it hard for her to swallow.

Thena is dead and buried in the ground at the back of the Cold Springs church. Sheila should take this rock out into the woods in the direction the old woman was heading when she died and fling it as far as she can into the marsh where it could be swallowed by mud and leaf mold and forgotten forever among the tadpoles.

It's a good idea, but Sheila knows she won't do it. She can't let it go. Thena kept the stone all this time for a reason.

With her very last strength, she carried it with her. That's reason enough for Sheila not to throw it away, even though it scares her. The least she can do is hang on to it and try to find out more.

TWENTY-THREE

The Stinging Trap

WATER SPLASHES INTO THE BUCKET. SHEILA PUMPS
until it's full, adds a cap of Pine-Sol, and swishes it all around
with a rag made from a man's undershirt. She holds the
bucket away from her body as she carries it into the house,
trying not to spill.

Her mother hesitates at the door to Thena's empty room.
Bonnie's hair is tied up in a scarf, and she wears a pair of
slacks rolled to the knees.

"We don't have to do it now," Sheila says.

"I'm not going to like it any better if we wait," Bonnie says.

Sheila lets her mother be the first to step into the room.
No one's been in there since Thena died. It's like an invisible

seal has been pasted over the doorway, and it's not Sheila's place to break it.

The whole house has felt off-kilter since Thena's death. Though the old woman had been less active in recent weeks and kept more and more to her bed, it was like a weight had been hanging on her end of the house. Now that she was gone, that weight had suddenly lifted, upsetting the equilibrium everywhere else.

Bonnie puts out her cigarette and steps through the doorway. She heads straight for the small window at the back.

"The first thing we need is some fresh air." She parts the curtains and wrenches at the window frame. It's not until she bends double, strain showing on her face, that the frame gives way, and a shower of dust and dead wasps billows into the room. She coughs. "Where's your sister with that broom?"

Footsteps stomp down the hall. "Hnh! Take that! And that!" shouts Angie as she thrusts the broom handle into the room, battling imaginary enemies.

Sheila snatches the broom away. "You're supposed to be helping us clean, not making more dust." She starts at the top of the room, flicking the bristles into the corners of the ceiling and swishing down cobwebs. Bonnie slides the curtains off the rail and starts a pile for laundry. Angie gets the job of collecting dirty dishes and shoveling pill bottles into the trash.

It's hard work, and Sheila's joints ache like she is a thousand years old, but she grits her teeth through the pain and keeps working.

Bonnie opens the old wooden bureau, pulling out the drawers and removing neatly folded clothes. She shakes out a blouse and holds it to her chest. "It's a shame she was so small. I don't think any of us can wear these."

When the clothes are sorted into paper grocery bags for the Christian Mission—except for a pair of wool mittens for Angie, who still has small hands, and a filmy scarf printed with roses that Sheila asks to keep—they start in on the cedar chest.

"Can I have my own room now?" Angie asks.

"If anyone gets their own room, it should be me," Sheila says. "I'm the oldest."

Angie picks up a pair of old-fashioned shoes, the leather cracked with age. "If I move down here, you can have the upstairs to yourself."

"Why should you get to choose who goes where?" Sheila says, taking the shoes and dropping them in the trash pile.

"Enough," Bonnie says. "You're both staying put. Sam's going to need his own space when he comes home."

Sam won't be home for another three years. Three years of listening to Angie snore, swallowing Angie's stink, sharing the same air, always pressed against each other, no room to breathe or think or imagine. It's not fair, but Sheila no longer expects life to be fair.

Bonnie sends Angie to the kitchen for tea, and they all rest for a moment, the cool mint clearing their sinuses and washing the dust out of their mouths.

Bonnie drains her glass and sets it down. "I'm going to put those library books in the car so they go back on the next trip to town." She collects the stack of westerns and romances. "You two strip that bed and drag the mattress out on the porch to air."

Sheila gets to her feet, but her heart gallops and stutters. She steadies herself against the bed frame and gulps down air. When the blackness finally ripples back from the edges of her vision, she folds the patchwork quilt and drapes it over the open lid of the cedar chest. The sheets go in the wash pile. She calls to Angie: "Come help me with this mattress."

Angie gets on the other side, and they lift. Something white flutters to the floor at Sheila's feet.

She turns the card over. A creature made of root and sinew glares from the paper, a crooked crown of worms hooked in his leaf-tangled hair. Sheila's hand twitches, and the red stain in the corner of his oily black eye shivers with malice.

Sheila feels sick, like the worms in his hair are hatching in her stomach, wriggling through her veins.

"What is it?" Angie has come up behind her and is trying to look over her elbow.

"Like you have to ask." She turns on Angie, suddenly furious, shoving the card in her sister's face. "Why would you put this . . . *thing* under Thena's bed? What is wrong with you?"

"I didn't!" Angie's face is flushed, and she looks genuinely surprised, but Sheila knows better than to fall for her lies.

"That's what you said about the card that turned up where my money was supposed to be."

"I didn't do that either!"

Sheila is barely listening. She is on a roll. "And that disgusting woman came back to me at the asylum."

"Wait, what?" Angie's face scrunches, her eyebrows drawing together in confusion.

"That card you gave me after the big rain. The one I tore up. It reappeared stuck to a tray I was washing at work." It's just like Angie to play dumb and hope that will be enough to get her off the hook, Sheila thinks. But it isn't going to work this time.

"That doesn't make any sense," Angie says. "How did it get there?"

Little stars explode behind Sheila's eyes, and her muscles surge with the need to *do* something. She feels stronger than she has in weeks, with the desire to control, to make right, to make Angie pay.

"Don't act like you don't know." Sheila lunges for her sister, but her rope snags on the end of the bed, snapping her mouth closed as she's whipped backward. Her mouth fills with the hot sourness of blood.

"I don't have anything to do with it."

Sheila swings her arm, trying to unhook the rope. "Why don't I believe you? Why do I keep finding these things everywhere?"

"I don't know! They used to stay put. Could be it's your fault they keep moving around. You're the one that finds them." Angie points at the card Sheila is holding. "That isn't even the one I put there."

"So you admit it. You did do it!"

"No! That's the Worm King. I would never put him under Thena's bed," Angie says. "I gave her the Truthteller instead. It's not a bad card. It wouldn't have hurt her."

"Then where did this come from?" Sheila pinches the card by the corner, only half aware that she is afraid to let her fingers touch any part of the King's inked body.

"He wanted to go there," Angie explains, "but I wouldn't let him. I put him back in the pack and left the Truthteller instead."

"What do you mean, 'wanted to'?" Sheila feels like all the anger that had filled her a moment ago is leaking away. She wants to hang on to it, but she's so tired, and none of this makes any sense.

"The cards tell me when they want to be put somewhere. I listen and do what they say. But the Worm King . . . He's powerful. And sneaky. You can't trust him. I couldn't do it. I didn't want anything bad to happen." Angie kicks the old mattress. "Do you think I killed her?"

"She was old. She was sick. She had to die sometime." Sheila's not sure she believes this, but if she lets herself think anything else, it means she believes that Angie's cards have real power—including over life and death.

Angie lifts the magnifying glass from the bedside table and peers through it at Sheila, like she's examining her. "It's not me, you know. It's not like I'm making it all up. It's not like I'm telling them to do what I want."

"If it's not you, who is it?" Sheila looks at Angie's eye, big and fishy behind the lens. It feels like she might be close to figuring something out.

Angie bends over and scans the rabbit face of the candy jar through the lens. "I don't know."

"Do you hear voices in your head?" Sheila asks.

"No! It's not like that. No one *talks* to me. I just feel it . . . like something deep down in my body is flipping the switches on my muscles and telling me what to do."

Sheila sighs. "I sometimes wonder if we ever get to choose anything."

The magnifying glass thunks on the bureau's top as Angie sets it down. "What do you mean?"

"This. All of this. Everything." Sheila waves at the room and the world around them. "Where we live, who we are, what happens to us. The parents we're born to and the family we live with. Who likes you, who hates you. Whether you're an airline stewardess or a night-shift aide at an insane asylum. If the bomb falls next week and we die before we get out of school, or we fall in love with someone who sweet-talks us into a backwoods hike where we're clubbed to death in a tent, or we live a long life and fade slowly in the back room of a relative's house."

"I choose." Angie plucks the Worm King from Sheila's fingers and pushes him firmly into the middle of the deck. "I decide what I'm going to buy at Butch's and whether I'm going to watch *Damnation Alley* or *The Parent Trap*. I decide what to draw and which comic books to read and whether I'm going to track Russian snipers along Marsh Creek or look for that Man of Stone at the copper mine."

"But the cards—you just said you don't control that," Sheila says. "Here, this time, you tried to do something different, and it still ended up being this Worm King, and Thena is still dead. How can you say you chose that?"

"I didn't say it works the way I want every time. That doesn't mean I'm not choosing. I'm still the one holding the pen. I'm still the one carrying the cards. Without me, they can't do anything." Angie grabs the mattress by the short end and tows it out of the room.

When Angie is gone and the room is still, Sheila shoves the bed frame aside. She gets down on her hands and knees and searches the floor underneath, feeling with her naked fingertips for a seam, a hinge, for cold air blowing from somewhere secret below. But there is no trapdoor, nothing but the husk of a spider and the plain bare boards.

TWENTY-FOUR

The Hollow Sister

THE GHOST BREATH OF WINTER HAS NOT YET reached the mountain, but the earth is tilting and the nights creep longer. The first-year fawns with their fading spots, the opossum brood gobbling ticks as they bumble after their mother in the dew-flecked grass, the hatchling turtles paddling in sun-warmed ponds have no scent of what is to come. Some will survive and some will die, as they always do. That is the way of the mountain.

But there is more than winter on the wind. There's the acid in the rain, the drops that sear and parch, the hemlocks crippled, the chestnuts exterminated, the new caterpillars stripping oaks at a voracious pace, the frog colonies that shrink and fade, their croaks and trills winking out forever. All while bottles, bags, and wrappers—impervious to insects, light, and decomposition—collect in the mountain's crevices, pile in her gaps, catch and clog in her veins. Given time, the mountain can erode these insults. But there's one invader burrowing under her skin that's an infection she can't shake, an itch that won't stop. His contamination spreads, poisoning her soil, leaching through bedrock to pollute her aquifers and fester in her deepest tissues.

From the west floats the dead whisper of her sister mountain, hollowed out, her bones replaced with struts, caverns scraped bare, tunnels gouged through substrata, guts threaded with snaking tubes. Her vast body violated and intruded, a whimpering shell.

The mountain's days of youthful fury and lava spouts are long cooled. No more the plumes of smoke and steam and hurling rocks, the rippled sheets of rage that cleared her slopes to start anew. Instead, the mountain shifts and reshapes. Blocks paths with deadfall, carves new channels, clears fresh routes. Tugs a rope here, drops an irresistible lure there, reels in that wayward shard of chaos with the blood-spot eye. Sends them all surging to a single point.

TWENTY-FIVE

The Dark Path Rises

SHEILA SNEAKS THROUGH THE LOCKED DOORS OF G Ward, gathering her rope carefully behind her so it doesn't catch in the closing door as she rushes inside. Immediately, she confronts a second set of doors. The one on the right is locked, but when she tries the door on the left, it opens onto steep, curving stairs, spiraling up.

Which is impossible. G Ward is on the top floor of the asylum. There is nothing above but the roof. She returns to the door on the right and raises her hand to shade the glare of the overhead lights as she peers through the tiny window. She can't see anything except a thick fog. So she takes the stairs.

Sheila climbs to a landing, around a corner, then up again. Pressure builds in her ears, like she is stuck in the middle of a yawn. Mechanical throbbing echoes faintly through the walls. There are no windows, so she can't judge how high she is climbing, how far she is above the ground, or where she is in relation to the rest of the building.

Eventually she reaches the top and faces another set of doors. These are unlocked, and she passes through. The throbbing grows louder. A long corridor stretches in front of her, lined at intervals with more doors. As she passes them, a wire-gridded window in the top of each door lets her see into blue-lit rooms where solitary men in pale pajamas are sleeping, sitting, talking to the walls, eating, dancing to unheard music, bouncing invisible balls. Pasted on the outside of the numbered doors are charts: grids with boxes to be ticked with Xs and Os for success or failure.

The men in the rooms don't seem to notice her, but as Sheila creeps down the corridor, her rope reacts. The usual pressure on her neck lifts as the rope seems to drift on unseen currents instead of weighing her down.

The next door she comes to, number 229, is different from all the others. Behind its small square of glass is a regular bedroom. Curtains hang over a window on the opposite wall that has been papered with a romantic floral design. A record player inhabits the corner, a poster for the movie *Pretty in Pink* tacked on the wall above. A fluffy Laura Ashley comforter stretches over the single bed.

There is no man in pajamas in this room. Sheila tries the door, and it clicks open. Men's voices rumble from a distant, unseen corridor, and she ducks inside, closing the door softly behind her. Hoping she can hide in here.

Now that she's inside, she knows this is not just any room. This is Juanita's bedroom. Those are Juanita's skirts and sweaters hanging in the closet with the folding doors, the green shirt that makes Juanita's eyes shine like acorns. Those are the books from Juanita's classes dumped on the table beside the bed: *Geometry I, World Geography, French III,* and *Romeo and Juliet.*

Sheila sits in front of the vanity. The men's voices are coming closer, but she barely hears them. These are Juanita's things: her hairbrush, her bracelet, her Jean Naté deodorant, sacred artifacts in the museum of Sheila's desire. Breath held, hardly daring, Sheila picks up the hairbrush as gingerly as if she's folding her fingers around Juanita's wrist and pulls the bristles through her own hair. Maybe she's imagining it, but it seems to give off just the faintest hint of Juanita's shampoo. All these items are so close to Juanita; they touch her skin every day, are present when she sighs and dreams, when she holds clothes against her shoulders in front of a mirror, when she dances by herself to the hi-fi in the corner, when she flops down on the bed sprawled in the heat, when she changes into her nightgown, when she curls against the pillow and sleeps, face flushed, hair curling against her temples. Even, she thinks, when Juanita steps out of the shower, water dripping from her wet hair, trickling in gentle rivulets over her shoulders, tickling her collarbone, and disappearing into the towel wrapped around the swell of her chest. The towel held with just a single tuck that could so easily come undone.

Sheila's hand shakes and she drops the brush back on the vanity next to a half-drunk bottle of grape Nehi and a little green book with gold foil trim and a key in a cardboard lock.

Juanita's diary. Where Juanita writes about her days, about her true feelings. Sheila's hand darts for the key. This is her chance to find out how Juanita really feels. To find out if all the things Sheila has imagined between them are possible. To know if she is seen by Juanita, if she takes up space in Juanita's head, in her dreams, in her thoughts.

What if Juanita . . . But Sheila can't complete the thought. Her blood rushes in her ears like the rain beating on the roof of her attic room during a raging storm.

The key is between Sheila's fingers, scraping against the lock, but she can't turn it. Because what if Juanita does see Sheila—the same way everyone else does, full of ridicule and scorn. Would it be worse to be seen and mocked or to remain invisible? What if Juanita writes only of her crushes on hateful boys on the sports teams and her worship of popular girls?

A droning like a siren rises in the back of Sheila's consciousness. A light shimmies on and off, flickering in the mirror in front of her.

If Sheila never opens the diary, she can hang on to her fantasy and pretend it's still possible. Her hope may never be fulfilled, but it also won't be denied. The key feels like a trigger under her fingers, a sudden motion that could destroy her.

But she has to know.

The lock turns, and Sheila folds back the diary's cover. Sheila is so nervous she can barely get her eyes to focus. Which is why at first she doesn't understand what she sees. On the first page, just for a moment, blurry sentences stretch from left to right. But before she can make out the words, they disappear. The page is blank and unfilled.

Sheila flips the pages forward and back, but they are all the same—all blank. She squints, scratches the paper, anything she can think of to call those half-glimpsed, fleeting words back into visibility, back into this world, back into her grasp.

"Come back," she whispers. "Come back, come back."

Footsteps rush in the hallway outside. Voices, louder now, closer, are shouting. "Code Eleven! Repeat, Code Eleven in room 229!"

As the door from the corridor bursts open, a hand takes Sheila's wrist, jerking her out of the chair, onto her feet, and into the closet just as two men rush into the room. One is a doctor in a white coat, the other a uniformed orderly. Sheila watches them from behind Juanita's winter parka.

The men scan the room, their shoulders dropping from alarm to disappointment.

"Nothing," the doctor says.

"Dammit, I thought we had this one." The orderly flicks a finger at the diary open on the vanity.

The doctor shakes his head. "Sachs is not going to like this."

The hand on Sheila's wrist tugs her farther back into the dark folds of Juanita's clothes. Sheila turns, and there is the boy. She can't see his face, but the shadow of his height, the darker smudge of his sweatshirt, and the dull white of the high-tops on his feet give him away. That and the faint red gleam from his eye.

He pulls, and she follows. The soft brush of Juanita's clothes against her turns coarse and fibrous as Sheila trails the boy deeper into a closet that never seems to end. Sleeves snatch at her, clutching her waist with greedy phantom hands, pulling her hair, holding her back. Fabric stretches across her face, invading her nose and mouth. Sheila swings her arms wildly, batting away the stiff satin taffeta of the dress Juanita wore to the homecoming dance, the tartan skirts clasped by jumbo safety pins, choked by the tangle of bra straps and slips, the strangling pantyhose. The air changes from citrus and cotton to something thicker, wet and suffocating, laced with mushrooms and mold.

Sheila stumbles over shoes that transform, becoming larger and harder. Her shoulder bumps the wall and it crumbles. Chunks break off and roll under her feet, grit trickles into her shoes, small things with many legs drop onto her hair and scuttle against her neck. The boy releases her hand, but she keeps following him. She's not going to let him leave her here in this darkness that makes no sense.

The ground slants, and Sheila's legs work harder. They are traveling uphill. Which, since they are already above the roof of the asylum, is impossible. But a faint seam of light is shining ahead. The path grows steeper and the ground becomes so slick that Sheila has to brace against the walls, digging her fingers into the crumbling sides as she struggles up the slope.

Then the boy and Sheila are climbing out of a narrow crack in the mountain's rocky side, out into the open where a steady downpour of rain washes the mud from her skin. Sheila squints through the torrent, trying to make out where she has ended up.

Her surroundings lack the heavy deertongue laurel that grows in the acid soil near the asylum. The air smells like her own side of the mountain, yet she doesn't quite recognize anything.

"Where are we? Where have you brought me?" Sheila asks the boy, her head full of questions. Her thoughts and feelings overflow like all the rotting leaves and crumbled squirrel bones thrust to the surface of the creeks in spring by days of extraordinary hammering rain.

She was at work, then she was in G Ward, and now she is standing on some unknown part of (probably) her own mountain with the boy who came out of nowhere to fetch her and lead her to safety. She can't seem to get all the events to line up so she can organize them. The edges keep sliding out of sync.

The rain slackens to a drizzle that patters gently on the leaves around them. Sheila wants to ask the boy more questions, but there are so many crowding at her. Each question she thinks of seems to require another question before it to make any sense.

While she's trying to sort these out, the boy asks a question of his own.

"Does she mean that much to you?"

Sheila doesn't have to ask who he's talking about. Of course he means Juanita. It's Juanita's bedroom she has escaped from. It's Juanita's diary she has tried to read.

"I know she's not perfect," Sheila says. "She sweats when she's nervous, and she laughs at the bitchy things Tammy Winchell says when she thinks she's being funny. She wears too much eye shadow and fills out the quizzes in magazines that tell you what kind of perfume matches your personality.

"But I don't care. I want to sit beside her. I want to turn the pages of the magazines with her. I want to watch her drink grape soda and hold the flash cards while she practices French vocabulary. I want to do anything with her."

Water runs down the boy's forehead and drips off the tip of his nose. "Have you kissed her?"

Sheila wraps her arms around her body, suddenly aware of her wet clothes sagging against her skin.

"Have you kissed anyone?"

Sheila's mind supplies a tangle of memories. Of being held down on the playground by Wayne Naugle, his curly hair, his flushed cheeks, his wet lips. His face moving closer to hers, his nasty grin. She shrinks back against the blacktop, but there is nowhere to go. She wriggles and twists, and then she is free, scrambling away with blood on her scraped knee and a few of his disgusting hairs caught in her fingers.

She shakes her head.

"You could kiss me," the boy says. "I wouldn't mind."

Revulsion, terror, fascination—how can she be feeling all of these at once?

Sheila rubs her cheek with her sleeve. "I don't want to kiss you."

"I know," he says. "But it's just for practice. So you'll know what to do when you get your chance with Juanita."

Sheila thinks again of Wayne, but the boy is nothing like him. The boy in front of her is slim and sealed and hushed. The boy is a secret behind closed curtains.

"I'll stop whenever you say," he says, as if he knows what she is thinking.

"Okay," she says, but she doesn't move toward him. Just holds still and closes her eyes, hands curled at her sides. She feels like a rabbit waiting for the blow.

When his lips touch hers, it's like he says. His sharp angles melt. His hard corners become soft curves. The scent of stone and rain and pine gives way to drugstore shampoo and pencil shavings.

It's strange and frightening to be so close to someone that the air between your bodies disappears, Sheila thinks. That invisible space that keeps you separate from others, that keeps you safe, pulls tight like a cinch. The air becomes an element outside the two of you, a pressure holding you together instead of keeping you apart.

A hand seeks Sheila's face and slides along her jaw to brush the damp hair from her cheek. A soft finger with a slightly too-long nail.

Sheila opens her eyes. The boy is gone. Juanita is here. Juanita is in her arms. Juanita's face is pressed to hers. Sheila can feel Juanita's thin shoulder blades under her hands as she pulls her close. She breaks off the kiss and drops her face into the hollow of Juanita's neck, lets Juanita's hair fall over her. The thud of Sheila's heart slows. She wants to rest here forever.

TWENTY-SIX

The Watcher under the Rock

ANGIE HASN'T BEEN BACK TO BUTCH'S STORE SINCE that day he almost ran her over, but the hole in the house left by Thena's death chases her out the door and across the mountain. The last time she was here, she left the Blood Double tucked under a box of crackers. She needs to find it again, to see if it has gone missing or switched on her like the others. To figure out what she got wrong.

But Butch's store is playing tricks on her. She can't find the crackers at all. The fifty-dollar survival knife is still on display, but the saltines are gone. She runs her hand along the shelves where the boxes used to be, wondering if someone could really have bought them all in just a few days.

"Damn flying squirrels got into them," Butch says, coming out from behind the curtain and making her jump. "They chewed holes in the boxes. Ate through the wrappers and crapped everywhere. I had a real mess to clean up. I stacked the rest over here. You want some?"

Butch doesn't sound like he's still mad at her. He sounds normal. Angie's trying to decide if that means she should ask him if he found the card when he says, "I was sorry to hear of Thena dying like that. That's a lonely way to go."

"Sheila found her in her nightgown, halfway out to the woods," Angie says.

"Folks will do strange things when they're at the end," Butch says, turning down the volume on his radio. "Your momma holding up all right?"

Angie takes a butterscotch candy from the counter. "I guess. She seems about the same. It's Sheila that's different."

"How so?"

Angie twists the candy wrapper, enjoying its squeak. "Like she's hiding something."

Butch hooks his thumbs into his belt loops. "She might just be sad."

"Maybe," Angie says. "It's more like she's got a secret."

"Huh. Nothing wrong with secrets as such. Sometimes they're a good thing."

"Yeah, but—" The radio squeals with static, and Butch tweaks the antenna. In the dead air between the bursts, Angie hears footsteps outside.

The man who stomps in is a stranger. But Angie knows right away that despite his military-green knapsack, he's not a Russian soldier. His neck is too skinny, his eyes too dark, his hair and beard too thin. Russians have blue eyes like the ice in Siberia, colorless blond hair, and square jaws like Dolph Lundgren in *Rocky IV.* And they don't smoke flavored cigars.

"You can turn around and leave that outside, pal," says Butch.

The man keeps coming. "It keeps the bugs away."

"My store, my rules." Butch's voice is sharp. "I don't want it stinking up the place. You don't like it, you can go somewhere else."

The man looks for a moment like he's going to argue, but Butch stares him down. The stranger retraces his steps to the door, and Angie hears the twist of his boot on stone as he rubs out the cigar. He comes back inside, but he keeps looking over his shoulder like he can't let it go.

"Not seen you around before," Butch says.

"I'm hiking. On the Trail." The bearded man stares at the goods displayed on the shelves as if they are taking all of his concentration. "It was good luck I was able to find your place way out here. You must not get much business."

"I do fine," Butch says, turning away and unpacking a case of beef jerky like he's not paying attention. But Angie knows Butch has eyes in the back of his head. The first few times she came to the store she tried pocketing some peppermint patties, and he always caught her.

On the radio, Willie Nelson sings about red-haired strangers and wild black horses as the man stalks among the store's cluttered shelves. He doesn't seem to see Angie— never acknowledges her by word or glance. But when he passes near her to get a closer look at the fancy survival knife, something rancid drifts up her nose.

The man wants toilet paper, which Butch has stocked in good supply. Lots of hikers want toilet paper. He wants matches, canned chili, a box of Lucky Charms. He piles it all on the counter, along with a two-year-old *Playboy* and a cherry soda.

"I'm short on cash," the stranger says. "Any chance you'd be interested in a trade?"

"Depends what you've got."

The man hesitates, then fishes something out of his knapsack and lays it on the counter.

Butch holds the watch by its leather strap and puts on his glasses to give it a closer look.

"Timex," the man says. "It runs good."

Butch presses the watch to his ear.

"It's worth more than all this." The man waves a hand over the goods piled on the counter. "But if you don't have the change, I understand. I just need my things."

Butch holds out the watch. "This looks a little small for you. Wouldn't you say this is a ladies' watch?"

The man licks his lips. "It's my girlfriend's."

"That right? She out there hiking with you?" Butch drops his eyes to the *Playboy*.

A faint pink stain creeps across the man's face. He shifts from foot to foot. "She doesn't—"

Butch folds his arms across his chest. "No deal."

The stranger stares at Butch for a moment, then snatches the watch. He pulls a few crumpled bills from his pocket and drops them on the counter. Butch takes the money and the man gathers his supplies and stuffs everything into the knapsack, except the cherry soda, which he tucks under his elbow.

Angie doesn't see what happens next—whether the man drops the bottle or it explodes on its own. She brings her arms up just in time to cover her face as glass and sticky cherry fizz spray across the floor.

The man keeps walking. Doesn't look around, doesn't say a word, only keeps walking out the door.

⚭

"NOT SO FAST," Butch says, catching Angie by the collar just as she reaches the door.

"Let go! He's going to get too far ahead."

"That might be for the best."

Angie looks at Butch like he's crazy. She can still see—or thinks she sees—the blur of the man's shape disappearing over the rocks on the western edge of the hill. "You know who that is! We can't let him get away!"

"We don't know that for sure," Butch says. "And if he is who you think, I'm not letting you hare off after him. What would your mother say? He's already killed two grown women, and you're just a twelve-year-old girl."

"I'm almost thirteen! And I'm not some dumb city kid. I've been training for something like this. I'm ready. You know I am." Her whole body tilts toward the door, straining to get closer to the man's trail.

Butch puts his body between her and the open woods, blocking her way.

"Come with me," Angie pleads. "We'll get him together. I'll track him, and you can help me take him down."

"Then what? What do you think you're going to do with him?"

Angie hasn't thought about that. The moment it all comes together is the moment the action ends in the movie. The Russian is captured and forced to surrender: end scene. Later you might see him weak and diminished behind steel bars. But the rest of the story is about the hero.

"There's something you need to realize," Butch says. "When you're out alone in the jungle—even if you're armed, even if the rest of your unit is in radio contact and only a few hundred yards away—when you step around that blind corner and come face-to-face with somebody whose only purpose in that moment is to kill you, to end you, to make you no more—it's not like in your movies. It's a mess, just a fucking mess. There are people whose job it is to take care of situations like that, and it's not mine. I had my days of that, and they are over."

Butch's voice is low and urgent like the bark of a dog at the sight of a snake. He has never talked to Angie like this before. She has never seen this other Butch who must have lived inside him all this time, asleep but still alive.

Angie opens her mouth, but Butch isn't done. "And I sure as hell am not going to put you into that."

Angie needs to take her time around this new Butch, act carefully. She lets the silence after his last words ring in the store, listening to the scratch of the chickens outside. "So what are we going to do then?"

Butch sighs, and all of the dangerous new Butch seems to glide out of him. "Much as I hate to say it, I guess I'm going to have to call the police."

"But you hate the police. You said—"

"Never mind what I said. If that man's our murderer, I don't see we have much of a choice. I don't know what he's doing still hanging around these parts. We're lucky he hasn't killed anybody else." He collects his keys from behind the counter. "I'll drive down to the Skyline Inn and use their phone. That's probably quickest."

"What will you tell them?" Angie follows him down the

path to the spot at the top of the dirt road where he parks his pickup.

"What he looks like, where we saw him, and how long ago." Butch heaves himself into the driver's seat.

"What will they do?"

"Hunt him, I guess. Find him. Arrest him." He roars the engine to life. "Don't just stand there asking questions. Get in."

Angie steps back. "Uh-uh. I gotta get back to the house. Sheila's home by herself. I got to warn her he's out there."

"Nice try," Butch says. "I'll drop you off. I'm not leaving you out here alone."

☙

BUTCH IDLES THE truck in front of the house. A dog barks but doesn't bother to leave the porch.

"That trooper I talked to seemed decent enough," he says. "They'll take care of it. So you leave it to them, you hear me?"

"I hear," Angie says, looking down at her lap. Scenes run through her head of at last showing the world what she can do. Scenes of her on TV explaining how she did it, how an overlooked, underestimated girl captured the most wanted man in the state and brought him to justice. Scenes where people finally realize how special she is.

The touch of Butch's calloused fingertip on her chin pulls her firmly back into the cab of the truck. Butch doesn't touch her very often. Their relationship is gruff, comradely. But he is turning her face to look at him, and the urgent, hidden, other Butch from those last moments in the store is back.

"Promise me that you'll stay home and take care of your mom and sister until they get that man in handcuffs." Butch's tired eyes search hers, waiting for an answer.

"If he comes here—" Angie begins.

"If he comes anywhere near your house, you grab Sam's rifle and put as many holes in the sonofabitch as you like. But you stay put, and you don't go after him."

"I understand."

He nods. "Good. Now what do I need to hear from you?"

Butch is her friend. Her best friend. And he needs her to say this. She can't refuse him.

"I promise," Angie says.

He drops his hand, and Angie climbs out of the truck, slamming the door behind her. As she nears the house, Sue and the other dogs spring off the porch and bound toward her. Butch reverses, and she can hear his old rust bucket banging over the ruts on the way down the steep lane.

Angie greets the dogs and follows them back to the quiet house. Inside, all is dark. She lied to Butch. Like her mother, Sheila is at work at the asylum. No one is home. Angie drops into a sagging chair and pulls the cards from her pocket. She holds the stack between her palms, settling into them, feeling if they are alive and ready.

A hum in her ears and a tingle in her stomach tells her that they are. She shifts the cards from hand to hand and closes her eyes, breathing deep and steady. In the hollow space inside her mind, she pushes out the thread of a question: *Is it ever okay to break a promise?*

Her hands stop shuffling, and she surveys the deck, feeling for the card that wants to surface, the one that is pushing to be released. *That one.* She pinches it between her fingers, then flips it over and opens her eyes.

The creature on the card is half man, half hound. The blindfold wrapped around its head droops onto its long snout, revealing part of its bulging eyes. It leans forward in pursuit, holding a forked branch between its three-fingered hands and carrying a quiver of acorn-tipped arrows on its spotted back. Its whip-thin tail vibrates with eagerness for the hunt, pointing straight out behind.

Angie bangs through the screen door and races up the stairs to her room. She drags a wooden stool over to the shared wardrobe, hops onto it, and starts feeling around under Sheila's sweaters on the top shelf until her hand connects with something hard.

She pulls out the confiscated knife. Angie has tracked Sheila's different hiding places all along. In a room this small there are no secrets. Angie didn't try to take it back earlier because she didn't want another beating. And because she knew it would be hers again in the end.

When she spotted the knife glittering on the bank of Marsh Creek like someone had dropped it when they stooped to fill their canteen, Angie knew that it had been left for her to find. Except for the red handle, it was identical to the one in Butch's store. The cards had brought it to her. Sheila could take it away, but Angie knew it would come back. And now this moment, this mission—this is what it was meant for.

Angie secures the knife at her waist and rockets back down the stairs, taking them two at a time. She's almost out the door when she backtracks to the kitchen. She grabs a clean dish towel from the cupboard and ties it around her head. She is ready.

She leaps off the porch, dodges through the garden, and vaults the woodpile beyond the rabbit hutch. Trees whip by in a blur as her feet pound across the rough ground. Her heart races, but it feels good, like she has eaten an entire bag of circus peanuts and could run like a deer for days.

She hits the stream at the edge of their property and realizes she doesn't know where to go next. The murderer is out there in the forest, but he could be anywhere. He could be hiding in some rocky den at the peak of the mountain or lying low in a dense patch of brush and briars.

Angie knows she can track him, but only if she can find something to put her on the scent. Going all the way back to Butch's store where she last saw the stranger and starting from there would take too long—plus she might run into Butch.

Maybe there's another way. Angie forces herself to be cool, to think things through like a soldier. What she needs is intel. And where does a soldier get that? From reports. But she's on her own. There's no one to give her a report about the conditions ahead. Unless . . .

She sinks onto a rock and pulls the cards from her pocket again. She never asks them more than one question a day and usually waits until they signal to her that they have something to say. But this is important.

The murderer is out there somewhere, getting away. Hiding himself deeper, stealing her chance, and she won't ever be able to find him again. Angie shuffles the cards. She's still breathing hard from her sprint, and she tries to quiet the rasp of it in her head so it doesn't drown out what the cards might want to say. She runs her fingers over their edges and sinks into the floating space where she can hear their faint voices.

Where is he? she asks.

She waits to feel the stirring that leads her to the card that wants to be drawn. But it's not happening. The cards in her hands feel like dry, flat paper instead of choices crouched inside a walnut shell ready to be cracked open and read. In this moment when she needs them most, the cards are withered and dead.

Why aren't they working? Angie wants to rip them all to fluttering specks. *Stupid*, she thinks. *Useless*. She clenches her fist around them, wanting them to be different, then drops them on the ground in disgust. Talons and tongues and horns and tails mock her as they fall and scatter.

But in that tumble, she glimpses the one she needs. She scoops the cards toward her, clawing them back from dirt and fern and rock. *He must be here*. She rakes through the cards, searching for the one she saw that she knows can help. The one she knows will have the answer.

At last she finds him.

"You," Angie says.

The Worm King sulks on the paper, black smudge and writhing lines, his red eye shining. A breeze ruffles the other cards, but Angie has no attention to spare. The Worm King is the only one that matters.

"Show me where he is." Angie's voice wavers, but she makes it strong. "Take me to him."

The Worm King lies flat, but Angie knows he can hear her. She feels like she is holding a baby rattler in the palm of her hand. She can feel the coiled potential, the toxic promise of a strike faster than the eye can see. Feel the delivery of poison, pain, and death. This is strength. This is power like Angie has never known. All that the cards have given her before is nothing to what she senses now.

Angie bends over, speaks right into the King's sullen face. "I mean it. I have to find him."

She wills herself to keep calm, like she is staring down the barrel of a Kalashnikov and can glimpse her tombstone at the other end. She mustn't let the King see she is afraid.

"You're going to take me there."

The energy in the cards shifts, seems to roll and tumble. A splash from the creek and she swivels her head. That must be it, his signal. But it's just a stupid rabbit kicking a shower of pebbles into the water as it scrambles up the bank and vanishes into a clump of ferns.

When Angie looks back at the card in her hand, the Worm King has turned his face away, and he is slipping off the side of the card. Only the faintest prick of red shows from the corner of his eye. He is leaving her for good.

"No! I'm not playing your games anymore!" Angie understands now why Sheila tore the Starved Woman to bits. She is tempted to rip the Worm King in half to show him that he can't get away with this.

But where would that leave her? She pounds her fist on the ground, and the mountain seems to shudder from the blow. More pebbles plop into the stream. The water smooths the disturbance away, the current surging down the valley. All that energy, always flowing in the same direction. But what if it could run the other way?

Angie presses her thumb on the Worm King's fleeing edge, pinning him in place. She speaks low, forming the words from deep inside her body. Someone sitting beside her wouldn't be able to hear her at all. But Angie knows the Worm King can.

"I always do what you want," she says. "All the time. This time, you do what I want. I need to find that man, and you're going to show me how."

As she speaks, fat drops of rain begin to fall, splatting on her bare head. One hits her in the eye, and she blinks it away. When she can see again, the Worm King has vanished from the card.

TWENTY-SEVEN

The Worm King

ANGIE SLUMPS IN THE RAIN BESIDE THE STREAM, THE blank card abandoned in the dirt at her feet. She has failed. For a moment, she thought she had understood something, had grasped some essential knowledge and put it to work for her. But maybe Sheila is right, and she's just playing pretend.

The stream swells with the sudden storm, carrying fish and leaves and broken twigs down into the valley and away. On the opposite bank, the rabbit is back, nibbling tender greens, its ears flattened against the rain.

"Stupid rabbit." Angie grabs a rock and throws it. She misses the rabbit, and the rock falls harmlessly into the undergrowth. Angie's not surprised—she didn't mean to clobber it, just make something pay for her frustration.

As it hops away, Angie notices a slab of rock behind where the rabbit was eating. The boulder is as big as an armchair, draped with a curtain of lichen and jewel-green moss. In the center, a long, deep crack cleaves the rock in two.

Angie snatches the Worm King's empty card and scrambles across the stream to the rock. If she turns sideways, sucks everything in, and wriggles, she can just squeeze through the gap. Inside the stone, it feels bigger than she expected, and the air smells cool and powdery. She can see very little, only smudged gray outlines and a faint green glow from the surface of the rock.

She shuffles a few steps into the darkness. The air stirring against her face and the distant sound of water dripping into a pool tell her that the walls don't end at the edge of the boulder. There is a passage ahead, a way forward, deeper into the heart of the mountain.

The Worm King hasn't let her down after all.

Angie tightens the knot of her headband, checks the knife at her hip, and marches forward. She has only traveled the length of a room when the tunnel narrows, the rough rock walls hemming her in.

As she wedges herself into the tight passage, Angie wonders if the Worm King is tricking her. If he is only pretending to do what she asked so he can lure her into the depths of the mountain and leave her there.

That thought brings the walls closer and seizes the air in her chest. She wants to strike out, to panic and run, but she gets a grip on herself. A soldier doesn't turn back because he's afraid. He completes his mission—and this is hers.

Angie's not sure how far she travels. After what seems like hours—though maybe it's days—of crawling on her knees through a cramped, winding shaft, the tunnel expands again. The ceiling rises, and she gets to her feet.

She steps out not into a natural cave, but a man-made dugout, narrow at the back where she has emerged and widening at the other end where daylight and birdsong filter through a brush-covered opening. If she stretches out her arms she can touch the walls on either side, where sap drips from the raw ends of severed roots. Boot treads crisscross the packed dirt floor.

This new cave smells not of cool rock and damp earth but like rank animal and overripe fruit. Angie gags and covers her nose with her hand, breathing carefully through her mouth. A nest of blankets is heaped in one corner, a battered *Playboy* and an army canteen within arm's reach. A crude shelf dug out of the wall holds an empty toilet paper roll, cans of beans, and a candle stub.

She's done it. She asked the Worm King to lead her to the murderer, and now here she is. There's no doubt in her mind that she has found his hideout. When she captures him, she will be a hero. No one will call her "cavewoman" ever again. If they do, it will be because she is the King of Caves, who tracked the bad man to his lair and single-handedly brought him to justice. Today is going to be the best day of her life.

A rucksack, bigger than the one the murderer carried into Butch's store, is slumped in one corner. Angie unclasps the buckles and rummages inside, finding a folding trail map, a plastic rain poncho, a metal spork and collapsible tin cup, and a nylon wallet that smells faintly of roses and licorice when she pries open the Velcro fastener. Angie is examining the face of a woman with short, dark hair smiling out from a

Rhode Island driver's license when she hears the snap of a branch outside. She drops the wallet and rushes to conceal herself in the mouth of the passage that brought her here.

But the tunnel is no longer there.

The back of the hideout is an unbroken wall of earth. Angie bangs her fist on the hard-packed dirt, half expecting it to crumble and let her through. But it stays strong and solid as if no opening had ever been. The sounds of movement outside are coming closer.

She is trapped.

Angie looks around the cave, but its tight confines offer nowhere to hide. She shrinks back into the deepest shadow, flattening herself against the wall. She draws the knife and holds it ready. Her mouth is dry, and she can barely hear the approaching footsteps over the roar of blood in her ears.

Her muscles tense, ready to spring the moment the man enters the hideout. She knows she will get only one chance. She has to attack before he spots her, before he even suspects she's here. She runs fight scenarios in her mind, fingers gripping the knife's handle so hard they ache.

But no one comes.

Did she really hear anything? Angie strains to listen, but it's hard to hear over her own ragged breath. Raising the knife in front of her, she eases past the bedroll and creeps along the wall to the brush-covered entrance.

The hideout is in the bottom of a deep, lush ravine. Just outside, two deer are browsing on a grapevine. The nearest one turns in her direction, regarding her with large, indifferent eyes. Leaves droop from its mouth as it continues to chew.

Angie lets out the breath she's been holding and relaxes her grip on the knife. Deer. Just a couple of deer. She scans the rest of the ravine. Warblers flit from tree to tree, and a chipmunk rests on a flat rock, clasping a seed between its paws.

Angie knows she's been lucky. But she's been stupid too. She can't let herself be trapped inside the cave when the murderer returns, not now that she knows it has no escape route. She lucked out this time, but he could return at any minute.

Just as she's about to climb outside, a gust of wind sweeps down the ravine and shakes the branches covering the entrance. Light dances across the hideout's interior and catches the tip of something papery white stuck in a crack running down the wall behind the bedroll.

Angie digs the tip of her knife into the jagged seam, and a wad of bills, wrinkled and dirty, falls to the ground at her feet. This must be Sheila's missing money—of course the murderer has taken it. She gathers the cash and stuffs it into her pocket.

The empty crack in the mountain's side gapes at her, as if it's waiting for something. Angie reaches into her other pocket and pulls out the empty card that used to hold the Worm King and slides it into the seam.

She parts the branches covering the entrance and crawls out into daylight. The chipmunk squeaks and darts into its burrow. The deer have moved on. Across the ravine, broken ferns and loose stones betray the murderer's route to and from his hideout.

Angie carefully replaces the branches over the entrance, trying to match their previous arrangement. She needs to find somewhere to hide where she can observe the entrance to the dugout but won't be seen when the murderer returns.

At the other end of the ravine, she finds a thick stand of chokecherry and spicebush. It's only about waist-high, but if she stays low, it should cover her. She scratches the ground, uncovering damp earth that she smears on her cheeks and forehead. She belly crawls into the thicket and turns around to surveil the path.

The space isn't big enough to stretch out, so she scrunches herself up and waits. She imagines the look of surprise on the murderer's face when he thinks he has returned to safety and she gets the drop on him. She imagines the surprise on the faces of the policemen when she brings her captive in.

She zeroes in on the path, picturing the unsuspecting murderer traipsing down the slope, completely unaware of the ambush waiting for him. She will hold off until he has completed all of his security checks. No, she will wait until he is pulling the brush away from the entrance. Or maybe until he is fixing his supper—that way his hands will be full. She will leap out from her hiding place and take him by surprise.

She will be at his side in an instant, as fast as a striking snake, one arm wrapped around his neck, the other threatening his throat with the sharp blade of her knife.

"Don't move," she'll say. "If you don't want to get hurt, you're going to do exactly as I tell you. Nod if you understand."

His eyes will bug out. He'll want to know who is doing this, who is holding him prisoner. He'll struggle to turn around, but she'll press the point of the knife harder against his neck and a shiny drop of red blood will appear. He'll tremble and swallow and nod to let her know that she has the upper hand, that he is in her power.

Or he will if he ever shows up.

Angie had no idea surveillance could be so boring. Her mouth is dry, her bladder is full, and water is seeping out from a hidden spring and soaking into her pants. She didn't eat much this morning, only leftover pie and a dill pickle for breakfast. When she left the house for Butch's she didn't plan to be out for so long, but now it's hours later, and she crawled all that way through the tunnels to get here.

Her belly is hollow, her thighs are numb, her neck is stiff, and she is bored bored bored. Her mind drifts away to a vision of *Hee Haw* singers and hospital romance, Evel Knievel and mushroom clouds. She falls asleep, her head lolling forward into the moss and acorn caps, her hand slack on the handle of the knife.

❧

ANGIE WAKES TO a cold drizzle. She is shivering, and the mud she smeared on her face is leaking into her eyes. Her head aches, twigs poke her lips, and grit swarms in her dry mouth. Pins and needles stab her right arm, and she can't believe how badly she has to pee.

If she doesn't get up and do something about it right now, she's going to burst like a pricked balloon. She clenches every muscle she can to hold it in and staggers to her feet. As she scrabbles at her waist and gets her pants down just in time, she wonders how long she has been asleep and if she has missed her chance to capture the murderer. She squats and the stream splatters on the leaves between her feet.

Which is why she doesn't hear the pelt of small rocks tumbling down through the ferns on the other side of the ravine. By the time Angie realizes the sound isn't the deer returning, the murderer is halfway down the far slope, zigzagging between saplings.

Angie hurries to get her pants back up, the elastic snarling around her damp thighs. She yanks at the wadded fabric and loses her balance, tipping sideways and snatching at branches to keep from falling over.

Luckily, the murderer has his head down to check his footing on the rain-slick leaves and doesn't look in her direction. When he reaches the bottom, he drops his rucksack near the entrance to his hideout. He bends over and digs inside the bag, muttering to himself. Angie can't make out any of the words, only a low rumble of sound from his throat.

Then the growl cuts off and his body goes still, like he's been hit with a freeze ray.

Angie doesn't know what she has done to give herself away, but she's certain he knows that she is there.

The man slowly rises to his feet, twisting around to scan the ravine, searching for what's not right, looking for the intruder. His eyes seem to zero in on where Angie is crouched behind the thin screen of leaves.

She shrinks back, her heart rabbiting in her throat. This is not how this was supposed to go. She was supposed to surprise *him*. He was never going to know she was there until the moment she dropped on him like a phantom. She holds her breath and forces herself to stay absolutely still, but she's having trouble convincing her muscles to do as she asks and not turn and run, run, *run*.

Even from across the length of the ravine, the murderer's gaze bores into her. Cold creeps over Angie's skin. She thinks of the murdered women's belongings scattered in his hideout like leftovers from a yard sale. Their sad watches and battered canteens. What will be left of her when he is done? What does she carry on her body right now that will become his next souvenir?

After several long seconds, he turns away. Angie relaxes. Maybe he didn't see her after all. Maybe she only imagined that he was looking right at her. But, even so, it's clear that he's now on his guard.

In a situation like this, Rambo would know what to do. Sometimes Rambo gets caught in a tight spot too, when it looks like he is out of options. But then it turns out that Rambo is so smart that he has prepared a cunning backup plan, and it all ends with him opening fire with his machine gun or tricking the enemy into a well-laid trap.

Angie is so far into her fantasy that she misses the moment when the murderer abandons the rucksack and bolts across the ravine, heading straight for her hiding place. He has seen her after all.

Angie draws the knife. She may not have a backup plan, but at least she has the knife. The knife the mountain gave her. Holding it makes her feel better—braver and stronger. It pours courage down her arm into her watery limbs and breathless ribs. This knife was meant for her, and it won't let her down. It won't let her lose.

When the murderer is only a few paces away, close enough for Angie to see the flecks of spit in his dirty beard and to choke on his dank animal smell, she springs out from behind the bush, letting loose the most terrifying battle cry she can muster.

The murderer stops, clocking the knife she brandishes wildly in front of her. He blinks, his flat eyes flicking over her, and growls. His own hands are empty, the long-nailed fingers bent like claws.

Angie shifts left, and he shifts left. She leans right, and he leans right, like a grotesque mirror. She can hear his breath, smell the burnt fruit of his cigar, hear her own blood pounding inside her skull as they circle each other, neither willing to strike first.

Angie waits for the slightest twitch that will give away his next move, the lunge that will topple her, the attack that she will have to repulse.

The man flexes his fingers like they're warming up to grab, but all he does is bend his knees and drop his weight a little lower. Angry snarls issue from his wet lips, but Angie can't make sense of a single word.

Whatever he's saying, he's still not coming any closer. Maybe he's scared of her. After all, he's unarmed, and she's the one who has a weapon.

"That's right," Angie says. "You better watch out. This blade will cut you to ribbons."

The sound of her own voice gives Angie a jolt of courage. Maybe this isn't going to be so hard. Maybe things can still come out all right.

Angie lunges, slicing the air between them.

The murderer swerves away from the jabbing blade. He shakes his head like he's dislodging a fly, and drops of water from his wet hair spray over her. He works his jaw, as if gnawing something between his yellow teeth.

Then he springs.

His weight slams into Angie, and they crash to the ground. And just like that, the knife is gone. Angie doesn't know how or where to, can't pinpoint the last moment she held it. It was gripped tight in her fist, her lifeline to getting out of this, and then it was gone.

The murderer is all around her, surrounding her, trapping her, smothering her. Together they tumble over rocks, thud into trees. He is so heavy. Angie tries to get free, get him off her, struggle to her feet, but each movement she makes, he blocks her. She is dizzy and breathless, and she doesn't know which way is up anymore. She just wants to get away. She shoves, she claws, she kicks, she wriggles and strains, but he is always there.

His face is in front of hers, stinking breath and bleeding lip. Then it's his back, his boot, his fist. She pounds on every part of him she can reach, but it makes no difference. *The knife*, she thinks. She has to find the knife. But she's running out of breath, out of energy. Her blows are getting weaker, her scrambles getting slower.

She still wants to believe she can win, but something deep in her brain is telling her the truth: That she is teetering much closer to the edge of her own life than she ever has before. That all of her battles on the school bus, in the lunch line at the cafeteria, in the locker room after class, were nothing more than bruises, scratches, and glancing blows. That, in fact, this stinking, growling, wordless man, not much older than her brother Sam, is the most dangerous enemy she has ever faced.

Out here, on the side of the mountain where no one knows she is, Angie is looking at two possible futures. One where she leaves the woods and sleeps in her bed tonight, and one where she is lying on the moss and stones, her eyes wide open to the sky, her breath still, her flesh cold, the worms making inroads at her toes.

TWENTY-EIGHT

The Brush-Covered Wound

SHEILA BREATHES IN JUANITA'S WARM SOFTNESS.
She feels like she has been granted everything she always
wanted. Holding Juanita in her arms is better than she
imagined. Juanita's presence is so warm and accepting. It's a
feeling Sheila never wants to end. She pulls Juanita tighter,
trying to keep her close, closer, never let her go. But as she
clings, Juanita's softness resists, grows harder, more angular.
Her back firmer, her shoulder blades sharper.

Sheila withdraws and feels again the rain misting on her
face, the scent of pine and stone. He is the boy once more,
and Sheila doesn't know why she is standing so close to him.

She backs away. "You tricked me."

"Yes," he says. "But now you know what it's like."

Sheila is trying to decide if she hates him or if she wants him to do it again when a shout carries to her through the thick mountain air. A moment later, it comes again, sharp and desperate. A cry of fear and bravado. Sheila's body recognizes the voice before her brain does: Angie.

"I have to go," Sheila says.

"I know. She needs you."

Sheila forces herself to look at him fully and not flinch from the red bloom in his eye. She asks her question without words, but he seems to understand because he says, "This is all I can do. You're on your own."

So she leaves him and runs in the direction of the shout. She looks back over her shoulder once, but the boy is fading, a blurry outline half filled with leaves and bark, his white shoes swelling with mushrooms, a cardinal's red wing blinking out his face.

She races over rocks, weaves around trees, ducks under branches, and hurdles logs, briars tearing at her hands and shins and thighs. The rope trails behind her, snagging on the sharp ends of everything. She loops it around her wrist to give herself some slack.

As she bolts across the mountain's haunch, tracking Angie's cries, Sheila searches for landmarks, for something that will tell her where she is and where she is headed. She skids to a stop at the edge of a steep, mossy ravine, startling a flock of wild turkeys that lumber into the trees.

A creature like something from one of Angie's cards struggles at the bottom of the ravine. It has too many arms, too many legs, and a filthy tangle of mismatched hair. It thrashes and snarls, rolling over rocks and banging into trees. It takes a moment before Sheila's brain is able to separate this seething mass into two people. To separate it into her sister Angie grappling with a bearded stranger twice her size.

Sheila launches herself down the slope into the trough of the ravine. She stumbles and slides on the wet leaves, barely staying on her feet as she tries to reach Angie before something terrible happens. As she gets closer, Sheila chokes on the smell coming off the man—not just weeks of fermented sweat but some intrinsic sickness, the bacteria in a spoiled jar of preserves, the tumor on the side of a fox that crawls with maggots while the animal staggers and licks and struggles to survive.

"Get away from her," Sheila yells, rushing at them. "Get off my sister!"

Sheila throws herself onto the man's back, trying to haul him away from Angie. He grunts when her weight hits him, but he's intent on his prey, his dirty hands gripping Angie's shoulders and banging her against the ground.

Sheila wraps her hands around his throat and digs in, her fingers tangling in his matted beard. She slaps at his face, seeking weakness, trying to get him to break his grip on her sister. She lands a lucky thumb in his eye, and the man roars and reaches around to strike her.

"Get away," Sheila gasps to Angie, as the man bucks and writhes. "Now!"

Angie crawls out of reach and collapses. "It's him," she says between panting breaths. "He's the murderer, the man they're looking for. I found him."

But Sheila barely has time to hear. The murderer shakes her loose and rounds on her. Leaves tangle in his hair, and his nose drips with blood. His eyes blaze with a ferocious light as he rushes toward her.

"Butch called the police," Angie says, clutching her side and trying to get to her knees. "They're on their way."

The man backhands Sheila across the face, knocking her flat. She tastes the iron salt of blood in her mouth as her chest seizes, seemingly unwilling to pump air anymore. Her vision goes dark as the murderer looms over her, snarling like an animal.

At the edge of her fading sight, Sheila sees Angie grab a fallen branch.

"Stay back," she rasps, but of course Angie doesn't listen.

Angie cracks the branch across the man's back. A shower of bark and bugs falls into Sheila's eyes, but the rotting wood snaps in two. The murderer topples, and Sheila scuttles out from under him just in time, leaving one shoe behind.

Sheila has to get them away from here, away from him, but she nearly wiped out running down the ravine's steep sides. The ground was mushy under wet leaves that hid spikes of stone and ankle-turning rabbit holes. If she and Angie try to run for it, the man will catch them before they make it ten feet.

The murderer lashes out and his hand closes on Angie's ankle. She shrieks and tries to break free, but his grip is strong. Sheila lunges forward to help, and the rope around her neck snags on a knob of root poking through the leaves and jerks her to a stop.

"No! Not now!" It's so unfair. She is always hindered, always prevented, caught and stuck. Tears squeeze out of her angry, bleeding face. She wrenches the rope free and hauls on it with both hands, pulling against whoever or whatever is on the other end. This time, she is going to pull it out by the root.

Her chest cracks open, unleashing a black vortex, a whirling maw that sweeps her marrow, extinguishing her consciousness and pain. It gains speed, gobbling her limbs and thoughts, spinning faster, spiraling down to the earth and up into her throat.

The rope flexes in her hands, sap oozing from between its fibers. Sheila's bare toes curl against the soil, into moss and bark and stone. The consuming current flows upward, infiltrating ankle shin thigh pelvis ribs, plundering her chest, striking out her arms hands mouth eyes. Her ears pop and fizzle, sound rushing into them, senses blazing.

She is not alone.

A second breath now rasps inside her skull, a second heart thuds beside her own. Sheila finds herself tucked inside her sister's straining body as Angie struggles in the murderer's grip. Some vibrating channel of communication that has always been clogged with static is now sluiced open and running freely, thoughts intentions desires flowing effortlessly between them.

Angie's fear presses on Sheila, squeezing in beside her, cramped and entwined like their shared bedroom. The man's filthy nails scrape at her own ankle, a barbed talon latched and ravening.

Angie's back is turned, but it doesn't matter. With her sister's mind inside her own, Sheila doesn't need to speak or even catch Angie's eye. They are one animal, one multibodied extension of the mountain as they coil the vine of Sheila's rope and loop it over the man's head, pulling it taut. He thrashes as the cord whips around him, swiping at the constricting bonds he feels but can't see.

The sisters twist and snare and tie. The air hums and the birds chorus in approval as Angie and Sheila zigzag and cross, feinting and fooling the fox while he snatches and snarls. They leap and gambol, always one hair out of reach, weaving him tight. When they finish, the bound man's eyes are two dots of fury, burning in his battered face.

The sisters flow apart, settling back into their separate bodies. Sheila feels Angie recede from her as the black vortex spins itself down. The rope is still around her neck, its coarse weight snaking behind her body.

Sheila bends over the murderer, and he lunges, spitting. His mouth hinges wide and he bares his teeth. She jumps back, and he bites down on her sleeve, just missing the skin beneath. The fabric tears as she shakes free and backs away.

She pulls Angie out of the man's earshot and whispers, "Was it true what you said? About Butch calling the police?"

"Yeah, but . . ." Angie looks around. "Do you know where we are?"

"I've been trying to figure it out, but I don't recognize anything. How did you get here?"

"He came into Butch's store. I used the cards to track him from our house after Butch dropped me off. They took me through all these tunnels I never knew existed. When I came out, I was in the back of his hideout over there. But when I tried to go back in, it was just solid rock."

A fat drop of leftover rain rolls off a leaf and splats on Sheila's face.

"Aren't you supposed to be at work?" Angie asks.

Sheila looks down at her work clothes. "I am. I was."

It seems like at least several days have passed since she crept through the doors of G Ward when she should have been rinsing breakfast trays. Then up the mysterious staircase and into Juanita's bedroom where she was rescued by the boy and dumped out on the side of the mountain.

"The police aren't coming, are they?" asks Angie. "They're never going to find this place."

"I think you're right," Sheila says. "What are we going to do with him?"

Angie points to the brush-covered wound in the mountain's side, where the murderer has been living like a parasite. "We could put him back in there."

❦

AS THEY DRAG the murderer across the rocky ground to the mouth of the dugout, Sheila kicks something buried in the leaves. She bends and picks up the red-handled knife.

She holds it out to Angie. "Isn't this yours?"

"I lost it." Angie can't meet Sheila's eyes. "I thought it would protect me, but he knocked it out of my hands."

Sheila scowls. "You should be glad that's all he—"

"I know," Angie says softly, cutting off the lecture. She takes the knife from Sheila and slides it back into the makeshift holster at her waist, and they heave the murderer the rest of the way to the cave. He struggles and snarls, but bound in the invisible rope, there's nothing he can do.

Angie tears the brush away from the entrance and looks into the dark mouth of the cave, at the heaped blankets, the rucksacks, the sad stockpile of food and goods.

"What about this stuff?" she asks.

"I don't want anything of his," Sheila says.

"I found your money," Angie says. "But there was other stuff . . . like, from those women, I think. Driver's licenses and things."

"It won't do them any good now," Sheila says. "Let it be."

Sheila stares down at the murderer trussed between them, his bleeding nose, his swollen lip, his eyes like murky swamps. Leaves and twigs are tangled in his hair, and his shirt has rucked up, showing skin as pale and smooth as the belly of a frog. She has no proof that he murdered those women, yet she knows it is so.

Sheila stoops to bundle him into the hole, but Angie stops her. She draws the knife and traces Sheila's rope backward from the knot behind the murderer's back and holds it in front of her.

"What are you doing?"

"I'm going to cut you free." Angie's brows draw together as she concentrates on making a clean, swift cut on something she can't see.

Sheila's arms fly up in defense. "No! You can't!"

Angie points at the bound man. "You don't want to be stuck with him, do you?"

"Don't you think I've wanted to cut it before?" Sheila says. "I don't know what will happen."

Angie seems to think about this, but she raises the knife again.

Sheila knocks Angie's arm so hard she drops the knife. "I said *no*."

It's not the dropped knife so much as the look of desperation on her sister's face that stops Angie from trying again.

"It'll be fine," Sheila says, though she has no idea if this is true. "Let's just do it. I'll take this end. You get his feet."

As Sheila bends to secure the man's shoulders, he slips a hand free of the rope and locks his fingers around her wrist. The touch of his filthy, broken nails flashes her into a starry velvet night, a woman lying with her broken face in the dirt, her tongue swollen with blood, her crushed lips trembling as she whimpers against the soil. Behind her, the dome of a tent, the shadows of trees. The night air is thick with the acid smell of fear, the warm copper tang of blood. In the glow of the moon, Sheila sees the man, blood flecking his face and beard, his eyes gleaming with delight.

He raises his arm and smashes a rock down on the broken

woman's head. The woman's body jerks, and her final breath puffs from between her bleeding lips.

Sheila twitches her arm free of the man's clutching fingers and shoves him headfirst into the hole. They struggle to get his shoulders past the entrance, and it takes both of them grabbing his boots and pushing at his kicking feet, but at last the murderer is entirely swallowed by the dark gash he has cut into the mountain's side.

Angie and Sheila collapse to the ground, gasping with the effort. Sheila presses her cheek against the raw dirt. The mountain's ribs seem to swell in and out, the echo of her own breath.

The ground beneath them begins to tremble. Softly at first, like a distant truck rolling over a bridge. Then the wind stops blowing, the birds stop singing, and the leaves stop rustling. The gentle tremor hums through their bodies like they are riding on the back of an enormous purring cat.

Sheila takes Angie's hand in hers, feeling the rough calluses of her sister's palm, the bones in her sister's fingers, the warmth of her skin. And they watch.

The wound in the mountain's side seems to swell, and the gap narrows until they can barely glimpse the man's boots in the gloom beyond. The broken roots that border the entrance stretch and begin to weave across the hole. The seam closes, and the roots stitch it tight.

Then the wind springs back into motion, breathing silt and mulch to fill the gaps. Moss marches across the naked scar, growing a carpet of seamless green. Blackberry canes spring from the ground in front, binding into an intricate screen. There is no bare patch on the mountain's side anymore, no hole scraped in her ribs. There is no man, and no murderer. Only the mountain and two sisters.

TWENTY-NINE

The Mountain Itself

EVER SINCE THEY BURIED THE MURDERER, THE rope around Sheila's neck has grown even harder to carry. Once the ground closed over the man's body, Sheila was afraid she wouldn't be able to leave the spot. Despite what she told Angie, she was worried that she might be chained in the bottom of the ravine forever. But when the mountain's wound was sealed, it was as if the rope had been pinched between two sharp edges, and Sheila fell back on her heels, suddenly released. But like an earthworm chopped in half, the other end of the rope regenerated, growing back thicker and heavier than ever before.

The rope drags behind Sheila as she pushes the mop back and forth over the asylum kitchen's floor. Its weight pulls her back as she climbs into her mom's car. It catches in the automatic doors when they stop at the IGA. It chokes her as she trudges out to feed the rabbits, and as she mounts the stairs to bed.

Every step she takes on the short climb over the ridge to Earl's tree stand is a battle, her muscles straining, sweat popping out on her forehead and the back of her neck. She has to stop several times, hands on knees, to gulp down air before she can take another step. When at last she arrives, she reaches for the block of wood nailed in the V between the two oaks and begins to climb. The cleats are narrow and far apart, and as she strains to reach the next one, the rope digs into her neck, jolting her back toward the ground. Her foot slips, and her ankle bangs against the rough bark. She hangs, twisting, scraping for a foothold, then hauls herself back up.

She winds the rope around her forearm so that it now weighs against her arm instead of her throat, and continues to climb. When she reaches the bottom of the tree stand, she pushes her head through the opening in the plywood floor. "Can I come in?"

"It's a free country," Angie says.

Sheila braces her hands on the edges of the hole and lifts herself into the tree stand, dropping the rope on the floor. Behind her, the plywood creaks, and she hears heavy breathing.

"What are you doing?"

"Twenty-two, twenty-three . . ." Angie presses her body off the floor and rests at the top. "Push-ups."

"I can see that. Why?"

Angie grinds out two more reps, her arms shaking. She collapses on her knees, red-faced and sucking in air. "You need to be able to do fifty to get in the army."

Sheila leans on the waist-high rail of the tree stand and looks out. From up here, she can see across the mountain's side to the distant valley and other blue-hazed ridges beyond. Animal trails crisscross the slope below. The leaves on the trees are beginning to curl with the dry yellow tips of late summer. Others have been stripped bare by hungry caterpillars and invasive moths.

"You really want to join up?" Sheila asks.

"I'll get to fight the Russians for real. I might even get to drive a tank."

Sheila turns away from the forest to face her sister. "You know those war movies you watch are made-up, right? That's not how it actually is. You'll have to sleep in the same room with a hundred people and eat awful food. You'll have to work hard—cleaning toilets and peeling potatoes and digging trenches. And I don't think they like girls very much."

"Maybe not," Angie says, getting to her feet. "But it's my choice."

"They won't take you until you're eighteen. What are you going to do until then?"

"They won't take me until they *believe* I'm eighteen," Angie says. "I've grown two inches since last summer. Butch says if they can tell I really want to get in, they won't ask too many questions."

Sheila realizes her little sister *is* taller—her eyes are almost level with Sheila's now, and some of the pudginess has fallen away from her cheeks. But there's more to the changes than that. Something about the way Angie moves has become more deliberate, less like a random collection of limbs and impulses. It's like someone has climbed into the vacant driver's seat of her body and finally taken charge.

Sheila traces her finger along the grooves some bored hunter has gouged into the railing. "You're going to do what you want anyways, aren't you?"

"If something bad is coming, I'd rather go out to meet it instead of waiting around for it to show up." Angie sights an imaginary target in the woods with her extended finger and fires. "Who knows—maybe I'll get assigned to guard the president when he comes to his mountain bunker. Then I'll end up right back here."

"Maybe," Sheila says.

"You didn't climb all the way up here just to tell me I shouldn't join the army. Do you want something?"

"Can't hide much from you," Sheila says. "Do you have that knife on you?"

Angie's face closes down, and Sheila recognizes the stubborn pucker of her lips. "I thought having a weapon would protect me. I didn't think he'd get it away from me so fast."

"That's not why I'm asking," Sheila says. "A lot of things didn't go the way we expected. You did the best you could. In the end, we figured it out."

"I guess we did."

After the mountain swallowed the murderer, the sisters had stumbled away in silence, their nerves alive to every crunched twig underfoot, every wingbeat of gnat and deer-fly. They still didn't know where they were, and yet, as they walked, the forest around them gradually became familiar again, as if slowly coming back into focus. Wordlessly they navigated deer trails and briar patches and deadfalls until they heard the distant cluck of the chickens and the dogs rushed out to greet them.

Angie had dropped to her knees and hugged Sue, letting the dog slobber over her face with her pink tongue. Sheila felt like there was something she ought to say then, before the moment was gone, but she didn't know whether it was praise or complaint or warning, so she kept quiet.

They'd passed the next few days in a careful, muffled hush, as if their ears were still ringing after the detonation of a massive bomb. They told no one about what had happened, not even when Bonnie mentioned the strange tremor that had rattled the windows at the Iron Mountain facility.

At first Sheila was grateful to Angie for keeping the pact of their silence. Sheila had feared Angie couldn't maintain it, that one night soon she would blurt their secret over dinner, flinging it out between the lima beans and the stewed apples, but she never said a word.

Now, it wasn't that Sheila doubted what had happened, but as the days flowed on and neither of them mentioned it, the events became less and less real, more like something half remembered from a dream. It was ridiculous that the act of talking about something, shaping your lips around words and forcing sounds out your throat should have any effect on whether something was real or not, but it seemed that it did.

A woodpecker slams its beak into a nearby tree, and the forest echoes with hollow drumming.

"So do you have that knife or not?"

Angie nods, and Sheila says, "I want you to cut this rope off me."

"You wouldn't let me," Angie protests. "You got *mad* at me."

"Because I don't know what will happen. I was scared. But I can't live with this. Ever since we buried that man, it's gotten heavier. It's choking me. I don't care what happens anymore—I have to get rid of it."

Angie withdraws the knife and hands it to Sheila.

Sheila shakes her head. "I want you to do it."

"Are you serious? I can't even see it!"

"I'll show you. I'll tell you where to cut." Sheila lifts the tail of the rope and holds it out with one hand. "Here. Grab it right here."

Angie extends her arm, and her breath puffs in surprise when her fingers close around something. "I can feel it!"

She raises the red-handled knife with her other hand. "It's not too thick. I should be able to cut through it no problem."

"Not there," Sheila says. "It has to be closer. You have to cut here, by my neck, or it'll just grow back again. You have to cut me loose."

Angie lowers the knife and stares at her sister. "What if I cut you? I can't see what I'm doing."

Sheila covers Angie's hand with her own and guides it along the rope to where it knots around her neck. "You can still feel it?"

Angie nods, her eyes big.

"Put the knife right there," Sheila says. "That's where you've got to do it."

Angie looks worried, but she does as Sheila says, carefully inserting the tip of the knife between the soft skin of Sheila's neck and the tension of the invisible rope.

Sheila holds her breath and tries to stay as still as possible. It feels like she can hear the flutter of every wren, sense the insects burrowing into the tree stand's warped planks, smell the clusters of walnuts ripening in their green husks. She trusts Angie, she tells herself, as the knife's blade shivers against her neck.

She remembers the channel that cleared between them when they fought the murderer, their movements flowing as one. Angie was now settled back in her separate container, but some remnant remained, some whispered shred of the space they had shared, their moment as a single animal.

"One . . . two . . ."

Sheila closes her eyes and tries not to flinch. She waits to feel the rope fall away. Waits to see if her life falls with it. Waits for the ground to shake, the sky to fall, for punishment, destruction, annihilation.

". . . three!" Angie slashes with the knife.

"Is it gone? Did you do it?" Sheila opens her eyes. The oak's leaves flutter; the woodpecker hammers another rotten trunk. A squirrel buries an acorn. The sky, the clouds, the planes overhead, the sun: it's all the same. It's all still there.

And so is the rope.

Sheila sags against the tree stand's wall. She should have known it wouldn't be that easy.

"I just sharpened it." Angie holds the knife to her face, examining the blade. She stops short of running her finger along the honed edge. Instead, she pulls the drawstring out of her sweatshirt and stretches it taut. She presses the knife against it and the cord splits cleanly in two.

"It's not your fault," Sheila says, looking at the dangling halves of string. She crosses to the hole in the floor and puts one foot through to the rungs below. She has tried. There's nothing to do now but go down. If she jumped from here, she wonders, would the rope catch her halfway, leave her swinging between earth and sky, dangling by her neck?

"WAIT!" ANGIE SAYS. "You could try the cards."

Sheila's feet hang in space. It's a long way down. "What are you talking about?"

"You could ask my cards what to do."

Sheila's not so sure this is a great idea. Each time she's encountered one of Angie's cards so far, she feels like she's stepped in a nest of rattlesnakes.

"I know they made you mad before," Angie says. "But they're not bad. They led me all the way through the mountain to the murderer. I couldn't have found him without them."

"That's not much of an argument in their favor."

"The Worm King helped us. Back in the ravine."

Sheila doubts that. But *something* had made the mountain close like a seam. She has no other choices, nowhere else to turn. She is stuck. So very stuck. Maybe the cards are cruel and unpredictable. But she can no longer deny they have power.

Sheila retracts her feet and climbs back into the tree stand. "How does it work?"

"I've never tried them with another person." Angie squats on her heels and produces the pack. Antlers and talons and teeth flick by as Angie shuffles the dog-eared cards through her fingers.

"Wonderful," Sheila says, crouching beside her.

Angie deals the cards face down on the floor of the tree stand. "You have to promise you won't get mad, no matter what card comes up."

"I promise," Sheila says. "Now what? How do I pick one?"

"You have to listen," Angie says. "One of them will be louder than the others. One of them wants to be heard."

Sheila listens. She hears a gnat droning in her ear. Angie's breathing, and her own. The creak of the tree stand's boards as a breeze sways the tops of the oaks. The sharp cry of a distant hawk. Her feet tingle from holding the crouch for so long while she stares at the blue lines on the backs of the battered cards that give nothing away. Her eyes water from staring, and she takes off her glasses to rub them. As she puts them back on her face, one of the cards wobbles, like the ripple of a pebble thrown into calm water.

"That one." Sheila touches her finger to the card, which has turned flat and blank and still again.

She turns it over.

The rounded hump of a mountain rises from the bottom of the card. Water rushes in one side and flows through a labyrinth of tunnels, spouting out the other side between two tall trees growing beside each other like a doorway. In a hollow chamber at the center of the maze, an enormous eye glows from the mountain's heart.

Sheila turns the card so Angie can see.

Angie swats at an enormous horsefly dive-bombing her head. "I didn't draw that."

Sheila tries to swallow the anger that's building in her chest. "You're not making sense. You're the one who said we should do this."

"I mean I drew every card in the pack with my own hand. Except that one." The horsefly attacks again, and Angie smashes it against the boards.

"How did it get in there then?" Sheila waves at the rest of the pack.

Angie opens her hand and lets the fly's body drop over the railing's edge. "You'd better ask the mountain."

ASK THE MOUNTAIN.

Angie's words repeat in Sheila's head as she lowers herself hand over hand back to the ground. At the bottom, she leans against the oaks. The rough bark knobbles into her spine. The climb down wasn't difficult, but she feels weak and is grateful to borrow strength from the trees.

Sheila had always been afraid something bad would happen if she ever tried to cut the rope and walk free. What she didn't consider was that it might be impossible to remove. She stares at the mountain card in her hand, a picture on a piece of paper. It doesn't seem like much of a solution.

She pushes away from the trees and sets out for home, stomping over rocks and not caring if briars tear her clothes. She can't believe she's been so stupid as to think there could be any way out. As she's crossing the rock pile near the old logging road, the tail of the rope snags on a broken branch and jerks Sheila off her feet.

She lands hard on her hands and knees, the impact traveling up her arms to her shoulders. Her head snaps back, and her glasses slide off the end of her nose.

Then she remembers.

She remembers so vividly it's like watching a TV show on the only clear station.

Sheila is six years old and on her knees beside a stream. She has come back to the mountain from thirteen months of living in town with her mom and Angie's father. She is home. She flings herself to the ground and presses her face to the cold seam between the rocks and whispers her story, dropping tears on the shaggy moss. The outside world didn't want her. She didn't belong to pavements and bricks and linoleum floors.

As an apology, an offering, a favor, the mountain shows Sheila a stone, a crystal seed beside the stream. Sheila plucks that grain of clear quartz from the raw black dirt. The air smells of pine and mushrooms, and her fingertips turn red from the shock of the cold as she washes it clean in the water running with melted snow.

Sheila holds the quartz to her eye and looks through a lens divided by fine lines of gold that splits the world into three sections. Through the stone, she scans the hemlocks, dormant blueberries, flattened ferns, and fallen stone walls. Almost without a thought, she pops the rock into her mouth and swallows.

It feels warm at first, as the crystal grain scrapes the tissue of her throat—like swallowing a peppercorn. Then it's gone, sliding out of reach of her mind, down into the invisible maze of her body.

What a strange thing to do, she thinks. *I wonder why I wanted to.* A sound in the thicket of nearby winterberry draws her attention. It's a rabbit, skinny and big-eyed, scrounging for something to eat among the frost-burned leaves of the winter forest. Six-year-old Sheila gets to her feet, pulls her sleeves down over her cold hands, and walks home, forgetting all about the stone.

THIRTY

The Sweetness You Trade For

EVERY YEAR ABOUT THIS TIME, SHEILA USED TO accompany Thena to this overgrown meadow ringed by trees where a hundred years ago a farmhouse stood. Now nothing remains except a pond crowded with cattails, the crumbling foundations of the old springhouse, and some wizened apple trees.

After Thena's leg withered and her heart slowed, Sheila made the trip alone to gather the curling leaves and feathery flowers of licorice tea. Though Thena's no longer around to peer suspiciously into the mug that Sheila brews, she can't bear to leave another glaring gap in the rhythms of the year on top of the haggard void that is Thena's vacant room.

As Sheila approaches the pond, sunning turtles and fat bullfrogs plop from the muddy banks into the safety of the water. When the rope's weight grinds on her and she stops for one more rest, a young buck on the other side startles to his feet, eyes bright and curious, before melting into the thicket of birch and bright-berried sumac at the forest's edge.

Sheila doesn't know why she's doing this, especially now when the journey is so hard, when every drag and tug of the rope slows her down. Thena is gone, Bonnie prefers heaping spoonfuls of whatever instant coffee is on sale at the IGA that week, and Angie doesn't drink anything that doesn't seethe with sugar. Sheila doesn't care for the musty, sweet taste of the tea, but it feels wrong to skip the ritual, to not make herself at least one cup.

Sheila shakes open her paper bag and wades rib-high into the sea of golden blooms, winding among the butterflies and bees and gnats and dragonflies. A scratch in her throat feels like the ghost of the stone she swallowed tickling her, even though there's plenty of ragweed growing here beside the tea, its sticky yellow powder coating everything in these last dry weeks of summer, clogging her head and dragging her down.

Thena always said the tea was a tonic, that it could heal wounds and cure infections. She had made Sheila drink pitchers of the stuff after Sam pushed her against the blazing woodstove when she was six and blistered her arm. Sheila picks at the rope's grip, adjusting its chafe around her neck. Maybe the tea will help her bear this burden, maybe it won't. It certainly can't hurt.

Sheila grabs handfuls of plants, plucks the choicest leaves, and drops them into the bag. She falls into a steady rhythm, bending and gathering, the harvest sun bathing her back and neck, filling her with honeyed warmth. The bees drone around her, and Sheila feels herself swell. Her mind drifts to Juanita, what she might be doing right now.

Sheila reaches for the next stalk, the leaves softly fuzzed in her hands. At this very moment, Juanita could be resting on her bed in her ranch house down in the valley. She'd be curled against the pillows, head bent over the diary balanced on her adorable knees. The white summer dress she wears slips carelessly off one shoulder. Her hair falls loose from its ponytail and whispers against her cheek, and the room smells of licorice whips and floral air freshener. The hi-fi in the corner plays something romantic and dreamy. Sheila can see it all, almost as if she's standing there in the room inches from Juanita's bent head, mere breaths from the soft skin of her nape. So close Juanita must surely know she's there. Any moment now, Juanita could look up and see her, could meet her eyes.

Feeling surges in Sheila's heart, lush and full. Her fingers itch to snatch Juanita out of the straight square walls of her house and transport her here to this meadow, these woods. She longs to share this bursting, entangled world that courses through her in vital, living threads.

Sheila drops the antler-handled knife and the bag stuffed with leaves and drifts to the edge of the forest. She searches for something to contain all that she feels. Everything the world is made from is available: soil and wood and root and stone and leaf and feather and shell and fungus and ferment. All of the ingredients, all possibilities are here. She needs only to put them together in the right order, like a recipe.

Briars tangle against her shins; vines grasp her ankle, then slide and release. Sheila gathers birch twigs, spiderwebs, a snail shell, and a handful of shimmering quartz sand. She follows the impulses of her body, lets her hands take over as they weave the twigs around the snail's vacant home, binding it with spiderwebs, forming an unfilled cup.

Her feet guide her back to the spring that feeds the pond, where she dips her creation and rinses it well. This is her chance to tell the truth, to pour out all that she has concealed and distorted. Her chance to make it whole and right again. To bring something into the world that has no lies.

She brings the vessel to her mouth and pours into its hollow heart not her thoughts but her whole body—all it knows and feels. Into it go her secrets, her love, and her promises—everything she needs to tell Juanita. When it's full, she sprinkles in the quartz sand and caps it all with more spider silk and moss. The woven bottle turns solid in her hand, preserved.

THIRTY-ONE

The Retreating Fog

SHEILA SWINGS THE MAUL OVER HER SHOULDER
and brings it down swift and hard. The log underneath splits
with a satisfying crack, and Sheila tosses the pieces onto the
pile growing beside her. Butch came by with his chainsaw last
week and cut the trees that fell in the spring rains into lengths
that will fit into their woodstove. But the trunk pieces are too
thick, and Sheila is splitting them into a usable size. Angie
attacks the smaller branches with a hatchet, chopping them
into lengths for kindling. She relishes the ache in her muscles
as the blade cleaves the wood.

Sheila throws down the maul and shakes her arms to
loosen her shoulders. "I got to rest for a bit," she calls to
Angie. "Come help me stack."

Sheila pulls on a long-sleeve shirt to cover her arms and starts collecting the split logs. Angie joins her, and they traipse back and forth to the woodpile that stretches against the east wall of the house. When they are both bent over collecting logs, Sheila says, "Do you remember when we were hunting mushrooms and you said you wanted Troy Eckheart to be your boyfriend?"

Angie shakes loose bark from a log. "I guess."

Sheila stoops to collect another log. "Do you really *like* boys? Like, want them to touch you and stuff?"

"You mean to kiss them and do dirty stuff with, like in the movies?"

"Yeah."

"I wouldn't mind," Angie says. "I mean, I don't know, but it seems like it's supposed to be fun?" She thinks for a moment. "Travis is really strong, and he kind of looks like he's bursting out of his uniform when he's playing baseball. Have you seen him bent over to bat, in those tight pants?" Angie mimics the stance, wiggling her butt.

Sheila makes a face. "You don't think that's a bit gross?"

"What? No!" Angie studies her sister. "Do you?"

Sheila fits a log carefully onto the stack, shoring up the column at the end. "Yeah, I do. Really gross, actually."

Sheila's not sure she wants to tell Angie this, but she has to tell somebody. She has to say it out loud to keep it from being a secret thing that she carries around like a worm in a peach, eating her from the inside. She might never tell anyone else, but she can try it out on Angie. If she can share with her sister the secret of sealing a man alive inside the mountain, she ought to be able to trust her with this truth.

"I don't like boys," Sheila says, making herself say the words. "I think if a boy touched me, I would gag."

She waits for Angie's reaction. For her to laugh or sneer or threaten to tell their mom and everyone at school. But Angie keeps stacking logs without breaking her rhythm.

"So if you don't like boys . . ." Angie fills her arms again, leaving the rest of the sentence hanging in the air like a question mark. She can't remember Sheila ever confiding in her. Her older sister has always been remote and secretive, like water trickling underground that you can hear and even smell, but never drink. That led Angie to think that Sheila was weak. Now she knows better. But she still doesn't understand her.

"There's a girl at school I really like. I don't think I can ever tell her." Sheila rushes the words out like she's trying to outrun them. When she was picking tea in the meadow, the truth seemed so clear, so easy.

Angie is bent over the woodpile, and Sheila can't see her face. The muscles flexing in Angie's back don't give anything away.

Angie slots the last log into the stack and straightens. She doesn't see what Sheila is making such a big deal about. Rules about who is allowed to do what with who have always baffled Angie, but she senses this is important to Sheila so she tries to get it right. "Like, you want to go on a date with her and kiss her and stuff?"

Sheila remembers her fantasies of pouring wine for Juanita at a fancy dinner, lighting candles and playing romantic music. She can't believe she is talking about this with her little sister. She wouldn't mind too much if one of Angie's nuclear bombs dropped right now and wiped them both out so that she never had to finish this conversation.

"Pretty much."

A green walnut breaks from a branch overhead and plops at Sheila's feet. Sheila can't stand the silence, the lack of reaction from Angie. She wants to shout, "So now you know. Are you disgusted? Am I still your sister?"

Instead, Sheila says, "Do you mind?"

For once, Sheila is asking for her opinion, almost treating her like an equal. Angie supposes that burying that man together had made some kind of link between them. And yet, she knows that they aren't going to be friends, not even now. They are too different. "What's it got to do with me?"

Angie is right. It doesn't have anything to do with her, not directly. Still . . . "People will say things," says Sheila. "Mean things."

"Nobody likes me anyways," says Angie. "What does it matter if they call you a lesbo? They already call me that, and it's not even true."

"Yeah, but in my case it probably is."

Angie thinks of the rumors, the nasty way the kids at school talk about her. The ignorance of people who think muscles and leg hair and a bad haircut mean something they don't. She shrugs. "I hear a lot of women in the army are like that. You're just helping me get used to it before I get there."

Sheila wonders if she has underestimated Angie all along. "You're not such a bad sister," Sheila says. "For a cavewoman."

Together they pull the tarp over the logs and secure the corners.

"What's her name?" Angie asks.

"Juanita Herman."

Angie calls up the faces of the older girls she has seen in the halls at school, earnest girls taping student government posters to the wall, girls wearing aprons in home ec class, girls in fringed jackets smoking in the bathroom, girls with mouth guards whacking balls across the hockey field. "Eleventh grade, brown hair, looks like she likes kittens and reads romance novels?"

That's not how Sheila thinks about Juanita, but she admits that it's probably true. "When you go back to school next week, will you give her a message for me?"

"What do you want me to say?"

Tell her that I want to run away with her. Tell her that I'm sorry I was too scared to talk to her. Tell her I think she's beautiful and special even if no one else can see it. Tell her I'm sorry we were never friends. Tell her if she ever wants me, I'll be waiting.

"Just give her this," Sheila says.

Sheila brings out the gift she made beside the pond. The miniature bottle rests in the palm of her hand.

Angie's fingers brush Sheila's palm as she takes the bottle and holds it up to the afternoon sunlight. A network of silver threads twines around the crystal quartz sides, and the mouth is stoppered with a spiky tuft of hardened moss.

The ghostly shapes of rabbits dance inside.

THIRTY-TWO

The Music of the Moss

SHEILA CLIMBS THE STAIRS TO THE ROOM SHE STILL shares with Angie under the eaves. Sheila's side remains spare and plain, one of Thena's western paperbacks broken-backed and abandoned on the rickety table beside her bed. The space seems smaller than ever somehow, all of her self and belongings crammed into just one corner, Angie spilling and overflowing. Sheila used to not mind how small it was as long as she could control it. Now she wonders what it would be like to stretch her arms wide and not brush them against the four walls.

She flicks the rope aside and crosses to Angie's half, which is still a mess, sheets tangled at the foot of her bed and the bare mattress scattered with candy wrappers and peanut shells.

Angie has pinned a sheet of paper to the wall with a hand-drawn grid marking her progress through some invented training regimen. Angie herself is outside, hupping around the henhouse, running drills with a fifty-pound sack of chicken feed hoisted on her shoulders.

Digging through Angie's sour laundry piled on the plank floor, Sheila unearths the doll a well-meaning but entirely mistaken relative gifted her sister for some early birthday. After hacking off all of the cherub's glossy hair and defacing her pink cheeks with black marker, Angie had tossed the baby into a corner and never touched it again.

Sheila turns the doll's scribbled face away from her and lifts the gingham pinafore. She slips her fingers inside the slit she cut in the doll's cotton back, seeking in the lumpy stuffing for the stone she hid after Thena's funeral.

There. She pulls out the smooth chunk of milky quartz she found bundled in Thena's dead hand. After burying the doll back under Angie's festering laundry, Sheila heads down the stairs and across the creaking porch. The dogs lazily lift their heads to stare after her with incurious eyes.

Acorns and hickory nuts crack under her feet as she makes her way into the woods. The poison ivy is thick and lush, its oily leaves crowding the path. The stone is heavy in her hand as she carries it, seeming to pulse against her palm like a small animal body with a beating heart.

When she is far enough from the house to not be seen or heard, Sheila crouches down and uncurls her fingers. Seeing the milky quartz stone in her hand, she has a brief, wild impulse to swallow it again.

After all, the mountain only wants to protect her. To keep her grounded, connected, her bare feet stepping softly along its spine. Here where it can watch over her, feed her with its streams and the fruits of its soil, keep the cycle turning round and round forever. If she stays, if she pleases it, the mountain will clasp her in protective hibernation.

Sheila imagines pushing the stone past her lips, choking it down her throat to rest heavy and cold in the pit of her stomach. Letting it grow with every passing year, every lost opportunity and every faded insult.

Or she could crack it open and find out what's inside.

Sheila balances the quartz on a wide, flat rock and lifts another stone, so big and heavy that she needs both hands to raise it over her head. She hammers it down on the milky quartz, crushing it like a walnut.

Splinters of white crystal scatter like shrapnel. The smallest shards fleck Sheila's skin with tiny cuts. A glinting scarlet seed remains at the center of the destruction. Sheila pokes it with her finger, and the red orb collapses to a puddle. The ruby liquid disappears into the bottom rock like grease soaked up by bread.

SHEILA REVISITS THE stream just above where the rotting log stretches across the water. She brushes acorn caps, leaf splinters, and glittering quartz sand from the top of a large flat rock. She takes off her top and bra and folds them on the sun-warmed surface. Her shorts and underwear follow, and then her glasses last of all, nestled on top of the pile. She faces the stream and feels her way carefully into the water.

Her toes curl around moss-slicked stones as she eases farther out, the current licking her calves. She wades upstream to a pool at the base of a rock. Here, the water laps her thighs, and her feet sink into deep, silty sand. Sheila lowers into the pool and leans back against the rock. The water pours through the cracks, rushes over ledges, trickles between gaps, murmuring in different voices.

The water is cold, and Sheila's insides bunch tight against her spine, trying to escape the chill. But soon she doesn't feel it anymore. The cold seems as natural as the air around her. She wonders why she has never done this before. All these years she has lived in these woods beside this stream. It has always been here and so has she, but they have never come together in this way. She's never stepped into the flow and met it face-to-face.

"You wanted me," Sheila says. "Here I am."

Her rope floats on the water's surface, lifting in the current, loosening the pressure on her neck. Sheila leans back, dips her head underwater, and soaks her hair. She means only to plunge quickly and rise back up, but once she is down, she doesn't want to leave. The current rushes past and slides away, but it's followed by the next, perpetually renewed. The water pours over her crown, brushes her forehead, caresses her eyelids, and sweeps away down her chin. Then it starts all over again.

Sheila opens her eyes and looks through the coursing water to the canopy of trees overhead. She is embraced, she is loved, she is no longer cold. Her skin glows, warm with delight. She can breathe, but she doesn't need to. Lightness commands her body, lifts her from the sandy bottom, and thrusts her to the surface.

Air fills her lungs, and water streams down her face. Sheila wipes the drops from her eyes, but the world stays blurred, smudges of green and gray for trees and blue for sky. She stands, and air whispers against her dimpling skin. The rope trails behind her as she climbs out of the water, heavy again.

Sheila squats on the bank, water pooling beneath her as she wrings out her wet hair and twists it over her shoulder. The water's caress still echoes on her skin, its tenderness and strength. Gnats whine in her ear, and a soft blue feather falls from a branch above. The water on her feet begins to dry, the patter of drops falling from her body onto the ground begins to slow.

Sheila leaves the stream, weaving between the hickories and beeches, their leaves turning gently golden. Late summer swallowtails flit among the branches, dancing to the music of the moss. The first rabbit leaps out from the shelter of the ferns to her left. Another parts a curtain of honeysuckle to her right. The rabbits hop quietly out of the undergrowth in ones and twos, spacing themselves evenly on both sides of the path, noses twitching in the radiant light.

Sheila knows better than to look for the boy. He is here in these silent, watchful columns. He has sent the rabbits to say goodbye.

☙

SHEILA RETURNS TO the house, her hair hanging damp against her shoulders.

She feels empty, washed out, flattened. She wants to be filled up. She opens cupboards, pokes into boxes and bags. Her hands seek what she wants, and for once she doesn't second-guess them, but lets her body choose, lets her body decide.

She dances around the rope as she gathers supplies, stacks them in her arms, and drops them on the table. A chipped plate with a yellow rose on one side. A tomato the size and weight of a man's heart, oozing red juice as she slices into it. She piles it onto thick slices of bread with plenty of salt, slathered with mayo, crunchy greens from the garden, sweet pickles on the side. She is so, so hungry.

The first bite of the sandwich sends sparks into her brain, out to her fingers, down to her toes. It fills her mouth with acid, salt, fat. The tomato is plush and full of satisfaction. It brings her warmth and energy and pleasure. She eats not greedily but well, savoring the sun and rain and soil and her own hard labor in the garden as she swallows the food down her throat into her bloodstream and begins to glow.

It feels like a new space is forming inside her ribs. When the sandwich is gone, down to the last crumb, and the plate is clean, Sheila rests her arms on the table and closes her eyes, feeling her body and limbs, all of her self. It all belongs to her. She has never had a meal so good.

After that, just because she wants it, fresh peaches from the farm stand sliced into a bowl with yesterday's biscuits crumbled on top. Finished off with a splash of cold milk and heaping spoonfuls of the golden sweet honey her mom traded two rabbits for.

The slither of peaches across her tongue is like being with Juanita. When Sheila finishes, she scrapes her spoon against the bowl. She licks out the last hint of honey and peach juice with a swipe of her finger. There is nothing more she wants just now. The rope hanging from her neck remains heavy, but she bears it easily. She is getting stronger.

Acknowledgments

A WISE PERSON ONCE SAID, "WRITING IS HARD. NO one should do it." I failed to heed that advice and therefore owe a debt of gratitude to the many people who supported me along the way:

To the Comets: Brooke Wonders, Dayna Smith, Rebecca Wright, Tim Susman, and special guest Megan Milks. I literally couldn't have done this without you. Magic is Real. Extra helpings of gratitude to Brooke for the title. Your prize is that you're now required to name every story I write from here on.

To my agent, Martha Perotto-Wills, for her insight and persistence; for really seeing Angie and Sheila and understanding where they belonged. And to James Mustelier and Molly Ker Hawn, also at The Bent Agency, for the parts they played.

To my champion editor, Elizabeth DeMeo, and also to Becky Kraemer, Nanci McCloskey, and the rest of the dream team at Tin House. A debut author couldn't wish for a more supportive publisher. Special thanks to Beth Steidle for a cover design that is both creepy and gorgeous.

To George Brown, Alison Green Myers, and everyone else at the Highlights Foundation who have given me so many opportunities and taken such good care of me over the years. I refill my well of Pennsylvania moss with every visit. And my stomach with carrot cake.

To mentors, teachers, and givers of sage advice: Karen Joy Fowler, Kij Johnson, Barbara Webb, Lynda Barry, Mike Allen, Margo Lanagan, and K. X. Song.

To Ashley Hope Pérez, for going first and showing me the way; for all the hours of book talks and story dreaming and merciless optimism.

To my mom for raising me barefoot on the side of a mountain and letting us read at the dinner table.

To public libraries and librarians everywhere, especially the Adams County Library in Gettysburg, PA. What you do matters enormously.

To Percy, who kept me going through the pandemic. I never imagined you and yet here you are. May the universe continue to surprise and delight. To Beatrix, for bookshelf adornment and constant companionship. And to the Squid, Heart of All Evil: rest in peace and wickedness.

To D, for everything. For *Molesworth* and *Jane Eyre* and *The Three Musketeers* and Jack & Stephen and reading aloud the whole way to the Grand Canyon. For believing in me and for always thinking this was something worth doing.

Reader's Guide

1. How would you characterize the relationship between Sheila and Angie? In what ways are they different, and are there ways in which they are the same?

2. How do the many communities surrounding them—both the people they encounter at school and elsewhere, and the plants and animals of the mountain on which they live—impact Sheila and Angie? What does this book have to say about the ways our surroundings can shape who we are?

3. What role does the mountain itself play in *Smother-moss*? How did author Alisa Alering make the world of the mountain come to life on the page?

4. Did you think the rope around Sheila's neck was real, imagined, or somewhere in between? Why do you think Alering created this image?

5. Who would you say is the most powerful character in this book? Are there ways in which different characters hold different types of power?

6. What did you make of the boy with the red spot in his eye? Did your opinion of him change over the course of the novel?

7. If you could have any one of Angie's monster cards, which would you choose? Why do you think these cards are so important to her?

8. In what ways do you think Sheila and Angie's lives will be—or already are—similar to their mother's or the old woman's? In what ways will they be different?

9. Both Sheila and Angie confront fears of theirs over the course of the novel. What does it mean, in the context of this story, to be brave?

10. How, by book's end, do you think Sheila and her sister have changed?

11. What do you think is next for these sisters?

ALISA ALERING grew up in the Appalachian Mountains of Pennsylvania and now lives in Arizona. After attending Clarion West, their short fiction has been published in *Fireside, Lady Churchill's Rosebud Wristlet, Podcastle*, and *Cast of Wonders*, among others, and been recognized by the Calvino Prize. A former librarian and science/technology reporter, they teach fiction workshops at the Highlights Foundation.